"I'm so sorry...

"Fun aprons are kind of my thing," Georgia said apologetically. "This is the manliest one I could find."

The manly apron in question was festooned with barnyard animals performing what appeared to be some sort of ballet. Cows leaped gracefully among sheep in tutus interspersed with a chorus of posing chickens. He pulled the apron over his head and turned to strike a pose.

"I mean, I think I'm pulling it off," he said, as Georgia's daughter nearly fell off the stool from laughter.

He felt a tug on the strings from behind him and turned his head to see Georgia tying the apron for him. "Thanks for being a sport," she whispered. "It's really good to hear her laugh again."

He leaned back a little to whisper in return, "No problem."

Georgia's eyes locked with his and for a moment... it felt like everything else in the room faded into the background.

Dear Reader,

One of my favorite parts of writing is that I get to weave little pieces of my own story in my books. My hobbies, places I've traveled or emotions I've experienced.

In *The Teacher's Forever Family*, I put more of myself on the page than ever before in a few different ways. From Georgia's love of baking to Malcolm's passion for rockhounding, these are activities that have been sources of joy for me throughout my life.

This book also delves into grief, something all of us experience at some point if we have the privilege of loving deeply. I think of grief as a path we walk, one that looks different for everyone and a path that is constantly changing. Georgia, a character who has been a source of wisdom and nurturing in previous books, is walking this path and finds herself stuck in a particularly narrow spot. It's tempting for her to look back, to where the way seemed brighter and more open. But when she finds someone who shows her the way forward, she has to choose to keep moving on.

I hope this story encourages you on whatever path you're walking.

Happy reading!

Laurie

THE TEACHER'S FOREVER FAMILY

LAURIE BATZEL

Recycling programs for this product may not exist in your area.

ISBN-13: 978-1-335-05155-4

The Teacher's Forever Family

For questions and comments about the quality of this book, please contact us at CustomerService@Harlequin.com.

Harlequin Enterprises ULC
22 Adelaide St. West, 41st Floor
Toronto, Ontario M5H 4E3, Canada
www.Harlequin.com

Printed in Lithuania

Laurie Batzel lives in the Poconos with her husband, their four two-legged children and their two four-legged children, Stuart the Corgi and Midge the Marvelous Rescue Pup. Her first book, *With My Soul*, was published in 2019, and her essays can be found in several editions of *Chicken Soup for the Soul*, as well as online at *McSweeney's Internet Tendency*, *Longreads* and Harvard University's *Tuesday Magazine*. When not writing romance that is equal parts swoons, sniffles and smiles, she can be found watching too much TV under too many blankets, testing the acceptable limits of caffeine consumption and perfecting her recipe for chocolate chip cookies. Learn more at authorlauriebatzel.com.

Also by Laurie Batzel

Harlequin Heartwarming

A Crystal Hill Romance

The Dairy Queen's Second Chance
The Valentine Plan

Visit the Author Profile page at Harlequin.com.

To anyone who has lost someone they loved:

Their light is still here, guiding you to everything that glitters in this world. Take it and pass along the joy.

Acknowledgments

To my family—my husband, James,
and my kids, Charles, Cameron, Cody and Caroline.
You are all my inspiration, my heart and my home.

To my agent, Stacey Graham, and 3 Seas Literary:
Thank you for going along this journey with me.

To the team at Harlequin Heartwarming, especially
Johanna Raisanen and Kathleen Scheibling,
I am so grateful for your enthusiastic support
and insightful direction.

To my parents, in-laws and extended family,
thank you for all your support and encouragement.

Finally, and always to CJ: Thanks for today.

CHAPTER ONE

WRITER'S BLOCK. The yips. A creative slump with a capital *S*.

Whatever the baker's equivalent was to all of these, Georgia Wright had it.

Normally this wouldn't have been an issue for her business. The small town of Crystal Hill and its occupants didn't typically stray far from the bakery classics when they visited Georgia's Bakery on the east side of the main drag, Jane Street. She could bake cream cheese–frosted cinnamon buns, glazed doughnuts and chocolate chip cookies with her eyes closed. But this time the standards were higher than usual, because she had been tasked with baking a wedding cake for Crystal Hill's equivalent of a royal wedding.

It wasn't just the fact that Georgia's cousin BeeBee, whom she loved like a sister, was the bride. That would be pressure enough to give her stress hives along the back of her arms. But the entire town had been invited to the wedding and subsequently had found themselves swept up in a matrimonial frenzy. Even though it was only September and the wedding wasn't until November 4, every single person in town was already talking about whom they were going to bring as their date, what they were going to wear and who was going to catch the bouquet. Wedding fever was everywhere, and no one was immune.

Well, almost no one.

Georgia shook her head and scratched her arms before turning on her giant mixer. It wasn't that she didn't like weddings. Her own had been lovely, small but elegant with a dessert-for-breakfast buffet that people still talked about eleven years later. It was a day she tried not to think about, however, since her husband had died in an accident nearly five years ago. A wedding was a celebration of the future, of the life a couple planned together. That night he had taken his motorcycle out for a ride, she had lost not only her love and best friend, but that future as well.

As happy as she was for Bill and BeeBee, Georgia couldn't wait for this whole thing to be over and for everyone to go back to their normal lives, where it didn't feel like every single man in town was checking her reflexes for bouquet-catching speed.

When the butter had creamed to a perfect consistency, she added the sugar and the eggs, one at a time. Baking was a meditative act for Georgia—it always had been since she was a little girl helping at the bakery when her mom ran it and it was called the Crystal Hill Bakery and Coffee Shop, a mouthful Georgia had changed when her mom retired and she took over. It cleared her head. The issue now was that baking was the stumbling block in her path. This wedding cake had to be absolutely perfect, both in taste and appearance. It also had to be perfect for Bee-Bee, a dairy farmer who had competed for—and won—the crown of the New York state dairy pageant a year and a half ago solely to afford adding Italian water buffaloes to her herd. An ordinary three-tier vanilla sponge cake with buttercream just wouldn't do the trick. Georgia's feelings over this being the first wedding cake she had to make since her husband's passing would simply have to wait.

Dropping in the dry ingredients and mixing until just combined, she added the chocolate chips to her fudge brownie mix before pouring the batter into the pan and sliding it in the oven. Georgia brushed her hands on her apron, then picked up her phone.

"Shoot," she said, then walked over to the swinging door that separated the kitchen from the bakery shop. "Silas, can you take over back here for me? I have to run down to Caroline's school for meet the teacher night. I shouldn't be long."

Silas Stephenson had retired after serving thirty years as the Crystal Hill high school principal and now worked part-time at the bakery because he had a sweet tooth a mile long and liked that the bakery was right next door to the antiques and jewelry shop over which he lived. He could lift the industrial-size bags of flour Georgia couldn't, and since he had been happily married for almost seven years to the aforementioned jewelry shop's proprietor, he was one of the few men in town who wouldn't be pestering Georgia to be his date to the wedding.

Slipping her apron over her head, she hung it on the wall hook next to the door and grabbed her purse off the hook next to it.

"Silas?" she called out again before walking through the door and slipping her phone in the back pocket of her blue dress. "Did you hear me say I was going out?"

Silas, who was standing behind the counter with his back turned to her, whipped around. His mouth was full of what Georgia guessed was a jelly doughnut, judging by the cascade of powdered sugar down his chin.

He nodded, then swallowed. "I heard. Although when I was there we called it interrogation night," he said with a grimace. "I do not miss those days. Parents coming in complaining to teachers, teachers coming in complaining to me, Ed complaining about my complaining about all of them when I got home."

Georgia pulled a napkin out from the stack next to the glass dome covering a suspiciously small stack of doughnuts and handed it to him. "I'll have you know, I have never complained once to a teacher at these things," she said proudly, then shrugged. "But when your kid is as sweet as Caroline is, what's there to complain about?"

"You got a point there," Silas said.

"And you have raspberry jelly there." Georgia indicated on her own chin, then shook her head. "It's a good thing you didn't ask for much of a salary. You're going to eat all my profits."

"I know," Silas moaned, dabbing at his chin. "But Ed has been on this Mediterranean diet kick ever since we went on that dinner cruise on Chef Bill's boat this summer. Now the closest thing I get to dessert at home is figs with sweetened balsamic vinegar. Figs, Gigi."

She tutted sympathetically, then pulled the lace curtains of the window to one side to peer across the street. "Is the coast clear?"

Silas nodded. "You're safe. I haven't seen Joe

Kim since this morning, and Renata's son is making deliveries across town."

"Phew," Georgia said, swiping a hand jokingly across her forehead. "The last thing I needed this morning was someone else asking me if I had a date to BeeBee's wedding yet." She screwed her lips up and wrinkled her nose. "I'll be so glad when this is all over."

"You still having issues with the plan for the cake?"

"Yes, and now I absolutely regret telling you about that," Georgia said. "I don't want it to get back to BeeBee that I'm stuck. She has enough on her plate already."

She shook her head sympathetically. BeeBee was far less interested in gowns and flower arrangements than the horn-growth rate of her water buffaloes. But as much as Georgia's cousin loved her muddy boots, she loved her town and her fiancé more, so when the council offered to close off the main shopping district so she could have her wedding at the town gazebo, she couldn't say no. She could, however, moan to Georgia repeatedly about wishing she and Bill had eloped.

"I'm sure she'll love whatever you make," Silas reassured her. "You're the best baker in the Mohawk Valley. Heck, the best baker in the state of New York, in my humble opinion."

"Thanks, Si," Georgia said, opening the door. Glancing back over her shoulder, she added, "And don't even think about touching those brownies when you take them out of the oven. I know exactly how many this recipe makes, and I will be counting."

The afternoon sun glinted off Crystal Hill Lake as Georgia walked to her car. Set below the foothills of the Adirondacks, the town's waters were known for their mineral-rich deposits. It had been foundcd as a mining hub over two hundred years ago, and while most of the operations had long since been shut down, the area had become a hot spot for tourists and city dwellers who escaped the oppressive concrete of Manhattan each summer for fresh air and small-town coziness. Closing her eyes and lifting her chin up, Georgia took a moment to enjoy the warmth on her cheeks.

That was a mistake.

When she opened her eyes, the owner of Larry's Dry Cleaning was standing in front of her. She jumped backward into the driver's side of her car and threw a hand over her heart. "Jeepers, you startled me."

"Sorry, Gigi," he said sheepishly. "Usually people smell the detergent on me before they see me coming."

She sniffed, then coughed. "It is a, ahem, very

powerful floral smell." Jerking her thumb over her shoulder, she gestured at the bakery. "Silas is at the counter if you need anything."

"Actually, it was you I was hoping to run into." Larry swiped a bead of sweat from his receding hairline with the back of his arm. "By any chance, do you have plans tonight?"

"I do, as a matter of fact," Georgia replied, feeling blindly behind her for the door handle. "Meet the teacher night at my kid's school. But I did hear the waitress at Mama Renata's—the pretty redhead—talking about a stain she couldn't get out of her apron. She said she had tried everything to get it out and nothing worked. I bet she would appreciate your expert eye. Just a thought."

She flung the door open and slid into the car, waving at Larry from the window as she drove down Jane Street toward the elementary school. The waitress at their local Italian eatery had mentioned the stain on her apron, although it was more of an offhand comment than a desperate plea for help. Larry wasn't a bad guy. All the men in Crystal Hill were nice. Whether it was something in the water—the town's running joke—or just coincidence, the women outnumbered the men in Crystal Hill by a fairly significant margin. Rather than fight against the tides, they embraced it. After all, the schools were highly rated and the streets were beautifully kept and decorated for each holiday season. It was good to live in a matriarchal Brigadoon that had sprung up in the shelter of the Adirondacks, and the men seemed to be happy supporting the women who made it all possible. Nice guys, for sure.

But when you had had Scharffen Berger's chocolate mousse for six years, it was hard to go back to chocolate pudding in the plastic container.

That's why it didn't matter how many men in town stopped by the bakery in hopes of "running into her." They could run ultramarathons and she still didn't plan on changing her mind. Georgia was never getting married again. Mike had been her high school sweetheart, quarterback of the football team and working his way up to assistant chief at the local fire squad before the accident. After the shock had come a sort of numb, gray feeling blanketing her entire world. Her only source of joy, her only reason for finding bits of color, had been her daughter, Caroline. It had been for her sake that Georgia had committed to processing the grief before it swallowed her whole. The key had been reminding herself of the bricks in her life that hadn't revolved around Mike: her work at the bakery and her love for her town. Unfortunately, both of those things were now centered around the idea of marriage.

As she drove, she flipped through the radio stations for a distraction from anything matrimonial. In between the twang of a country song and a heavy metal scream in a language that sounded perhaps like Swedish, an ad seemed to speak directly to her.

"Do you love to bake?" it asked presciently.

"Why, yes I do, disembodied radio voice," she answered with a chuckle.

"Do people constantly ask for the recipes of the desserts you bring to potlucks?"

She turned the corner between the town rec center and the old stone library. "Only if they're new in town and haven't been informed all my recipes are top secret."

"Are you looking for something to stimulate your creativity?"

"Okay, now this is getting eerie," she replied.

"Then you should apply to the Food Network Regional Baking Champion contest," the voice proclaimed excitedly. "Each week the website will post a different recipe challenge. Make a video of yourself baking your recipe, then submit it online. Your videos must be entertaining and your recipes original creations. Go to our website for more details and follow next week as we announce the special guest hosts of the contest."

Her smile faded as she put the car in Park. That all sounded great—except for the fact that she couldn't even come up with a new recipe for a wedding cake she had months to prepare. Plus, when she baked, she concentrated so hard on the process, talking and being entertaining wasn't an option. Caroline called it her "baking coma." There was a lot she would do for her business, but nothing was more important than her town and her family. BeeBee's wedding cake deserved all her focus.

Actually, right now she needed to focus on running because, as usual, she was ridiculously late.

CHAPTER TWO

MALCOLM GULLESON WANTED to hide.

Not from the kids in his third-grade classroom, though. They were his favorite part of the job and the entire reason he put up with all the paperwork and planning and bureaucratic nonsense that came with it. If it weren't for the kids, he never would have taken a job that started early in the morning and then occupied most of his evenings with after-school committees, classroom budget submissions and license-certification requirements.

Kids made him laugh literally every single day. He would never say it out loud, of course, but third grade was his favorite age to teach. They were young enough to be completely unhinged by glee and wonder while old enough to have distinct passions and opinions of their own. This was his first year teaching at Crystal Hill Elementary, but the kids had already made him feel at home, giving him the nickname Mr. G and bringing treasured rocks from their driveways after he told them that he was what people in the geology field called a "rockhound."

Today was meet the teacher night, but it wasn't the parents from whom he needed respite, either. It was always nerve-racking, finding the balance between encouraging anxious parents that they were doing enough to keep their child on track and reminding others that third grade was a little young to be putting together a college application profile. After all, his main concern was their child becoming an enthusiastic learner rather than a junior neurosurgeon. He wasn't a parent himself yet, a personal sore point, but he knew the most important thing they all shared was the desire for the child's happiness.

In a town like Crystal Hill, where the natural scenery was second to none and the people seemed to rally around each other in times of need, raising happy children was probably easier than just about anywhere else. That was one of the reasons why he had chosen this area to settle down in after leaving his last job teaching at a school in midtown Manhattan.

A knock sounded on the door of his classroom, followed by someone who was the source of his need for refuge.

"Hellooo," a high-pitched female voice sang on the other side. "Mr. Gulleson, it's me, Miss

Chattelsmith. Remember, from orientation? I just wanted to see how you were making out." The last two words were punctuated by a throaty giggle at a decibel that would send his parents' Samoyed, Roger, into howling fits. "I mean, how you were doing on interrogation day. A bunch of us are going out for pizza at Mama Renata's afterward. Wanna join?"

Mmm-hmm. He wasn't falling for that again. The last time Miss Alyssa Chattelsmith had invited him somewhere with "a bunch of us" other teachers, the bunch mysteriously was nowhere to be found and it ended up being the two of them at Big Joe's Diner. Fortunately, he had been able to beg off after a single cup of coffee using an early-morning practice with the junior high cross country team he assistant coached as an excuse.

"I'm, uh, busy," he called through the door. "Thanks for the invite, though. Got my next parent coming soon, so I should get back to preparing my notes."

"All right, but I'll be back!" she trilled, and only when the sounds of her heels clicking on the tiled floor grew distant did he feel safe enough to stand and open the door a crack for his next parent.

Alyssa was nice enough, but there were two reasons he was avoiding her frequent invitations for coffee or pizza or swing dancing at the rec center. The first was that she was twenty-four, and while a six-year age difference wasn't insurmountable, she was a *young* twenty-four to Malcolm's thirty, soon to be thirty-one. He had lived in tiny apartments and traveled the world, and now he was looking for someone to settle down with, someone he could start his own family with as soon as possible, without having to wait for them to do any wild oat sowing or game playing. Malcolm didn't want just a girlfriend.

He wanted a wife.

But between arriving at work early to plan lessons, staying at work late for after-school tutoring or coaching on the weekends, there wasn't ample opportunity, time or energy to meet anyone who wasn't a teacher or a parent of one of his students. This, on top of being in a new town and knowing no one, was making his search for Miss Right a bit more complicated than he would have liked.

The second reason was even more of a deal breaker: He would never, ever date anyone involved with his work. Again. The last time had ended in such a disaster that not only had he left the school where they'd worked, it had forced him to adopt sky-high boundaries when it came to mixing his job and his romantic life. It was a sacrifice he was willing to make, because being a teacher would always come first for him. Education had been a key foundation of his family's life, ever since his first toy was a tiny alphabet block, the legacy his incredible adoptive parents had instilled in him, and he wouldn't let them down.

Unfortunately for Malcolm, Alyssa wasn't his only coworker with romantic designs on him. The music teacher, Miss Harrison, had a habit of mysteriously breaking out into renditions of "Till There Was You" from *The Music Man* every time he walked by her classroom, and that was decidedly not on the elementary music syllabus.

There was another knock on the door, softer this time.

Malcolm checked his watch. Hopefully this was his next parent. It was already five minutes after their scheduled time, and if they were any later, he would be off for the rest of the day. He looked up at the door, smiling first at the little girl hovering around her mom's long, flowing skirt. Caroline Wright was the next name on his list, so the woman had to be her mom. His eyes traveled up from Caroline's curly reddish-gold head to a woman with a warm smile and the brightest blue eyes he had ever seen.

Malcolm's throat dried up suddenly. He coughed into his elbow, then stood. "Sorry about that," he said hoarsely, giving a small shake of his head. "Just a little tickle."

The woman frowned and dug into the large emerald green bag over her shoulder. "I have some cough drops in here somewhere," she said, peering deeper into the bag as she searched. "Your voice must be worn out from teaching, then having to talk to parents all evening. I have a juice pouch if you need one." She looked up from the bag and blinked those mesmerizing eyes.

He couldn't help returning her smile. "Tell me you're a mom without telling me you're a mom."

"Guilty," she said with a laugh, ruffling Caroline's hair with one hand. "I could survive a zombie apocalypse for at least a week with just my purse. Longer if I could forage from the glove compartment of my car."

"Good to know," he said. Reaching back for his stack of papers, he shuffled them on the desk, then set them down on Caroline's small desk in front and walked past the chalkboard with his hand extended. "I'm Mr. Gulleson. It's nice to meet you."

"Georgia Wright, Caroline's mom," she answered. Her small hand disappeared in his, and he squeezed it gently before bending down to greet Caroline. "One, two or three today?"

She squinted one eye, then nodded thoughtfully as she spoke. "Three, please."

Of course she chose the most embarrassing

option. Normally Malcolm had zero qualms about doing whatever ridiculous antics would make the kids in his class laugh or feel more at ease. But if he was being completely honest, he had really been hoping she would pick one or two, given that her *very* pretty mom was right there watching his every move.

"Three it is, then." He put one hand on his hip and thrust the other into the air as if he were twirling a lasso, galloping in a circle in place as Caroline mimicked his movements, giggling the entire time.

After they had finished and he directed the little girl to her desk, where there was a coloring book and crayons set up, Malcolm turned back to see Georgia staring at him with her eyebrows all the way up to her strawberry blond hairline.

He sighed and rubbed the bridge of his nose with two fingers. "Yeah, so I give the kids three options for greeting me when they come into the classroom. One is a high five, two is a fist bump and three is cowboy dance party." He lowered his hand and shrugged. "Guess which one is the most popular and will also result in me needing a hip replacement by the time I'm forty."

Georgia crossed her arms and looked as if she was trying very hard to suppress a smile. "Seems like it's kind of a self-inflicted injury, though."

"Anything for the kids," he said truthfully. Gesturing to the grown-up–size chair next to his desk, Malcolm said, "I know all parents have a thousand places to be, so have a seat and we'll get right to it, Mrs. Wright."

Georgia nodded gratefully and spread the long skirt of her blue dress out underneath her legs as she sat down. With the motion, he noticed that she didn't wear a wedding ring. Malcolm silently chastised himself for assuming that a parent had to be married. He taught his students all the time that words mattered, and as he held additional teaching certifications in science, accuracy mattered most of all.

"Obviously, we're only two weeks into the school year, so I'm still getting to know all my students," he said as he reached back and sank into the swivel chair behind his desk. "I operate on the belief that parents are the experts on their children, so I like to take these events as a way to get the inside scoop on how I can help them best. So far Caroline doesn't seem to be struggling with any of the materials we're reviewing from the second-grade curriculum. I've been very impressed with how she seems to be friends with everyone in the class."

"Well, this is a small town, so most of these kids have known each other since preschool," Georgia said. "She's never had a problem making friends. If anything, she might have to be reminded every now and then that she's not running for mayor. Yet," Georgia added with a chuckle.

"She would certainly have my vote." He smiled. "Maybe I can get her to introduce me to the town. I only moved here a month before new teacher orientation, so I'm still getting my Crystal Hill sea legs. You run the bakery on Jane Street, right? One of the parents brought in doughnuts from your shop last week for a birthday. They were the best I've ever had."

"Thank you," she said. Her cheeks flushed, and she pushed a curl behind one ear as she ducked her head. The expression was endearing, and Malcolm had to drag his hand across his face to wipe off the goofy smile and rearrange his features into teacher mode.

"Is there anything specific about Caroline that you feel I should know as her teacher?" he asked, leaning forward on his elbows. "She does seem somewhat reticent about raising her hand to answer questions, so if there is any way to draw her out a little more during classroom discussions, I'd really appreciate the Caroline cheat code."

Georgia chewed on her lower lip, her eyes lifting to the poster behind him depicting the water cycle. "Well, she loves animals," she offered. "Could that help at all?"

"That's technically more biology, which we won't start until spring," he replied doubtfully. "It's good to know for the future, though."

She seemed almost to shrink back into herself, much like he noticed Caroline had, particularly when he went over the science units in the syllabus. He had to fold his hands in his lap to keep from reaching out for her hand to comfort her. She was beautiful and made doughnuts that had literally featured in his dreams since he had them, but this was one boundary he refused to cross. Dating a parent wasn't forbidden in the school's rules; it was, however, strictly against his own personal code of conduct. No fellow teachers, school nurses or parents of students. But he knew parents tended to be harder on themselves than anyone else, so he hastened to find some way to put her more at ease.

"Don't worry," he added in what he hoped was a reassuring tone. "Quiet isn't a bad thing. I won't name names, but I wish at least one of the boys would learn the fine art of zipping the lip."

She laughed, seeming to relax. "I won't say who, but I think I know which one you mean. I guess I'm just a little flummoxed. All her other teachers knew her since she was a baby, so this is the first time I've actually done this with someone new."

"Flummoxed." He gave a thumbs-up. "Great vocabulary word. No worries, Caroline is going to have a wonderful year."

"I hope so," she replied, turning her head back quickly to look at Caroline. "But the school has my contact information, so if there are any issues, please reach out as soon as possible. Really. I'll do anything for my girl. She's—she's my whole world." She looked back at him with eyes that shone with genuine emotion.

Malcolm adjusted his collar again as she fixed those eyes directly on him with a new intensity. The color really was remarkable. They sparkled like gemstones, but not sapphires, which were a darker blue. Turquoise was closer, but it wasn't a faceted gemstone that reflected the light in the same way. Blue zircon, maybe? Oh no, he was rock ruminating again. Even his parents, who had encouraged his interest in geology ever since he started his first rock collection out of driveway gravel, occasionally glazed over when he started fixating.

"Just let me know what you need," he promised, nodding his head back at Caroline to remind himself of his true purpose here. "I'll do anything I can to help her engage with the material."

She nodded and reached up to absently fiddle with a pendant around her neck. The stone caught the light.

Malcolm recognized the stone instantly, and his smile widened to match Georgia's.

CHAPTER THREE

"AND I JUST sat there," Georgia explained to the women sitting in a circle of folding chairs in the basement of the church rectory. "All I gave this nice, hardworking teacher to go on with my child was 'she likes animals.'" She slid into her seat, her cup of lukewarm coffee clutched in both hands over her lap.

It had only been a day since her meeting with Caroline's teacher, but Georgia couldn't stop feeling like she had failed a parenting pop quiz.

Agnes Rhinegold, the leader of the grieving widows' support group, touched her lightly on the arm. "First of all, remember to give yourself grace," she said gently with affirming murmurs emanating from the circle. "Parenting doesn't come with a playbook, especially parenting after a loss. But since it seems to have struck a nerve with you, why do you think you didn't tell the teacher about losing Caroline's father? Wouldn't that be something he should know?"

"I think so," Georgia said hesitantly. She took

a sip of coffee out of habit more than thirst and wrinkled her nose. Blech. It was lucky this was such a great support group, because she certainly wasn't coming for the refreshments. "All her other teachers already knew about Mike, and they didn't bring it up, I think because they didn't want to upset me. You all know how it is—most people are so awkward around young widows or widowers that they feel like it's best to just say nothing at all. I guess it's what I'm used to by now."

"Are you sure that was it?" Agnes pressed. "You said you've been talking about Mike more, especially around Caroline. What was different about this circumstance?"

"I mean, Caroline and I talk about him," Georgia specified. "You know, his rabid love of sports, how he always wanted to be a scientist. I want her to think of him as a real person, not just some picture on the wall." She shook her head. "Maybe because this was a new teacher, I wanted her to have a chance to start fresh. You know, to be a normal kid in class, not one that the teacher feels like they have to tiptoe around certain subjects with. There's just so much pressure to get everything right since I'm on my own here. I can't mess this up."

"I know what you mean," Bryony Wills interjected. She had only just joined the group a few months ago, after her husband had passed away from a long battle with cancer. She was heavily pregnant with a baby they had conceived from the sperm he had frozen before chemotherapy. Rubbing her belly, she shifted in her chair. "I feel so awkward when I have to explain my situation to someone I've never met before, and I'm a grown-up. What's my kid going to say when he or she is going to school? Then I feel bad for worrying about it when I'm lucky to even have this part of him. Thank goodness for science and our oncological fertility specialist," she said with a catch in her throat.

Georgia nodded. Science had always been more Mike's thing than hers, but she had several friends who had conceived through IVF and was in awe of the people who made those babies possible.

"Ultimately, the loss is part of your story," Agnes said. "You get to choose how much of that story you share with the world and when."

Georgia turned those words over in her head on the way home. In a small town, it seemed like everyone already knew everyone else's story. In a way, it was comforting, especially with something difficult and sensitive. Not having to rehash it over and over again was a gift, especially in those early days. However, it also meant that the narrative was perpetually out of her control. There was something to be said for starting fresh, for a completely blank canvas on which to create. And creating was her and Caroline's favorite part of baking. Even as a fussy toddler, she had been mesmerized every time Georgia got out the icing bag and piped lines of sugar roses along the white expanse of one of her cakes.

She put her head back against the seat and groaned. As much as the support group had helped her sort through her emotions over the years, even they couldn't help her figure out what to make for BeeBee's wedding cake. She had even tried making a French croquembouche this morning, but French pastry didn't fit with BeeBee's rustic personality and Bill's restless spirit.

A familiar voice came on the radio, and Georgia leaned forward to turn the volume up.

"Bakers across America are starting to fill out their applications to be regional baking champs on the hottest new Food Network competition," the announcer she had heard yesterday was saying.

"Well, good for them," Georgia responded sarcastically. "Must be nice to actually have ideas."

"The grand prize winner at the end of the four-week event will be featured on national television this spring with their featured dessert and will get to meet the guest hosts of the show, Chase and Anthony, from *Desserts Around the World*."

Georgia's head snapped up. Chase and Anthony were her favorite Food Network personalities. The two had met when Chase was an anchor on a local news station doing a report on ice cream shops of upstate New York. Anthony, only five at the time, had crashed one of the shoots, and the pair was so adorable they ended up being signed to host their own show. It was her and Caroline's favorite comfort watch—whenever they were sick or stressed, they rewatched old episodes to make themselves feel better.

She pulled up in the driveway at her house. Silas was watching Caroline, which meant that she would have fallen asleep on the couch next to him while *Antiques Roadshow* blared on PBS at rock-concert volume. Silas liked to guess whether the appraisal amounts of the objects went up or down and often shouted his estimate so loud that he ended up missing the answer.

She opened the door quietly and closed it behind her. Harley, her enormous Maine coon cat, padded across the foyer to greet her. The house was in its usual state of disarray, with the clutter of Caroline's school stuff scattered in various piles Georgia kept meaning to put away before getting distracted by something else more urgent and the boxes of her new business cards for the bakery stacked in a corner by the stairs.

She sighed and took off her shoes, too weary to do much else.

"Twenty-five hundred, easy," Silas yelled from the living room.

Georgia walked around the corner into the kitchen and stood with her hands on her hips as Silas sat on the couch in the adjoining living room and pointed at the television. There was no sign of Caroline, though.

"What did you do with my daughter?" Georgia asked, dropping her purse on the table and walking into the living room.

Looking startled at the sound of her voice, he switched off the TV before turning to her with his hand over his heart. "Gigi, goodness. You're home earlier than I thought you'd be," he said, then checked his watch and grimaced. "Never mind. I've been in a *Roadshow* time vortex." He inclined his head at the now-black screen. "That was a good one. They filmed it at an estate on the Gold Coast. Caroline's asleep in her room. She seemed pretty tuckered out from the school day."

"Oh." Georgia flopped on the rocking chair in the corner. "That's too bad. I wanted to tell her about the Food Network competition thing I keep hearing ads for. Chase and Anthony are going to be the guest judges."

"Are you going to enter?" he asked. "You love their show. Plus, nobody bakes like you."

"I don't even bake like me right now," she said glumly. "I would love to, but I'm still stuck on BeeBee's cake. I'm pretty sure Sisyphus didn't look at the boulder he had to roll up the hill and go, 'You know what this needs? Another rock.'"

"Maybe you could use this contest as a way to get those creative juices flowing again," Silas suggested, pushing his hands on his knees and standing up from the couch with a groan. "Ugh. I think there's a Barbie doll somewhere under that cushion I was sitting on for the last hour."

"You know, that's not a bad idea," Georgia replied as she rocked the chair back and forth. "Maybe what I need is a distraction from the wedding—I mean, the wedding cake. It's like when you're looking for one thing and you just can't find it, so you go do something else and that's when you realize where you left the thing."

Silas, who had been digging between the couch cushions as she talked, suddenly withdrew a blond Barbie with its arms sticking up. "If by the thing, you mean the doll whose hands are now imprinted in my buttocks, then yes. If you mean metaphorically, yes to that, too." He chucked the doll to Georgia and shrugged. "What have you got to lose?"

CHAPTER FOUR

MALCOLM WALKED DOWN Jane Street toward Georgia's Bakery on a mission. Unfortunately, the mission had nothing to do with procuring another one of those delicious doughnuts, although if one happened to call out his name while he was there, it would be rude not to answer.

This was a teaching-related mission. Even though it was Saturday, the thing about his job was that it seemed to invade almost every hour of the day and week. He laughed every time he heard people talk about how nice it must be to have a teacher's schedule with summers and holidays off. He supposed that would be nice, if those off hours didn't also include answering emails and calls to fill out questionnaires for pediatric ADHD assessments, lesson planning or trying to figure out the latest software platform he was using for his classroom that year. He knew other teachers put these things off for their planning periods during school hours, but even his planning periods seemed to fill up fast with demands for his time, and drops in a bucket soon became a deluge.

Plus, when it came to concerns about his students, he didn't want to waste any time.

It had been over a week since meet the teacher night at school, and he had noticed something about Caroline Wright that made him curious. She had begun to raise her hand and participate in classroom discussions with excitement for learning about everything…except science. Having done his senior undergrad project on engaging female students in STEM learning, he knew the statistics for young women entering the hard sciences were still abysmally low, even though they were starting to improve. The key was early encouragement, to catch signs of insecurity or reticence as soon as they started to show. Caroline was a bright student with potential to excel in anything she chose, and he refused to let her self-limit.

His hypothesis had formed during their first science lesson on the water cycle. He had started the lecture with his typical chant, "When I say H_2, you say—" and the entire class was encouraged to scream "O" at the top of their lungs, something third graders rarely had problems accomplishing. But Caroline didn't scream along. Thinking she might have been dehydrated, he stopped the chanting with a clap of his hands.

"While we're on the subject, let's take a water break." He had encouraged everyone to grab their water bottles and take a good long sip, which she did. "Okay. Now can anyone tell me what the first step in the water cycle is? Bonus points if you use the scientific term that starts with the letter *P*—" He had held his hand up, instantly regretting that choice. "Jeremy, I can already tell what you're thinking, and I'm going to stop you right there. This has nothing to do with the bathroom and everything to do with the natural process where water comes down from the sky. It's…raise your hands if you know it."

Everyone in the class had raised their hand—everyone except Caroline. Okay, so maybe she was having an off day or not feeling well. But at recess, she played happily with the other kids, squealing with her best friends as they took turns going down the hot slide in the early-afternoon sun. Later during the math lecture, she volunteered to go up to the board to solve the problem of the day. So she wasn't intimidated by the *M* in STEM, that much was for sure.

But the next day, it was the same reaction to the science lesson. Taking Georgia's tip about her love of animals, he brought out his bearded dragon puppet to perform the water cycle rap, aka *Condensation Nation*. Sure, he wasn't Lin-Manuel Miranda or anything, but this rap had taken him weeks to craft over the summer, and he'd even had one of his friends who was a professional DJ in the city lay down a beat to go with it. Yet she remained impassive at best. The only one to show less enthusiasm for his performance was Newton the actual lizard, who Malcolm suspected found the whole thing slightly demeaning to his species.

If not even Rap Master Beard-o could get her excited, it was time to ask for help. Hence, today's mission. He pushed through the door of the bakery, determined not to get distracted by the incredibly delicious smell of fresh-baked yeasted bread that hit him as soon as he walked in.

Georgia's wide smile that greeted him from behind the counter, however, was so dazzling he almost forgot his own name, let alone his purpose in coming here today.

"Mr. Gulleson," she said warmly. "It's nice to see you here. What can I get for you? We have fresh maple-glazed toffee chip scones that are minutes out of the oven."

His mouth watered at the sight of the cinnamon-colored frosting on the crumbly pastries, but then he shook his head. "I'm actually here to talk to you about Caroline. Do you have a minute?"

She wiped her hands on her apron. "Sure. The morning rush won't start for a few minutes. Have a seat, I'll bring you some coffee. On the house."

He pulled a chair out from one of the center tables and motioned for her to sit. "No need. I'll be ordering pretty much your entire case and a vat of coffee to go."

"Uh-oh." She sat in the chair and gave him a worried frown. "This must be bad. Either you're trying to placate me by buying all my baked goods or you have to self-medicate with enough sugar to take out an army of hummingbirds. Spit it out, Mr. Gulleson. What's going on?"

Darn it, she was pretty and funny. This was only getting more difficult. "Caroline is doing great in school." He started with a positive. "But I'm concerned about her lack of participation during our science lessons. She goes from actively raising her hand, smiling and laughing, to giving one-word answers, and that's only if pressed. Her answers on the worksheets are exemplary, so she knows the subject. I'm a little perplexed by it, so I was wondering if you had any insight as to why she's seeming to clam up during science time only."

"To be honest, science was always my least favorite subject in school," Georgia said. "I always leaned more toward the creative side of things, like art or writing or— Oh, no," she exclaimed, clapping a hand to her head. "This is all my fault."

Malcolm leaned forward on the table and put a hand up. "Don't blame yourself," he said. A desperate need to comfort her overtook him. "This isn't a big deal. I just wanted to bring you in to talk about it before it becomes a problem."

She shook her head and slumped down into the chair. "That's nice of you to say, but I should have seen this coming. She's always been a mama's girl, helping me at the bakery and with deliveries. We do everything together. I'm sure at some point I subconsciously passed on my dislike of all this stuff to her," Georgia said, waving her hand at him.

She looked utterly miserable, which matched the way Malcolm felt at the moment. He had approached this all wrong. This was his eighth year of teaching; he knew better than to come at a parent so directly, even with a compliment sandwich. Moms like Georgia took on so much responsibility and then internalized the smallest complication as a failure. *Rookie mistake, Gulleson,* he chastised himself before standing and walking around the table to kneel in front of Georgia.

"Hey," he said softly. "You did nothing wrong. Sometimes it takes time for the light bulb to click with certain things. Sometimes it's just not their bag, and that's okay, too. Your daughter is a smart, wonderful kid, and that's definitely a reflection of the care she receives at home. You're doing a great job."

She took a long, deep breath, then looked him in the eyes. "Thanks," she said softly. "I didn't realize how much I needed to hear that. Especially since I'm doing this all on my own. It gets really overwhelming."

Aha. So she *was* a single mother. He fought back the rising tide of relief. Not that he was going to ask her out or anything. While dating a parent wasn't expressly forbidden, either, it fell along the same lines of potential chaos as dating a fellow teacher. The possibility that it could interfere with his ability to teach effectively was enough to make it off-limits for his own code of conduct. Everything he did was for the kids, even if it made his own dream—finding a partner to have a family with—a little harder to reach.

Rising to his feet, Malcolm crossed the room to adjust a napkin dispenser on a table that had been bothering him since he sat down. For the son of an engineer and a physicist, the house rule had always been *if it's not a right angle, it's a wrong angle*. Everything in his world had revolved around his parents' passions for science, from the family vacations to the meals his mom had arranged to look like protons. Then inspiration struck and Malcolm indulged himself in a congratulatory grin before turning around.

"I've got it," he said, turning his palms upward. "To quote Archimedes, 'Eureka!'"

Georgia's face brightened hopefully. "What is it?"

"You said she loves to help you in the bakery and does everything you do, right?"

"She's a mama's girl, always has been," Georgia said proudly.

"What is baking if not science with a utilitarian and delicious purpose?" He went back to his laptop on the table and started looking up chemical formulas in baking. "Leavening agents are simply chemical reactions. The way temperature and humidity impact a bake could be correlated to environmental studies…somehow, I'm sure."

"There's just one problem," Georgia said, cringing. "I don't really understand any of that stuff. I learned to bake with my mom, who learned from my grandma. Baking is intuitive to me. By the time I learned any of this stuff, it will be too late."

"Okay, so I can help you with that," he said. Malcolm leaned against the counter and gestured to the glass container to his right. "I mean, I'm not a baker, but no one researches better than me. Give me a few days, then I could come over and explain the science behind the recipes while you two bake together. Let's see if something sparks," he said, then a hot flush spread on the back of his neck and he rubbed beneath the collar of his button-down shirt with one hand. "I mean, if something sparks her interest."

Georgia's light eyebrows knit together, and she tipped her head to one side. "You'd do that in your spare time for just one kid?" she asked, her voice raising with incredulity. "I knew teachers were superheroes, but this is going above and beyond. The thing is, I don't even use recipes all that often. I've been baking the same standards for so long that I could probably do it blindfolded." She rolled her eyes, then added, almost to herself, "That would make an interesting presentation for the baking contest..." When she trailed off, her eyes narrowed as if trying to see something in the distance, then she looked up and pointed a finger at him. "You could actually help me in more ways than one." For the first time since they had started talking, she flashed that brilliant smile at him.

Malcolm swallowed hard. "Anything," he said hoarsely. As she rose and walked quickly toward him, her full skirt swinging around shapely legs he should not have been noticing, the open-ended nature of his acceptance began to feel like a dangerous promise. As she walked past him to go back behind the counter, the tantalizing smell of vanilla hung in the air. This was the kind of woman he really would do anything for…except she was his student's parent, and therefore, *anything* had its limits.

"How would you feel about filming these demonstrations for a national baking contest?" she asked, pouring coffee into a large to-go cup and handing it to him with those wide blue eyes looking imploringly back at him.

Filming himself baking? Certainly, out of all of the out-of-the-box things he had done for his students, this was a first. This was well out of his comfort zone. Doing a lecture about geology for his teacher Instagram account? No problem. Filming workouts for the kids on the track team to practice at home? Easy-peasy. But this was something he had never done before. He would rather she had asked him to do his cowboy dance on national television.

Then Caroline burst through the back door of the bakery, a streak of maple frosting dashed across her cheek.

"Please say you'll do it, Mr. G," she begged, standing next to her mom and pushing up from the counter with her hands as she jumped up and down.

Now, how could he say no to that?

CHAPTER FIVE

THE SECOND MR. GULLESON agreed to her plan, Georgia regretted asking him.

She was in the middle of the worst baking slump of her life, for one thing. Entering a competition in which creativity was stressed as one of the large qualifiers was just setting herself up for failure. Her hope had been that the contest would somehow motivate her to get out of her comfort zone and come up with the perfect idea for BeeBee's wedding cake while also giving Georgia a chance to meet two of her favorite Food Network personalities. Your classic two-birds-with-one-baking-stone scenario. If this didn't work, however, she would still be in a slump and now everyone would know it.

The even bigger source of her baker's remorse was asking Mr. Gulleson to be part of the demonstration. He was cute. Very cute. So cute he should have been carrying a shield with a big white star on it instead of a class roster sheet. His dark hair was cropped short and the eyes behind his wire-rimmed glasses were the same midnight black. He reminded her a little bit of Keanu Reeves and she wondered if, like Keanu, he had Asian heritage. He wore a plaid button-down shirt and khakis that showed off a trim figure. He was under six foot, maybe a few inches taller than her own five foot six, but that was probably a good thing for an elementary school teacher who spent all day around tiny humans. Everything about him was tidy and neatly pressed. Georgia was suddenly very conscious of the thin dusting of flour on her skirt.

She could not, would not have a crush on her daughter's third-grade teacher. She had already touched her hair twice in the last five minutes and there had definitely been some eyelash batting. He was not going to get any less cute or any less off-limits the more time they spent together, so why on earth had she asked him to be her partner in the baking competition videos? Sure, him explaining the science behind the baking process as she demonstrated the recipe would be a great hook for the contest, plus the fact that most of the viewers voting would be women meant a little male eye candy would go a long way in terms of getting her to the final round. But none of that mattered compared to her daughter's well-being. Fortunately, it wasn't too late to reverse course.

Georgia opened her mouth to tell him never mind, but before she could get the words out, small arms wrapped themselves around her waist.

"Mom, this is going to be so much fun," Caroline squealed. "Mr. G is going to make baking videos with us? I can't wait to tell Kylie and Taylor!"

"Um." Georgia looked back at Mr. Gulleson, then tugged Caroline toward the coffeepot on the back counter and bent down to whisper to her. "I think I spoke too soon, sweetheart. It was just an idea I was throwing around, but now that I've thought a bit more about it, maybe we should slow down a little."

Caroline frowned, her bottom lip poking out in what Georgia called her "sad monkey" face. "Why? The contest sounds great and Mr. G is really funny. He'll totally help you win."

"The contest isn't what's most important," Georgia said. "What Mr. Gulleson and I are most interested in is getting you more excited about learning science. Maybe we could just arrange for some after-school tutoring. Here. Without me."

"Sorry, I couldn't help overhearing." Mr. Gulleson spoke up as he launched himself off the counter and turned to face them. "Teachers' ears are extra sensitive, especially when it comes to people whispering about them." He winked at Caroline, and Georgia's heart rose like a perfectly cooked soufflé.

"It's just that I hate to take so much of your time with something like this." Georgia straightened up to gesture at him. "It would be a couple hours once a week, maybe more if you needed to go over the recipe information ahead of time. The ad said the contestants needed to post a video of each challenge every Friday for the next month. We couldn't ask you to do that."

He shrugged. "I'm new in town, so I don't really have anything else going on," he said. "Plus, I'd get to sample whatever we baked, right?"

Georgia grimaced. "Don't get too excited about that. The ad said they wanted creativity in the challenges. That means you're more likely to be a guinea pig for new recipes, and I make no guarantees about how good they'll be." *Especially now that I'm in the world's worst slump*, she added in her head.

"My mommy's cookies are the best in the world," Caroline added proudly and unhelpfully. "Plus, if we win, you just said we might get to meet Chase and Anthony. That would be so cool. We watch their show all the time." She turned to Mr. Gulleson, who looked over at Georgia.

"I promise you wouldn't be imposing," he said. "When I taught overseas, I actually had to stay with one of the students' families for a few weeks while I waited for an apartment to open up, and we did all kinds of science experiments at their kitchen table. It really brought the lessons to life in a whole new way, so I think this could be a way to get Caroline interested in the practical applications of science. Besides, you'll be more lively company for Friday evenings than Newton."

"Newton?" His dog, maybe? He seemed like the kind of guy who would have a big golden retriever. Not to mention a beautiful wife. No way this guy was single.

"Newton's our class pet, a gecko. He comes to my apartment on the weekends. He's not much of a sparkling conversationalist. Then again, neither was his namesake, Sir Isaac Newton, if contemporary records are to be believed."

Darn it, he was funny, too. The only recipe she saw here was one for disaster. Georgia looked down at Caroline's pleading face. "Will you listen to Mr. G while we're making the videos? That's the only thing that matters to me."

"I will, I promise," Caroline said.

Georgia screwed up her face, trying to find some other reason to back out and coming up empty. "Then I guess we're doing this. I'll go online tonight and fill out the application. The ad on the radio said it kicks off next week, so as soon as I see what the first challenge is, I'll start working on a recipe."

Ugh, that was going to be painful. She hated sitting down and figuring out the exact measurements, writing down step-by-step directions. Baking was—during her normal non-slump days—joyful and freeing for her. She'd been doing it since before she could even read the recipes in her mom's tattered cookbook. Maybe there was something in there that she could tweak for some of the challenges. It had been years since she'd cracked it open.

"Here's my cell phone number," Mr. Gulleson said as he leaned over the table and wrote on the back of a napkin. He folded it and handed it to Georgia with a wide smile. The man even had perfect deep dimples like a movie star. If he was single, the other teachers were probably swarming him every second of the day. Male elementary teachers were a rare enough breed as it was, and to find one this good-looking? That was like finding the Holy Grail in the mug aisle at Target. It just didn't happen. "Why don't you call me and let me know when you need me."

Georgia put a finger over her lips to stop the sigh from escaping. No. She would not be needing anything from him or any man other than a purely professional transaction. She would simply have to keep reminding herself that he was Caroline's teacher. That was all.

"Thanks," she said, taking the paper out of his hand. Their fingertips brushed lightly for a whisper of a moment, and the tingles reverberated through her even after he had closed the door behind him, his arms filled with a box of scones and several doughnuts.

Fortunately, Caroline's nonstop stream of chatter kept Georgia from focusing too hard on unsuitable tingles.

"I can't wait to see what the challenges are going to be," she said from the corner booth. "If you win, can I come and meet Chase and Anthony?"

"Pump the brakes, kiddo," Georgia answered, tossing her daughter a raised eyebrow as she steered her through the back door of the bakery. "Are you sure you're okay with Mr. Gulleson coming over and helping like this? Because if it's weird or embarrassing to have your teacher come over, I can text him and call this all off. This is just to get you more involved with science. I don't care about winning."

"I want Mr. G to come over," Caroline said instantly. "He's really funny and nice. You'll definitely win if you have him on the videos. I heard one of the other teachers say that he's a tasty snack. That means he knows all about good food, right?"

"Erm, right, that's exactly what that means," Georgia said, choking back a laugh. Sometimes it was really good to be reminded that kids heard *everything*. "Don't get your hopes up about winning, though. I'm just hoping that this will motivate me to get some ideas for Cousin BeeBee's wedding cake."

Caroline tipped her head to one side and pursed her lips thoughtfully. The expression was so like her dad's, prompting that bittersweet combination of grief and joyful memories that still caught Georgia by surprise even five years after losing him. The pain didn't lessen over time and Georgia didn't expect it to, yet it changed continually. What had once been a darkness weighing down every other emotion was now more like living in the moment just before sunrise. The world around her still felt shadowed and dim, yet glimmers of happiness were able to pierce through the barren branches and make their way inside her. The tears still flowed when she and Caroline talked about Mike, but so did the smiles now.

"What about an ice cream cake shaped like her water buffaloes?" Caroline finally suggested.

Georgia laughed. "Bill already put the kibosh on any and all wedding cakes shaped like

BeeBee's animals," she said before adding, "Although he didn't say anything about *cookies* shaped like water buffaloes. I might have to mention that loophole to BeeBee at our tasting next week. Now, why don't you go wash that icing off your face before you start attracting flies."

Silas came out of the pantry in a rush, surreptitiously brushing crumbs out of his mustache. "What are we giggling about over here?"

"Well..." Georgia hesitated. "I spontaneously decided to enter a Food Network online baking contest with Caroline's ridiculously good-looking teacher as my recipe demonstration partner because of her complete lack of interest in science and my apparent desire to humiliate myself in front of the entire internet." She folded her arms over her chest. "Other than that, nothing new and exciting."

"Ooh, is that the new teacher everyone is talking about? The one they call Mr. G, which, if the whisper network is correct, is short for Mr. Gorgeous?" Silas leaned on the steel counter and put his chin in his hands. "I heard he looks exactly like that actor in that movie? The bad guy from the Jane Austen remake on Netflix? Not that I've seen it one or five times."

Georgia smiled and shook her head. "Never change, Si." She pushed the door open and did a quick assessment of the case in front. "We're running low on black and whites. Is the next batch cool enough to frost yet?"

"I was just checking on those before you came in," Silas said with a wink.

"And by checking, do you mean eating?"

"It's called quality control," he said, standing upright indignantly. "I'll go back and get those started, but don't think that means I'm giving up on a full report about your encounter with Professor Hot—"

"Caroline, you're back from the bathroom," Georgia said loudly, throwing a glare at Silas, who promptly backed into the kitchen without finishing his sentence. "Go ahead and get started on your homework. I'm going to look up the recipe prompt for the competition this week so I can start planning what I'm going to make."

"You mean what you and Mr. Gulleson are going to make," Caroline said as she pulled a worksheet out of her folder. She started to write her name, then looked up. "I promise you'll like him, Mommy. All the lady teachers at school do."

A hoot of laughter sounded from the kitchen, and Georgia buried her head in her hands.

Not liking Mr. Gulleson was the least of her worries right now.

CHAPTER SIX

MALCOLM HAD OFFICIALLY fallen into one of the great traps of history, on par with engaging in a land war in Asia during the winter.

He had begun a staring contest with a gecko.

Scientifically, he knew that most geckos didn't actually blink at all. With a clear membrane that covered their eyes to keep them moist and an agile tongue that could actually reach the eye if necessary, there was no endgame here that allowed him to win. And yet, here they sat, Malcolm on the small rocking chair that had furnished every apartment he had lived in since college and Newton the gecko in his tank that, with its faux-rock caves, skulls and even a few succulent plants, was far more decorated than the blank walls of his apartment.

He had furniture, of course. The aforementioned chair, a bed and, most importantly, shelves for his rock collections that, despite having grown quite extensive over the years, were neatly categorized and labeled, each mineral and gemstone in its place. Efficiency was the soul of the scientific method, and everything in his life was in its place. Everything except one box that had come back with him from his year teaching abroad in China. He had yet to figure out a category for its contents, so it remained packed and stowed away in a corner of his bedroom so as not to cause clutter.

Newton continued to challenge him with his black-hole eyes, as if daring him to recognize the fact that he was almost thirty-one years old and remained unmarried, childless and still living in small bachelor-pad apartments.

At that thought, Malcolm gave up and blinked. "You win this time, Professor," he said to Newton before shaking papaya-flavored gecko food out of the package and into the dish in Newton's terrarium. It was a far cry from the lizard's natural diet of mealworms, flies and other insects, yet feeding live creatures to a reptile was simply a bridge too far. Plus, Newton was on a special medication for an immune deficiency, and it was much easier to get the pill into a treat rather than risk losing a finger shoving it directly into the lizard's mouth. He sighed and put his hands on his knees to push to a stand.

He didn't even *like* reptiles all that much. You couldn't take a gecko for a walk around the neighborhood or get hours of entertainment watching them chase a laser pointer. They just wandered around their little habitats, stared unnervingly into your soul and slept for long periods of time in their little caves. Malcolm kept a picture of his parents' dog, Roger, as his screen saver on his laptop as another reminder of what he had to look forward to someday. Someday when he had a house with a yard. A wife, a child.

Someday needed to hurry up and get here *yesterday*.

Crossing the room, he picked his phone up off the charging station on his small work desk and marked the monthly medication as completed on his calendar app with more than a little satisfaction. Was there any better feeling than accomplishing a task, no matter how trivial, and then crossing it off your list? If there was, he had yet to discover it.

The next item on his calendar for today made his smile widen. This evening he was going to Georgia's house to help her and Caroline with their video for the cooking show challenge. Ever since they had talked at the bakery he had been studying the chemistry of baking, swapping his *National Geographic*s for *Cooking Illustrated*. While technically he had never actually baked anything, he didn't anticipate running into too much difficulty. It was science. If you followed the list of directions in the recipe precisely, the dish should come out baked as intended. Easy squeezy.

The challenge for him was going to be engaging Caroline with the actual science behind the recipe's success. All his attempts to get her to actively participate in this week's science topic had been met with nods and one-word responses when in every other subject she was excited and downright chatty. There were studies that suggested girls were conditioned as young as elementary age to believe they weren't naturally as capable at STEM as boys. In the past, he had definitely observed that to be true with math, but that was his best guess as to why she seemed intimidated by the subject.

Well, that changed today. Malcolm loaded up his messenger bag with the children's book about Marie Curie he would "accidentally" leave behind and the set of carved wooden mixing spoons his mother had insisted on sending to him wherever he went, even all the way to China. She knew very well he didn't cook, and yet she had always claimed one day they would come in handy. After swapping out his teacher's uniform of button-down shirt and khakis for jeans and a T-shirt that said Geology Rocks, he was ready to go.

"Be good while I'm gone," he said to Newton, putting his finger on the outside of the tank.

Shouldering his bag, he locked the door behind him and clattered down the outside entrance steps of the apartment he was renting. It was on the third floor of a very old house conveniently across the street from the school. This was the first job where he'd been able to walk to work, and it was a privilege he didn't think he would ever take for granted. It meant mornings where he caught the first light of dawn slipping out between still-darkened trees and finding the secret dewdrops on the grass like hidden diamonds. It meant time to make lists, to plan. To dream about the hopefully not too distant future.

As he crossed the road and hopped over the curb onto the sidewalk that led around the school to a small residential cul-de-sac, Malcolm's thoughts wandered to the items on the checklist of his life. First on the list was finding a house available in a neighborhood exactly like this one. That way when he accomplished the next and most important item on his list—getting married—they wouldn't have to wait to start a family of their very own. When you knew exactly what you wanted, having to wait for it was a special kind of torture. Like smelling chocolate chip cookies in the oven as they baked, knowing that they still had to cool for a few minutes before they could be eaten without incurring a seriously burned tongue from molten chocolate.

Thinking about chocolate rounded him back to the purpose of this evening's activity. They were making brownies, one of his favorite treats. Growing up, he had thought his mom was the best baker in the world. Eventually he realized that the homemade brownies he loved so much were actually courtesy of Betty Crocker mixes, but that didn't diminish his affection for them. On the contrary, it meant that whenever he was at the grocery store and saw that signature red box, he thought of his mom standing at the stove with a metal mixing bowl and the wooden spoon she let him lick the batter off when she was done. She and his dad had instilled in him from the beginning that family was the most important thing in life.

Unlike the later revelation of the brownie mix, Malcolm had always known he was adopted. Pictures of his parents traveling to the orphanage in China to pick him up had been placed on the mantel above the fireplace for the world to see the moment their family had been created. Not to mention the fact that both his parents were tall redheads with pale skin that burned instantly in the only five minutes of heat Minnesota got in the summer. His adoption had been closed, which meant his adoptive parents knew nothing about his birth parents; however, his caregivers had told the Gullesons they believed Malcolm to be only half Chinese, judging by some early genetic testing. He had always loved hearing the story about their journey, how they had waited for years, then finally received the news that they were matched with a three-month-old baby boy. How they had sent a care package with a small stuffed panda bear he still kept with him wherever he traveled and how grateful they were to his early caregivers, who had showered him with love and affection until his parents came to bring him homc. It was his favorite bedtime story, and he couldn't wait until he could tell his own child the story of how their family came to be.

He just had to meet the kid's mother first.

Checking his phone for the address Georgia had texted him, Malcolm curved along the sidewalk, stopping in front of a sunshine-yellow Cape Cod with white shutters and potted marigolds lining the path like small floral torches. He rang the doorbell and took a step back to admire a dancing rainbow flung onto the white door by the sunlight refracting through the glass wind chimes hanging from the porch. He smiled, thinking about how much fun it was going to be to teach that section to this group of kids. Explaining to them how light traveled in a straight line until it met the rectangular shape of the prism, which refracted the light into the colors, was an abstract and, some educators argued, overly advanced concept for third graders to grasp. But every year he taught it, the children would gasp at the sudden transformation. Every year he knew at least one kid would be inspired to learn more about science because of the beauty of that experiment. That was why he spent his precious hours off doing things like recording explanations of the science behind baking. Making a difference, one kid at a time.

The door swung open, and Georgia appeared behind the screen. She was wearing makeup this time, and the sparkles on her eyelids and cheeks reminded him of the tiny druzy crystals you could find on certain types of rocks in this area. Between the makeup and the halo of the light behind her golden hair, a shimmer surrounded her. Malcolm swallowed hard. Like a magpie, he had always been drawn to shiny things.

"Mr. Gulleson, it's good to see you," she said, waving him in with one hand while holding the door open with the other. "Caroline's so excited that you're helping us with this competition video. She's been talking about it nonstop for the last week."

"Call me Malcolm," he said as he stepped through the door, then nearly tripped on a pair of roller skates in the middle of the foyer. "Whoops,

I almost sprained my foot wrist there." He chuckled to himself.

Georgia gave him a quizzical expression. "Foot wrist?"

"My ankle." He picked his foot off the ground and wiggled it in the air. "Sorry, you teach elementary school for long enough, you start to lose some of your grown-up words. At my last doctor's appointment, I told them I had some clicking in my legbow, and the doctor started to check me for signs of a stroke until I pointed to my knee."

Georgia laughed. "I get it. When Caroline was a baby, she needed to be rocked so much that I'd find myself swaying side to side in the bakery even when I wasn't holding her. The things we do for our kids," she said with an exaggerated roll of her eyes.

"Like entering a baking competition with a third-grade teacher whose culinary skills are limited to toast and microwave popcorn?"

"Exactly." She pointed a finger gun at him, then cocked her head to one side. "Although the competition is as much for me as it is for her— Oh, watch out for the vacuum cleaner," she warned him.

Malcolm dodged the vacuum in the middle of the doorway only to back into a laundry basket sitting in the entryway to the kitchen. His heart nearly stopped when the clothes inside it started to move, but it resumed its normal rhythm when they emitted a disgruntled meow and an enormous orange cat with tufts of fur puffing around its ears picked its head up from under the pile of clothing.

"That's Harley," Georgia explained, nodding at the cat. "Her favorite thing in life is to wait until I've just taken clean clothes out of the dryer, then make a nest. Sorry about the clutter," she added. "Between the bakery and running Caroline to activities and helping my cousin with wedding plans, I just can't get on top of the housework. Cards on the table—I'm not the most organized housekeeper to begin with, but life is especially crazy right now."

Malcolm nodded. "Understandable." As he walked into the kitchen, however, he had to stuff his hands in his pockets to stop himself from going into hyper-cleaning mode. He didn't know how anyone could function with stuff just lying around. The kitchen, at least, was tidy, he noted with no small amount of relief. Georgia had set out a mixing bowl and ingredients on top of an island, and the black cooktop was wiped clean below a cheery tile backsplash with a sunflower design. On a stool in front of a round kitchen table, Caroline perched behind a tripod with a phone set up to record.

"Hi, Mr. G." She waved cheerily at him, then pointed at the sink behind the island. "Don't forget to wash up."

"Thanks, Caroline," he said. After washing his hands and shaking them dry, he turned to see Georgia holding an apron in front of her with an apologetic wrinkle of her face.

"I'm so sorry," she said. "Fun aprons are kind of my thing. This is the manliest one I could find."

The manly apron in question was festooned with barnyard animals performing what appeared to be some sort of ballet. Cows leaped gracefully among sheep in tutus interspersed with a chorus of posing chickens. *Manly* was definitely not the word he would have used, but Caroline's stifled giggle from behind him was all the motivation he needed. He took the apron and pulled it over his head, turning to strike a pose for the little girl.

"I mean, I think I'm pulling it off," he said as Caroline nearly fell off the stool.

He felt a tug on the strings from behind him and turned his head to see Georgia tying the apron for him. "Thanks for being a sport," she whispered. "I worry so much about her, but when she laughs, it makes me feel like everything's going to be okay."

Was there a time when everything wasn't okay

for them? Aside from her Marcel Marceau impression during science lectures, she seemed to be a happy kid with lots of friends. This was the other reason he devoted his out-of-class time to things like this: You never really knew a kid's full story from the time spent with them in the classroom. He leaned back a little to whisper in return, "No problem."

Georgia's eyes locked with his, and for a moment, it felt like everything else in the room faded into the background. He was close enough to smell the lingering scent of vanilla on her own pink-checkered apron, so close that he could see the freckles above her upper lip. She was so pretty…and so not the woman he needed to be thinking about that way.

Straightening up, Malcolm cleared his throat. "So, uh, how are we doing this?"

"Well." Georgia tucked a curl behind one ear, avoiding his gaze. "I'll do the baking, you do the teaching. Caroline is going to record the video as a live stream to the Food Network social media page. Sound good?"

"No, I mean, like, what recipe are you using?" He took two steps, then leaned over to pick up the messenger bag he had set down on the table behind Caroline. "I printed out one from *Cook's Illustrated.* They do a nice job of explaining the science behind everything."

Georgia shrugged. "We can use that if you want. I don't really use actual recipes that much anymore."

Caroline made a small noise.

"Bless you," Malcolm said offhandedly, rubbing his forehead with his hand. "What do you mean, you don't use a recipe? How do you know what measurements to use?"

Caroline seemed to sneeze again.

"Bless you," Georgia said this time before turning narrowed eyes back to Malcolm and planting her hands on her hips. "Um, I've been baking my entire life. It's intuitive."

"It's science," Malcolm argued. "Science isn't intuitive. It's a process. You perform experiments based on hypotheses with precise parameters and measurements. If you just toss around acids and bases willy-nilly, you never know what caused the subsequent, but inevitable, explosion."

"Excuse me, sir," Georgia argued, irritation hardening the soft tones in her voice. "I have never once had an explosion in my kitchen. Okay, one time, but that's how you learn not to leave Pyrex on a hot stove." She shuddered. "It was my good speckled one, too."

He could tell she was fighting annoyance with him as much as he was fighting his attraction to her. For some reason, this made pushing her buttons even more irresistible. "I'm just saying there's a right way to do things."

Her nostrils flared, and it was the cutest thing in the world.

Caroline made her noise even louder this time.

"Bless you," Georgia and Malcolm said simultaneously.

"I'm not sneezing," Caroline whispered. "I'm recording."

CHAPTER SEVEN

GEORGIA WHIPPED HER head around so fast a curl flew out and stuck to the brand-new lip gloss she had bought for these videos.

"Hi, guys," she said in the voice that Caroline called her "nice phone voice." "We're live streaming for the Food Network's Regional Baking Champion contest. I'm Gigi and this is science teacher Mr. G."

The words came out before she had time to realize how cringey and cutesy their names together were. Out of the corner of her eye, she saw Malcolm wordlessly mouth "Gigi?" and gritted her teeth into a forced smile.

"For today's baking challenge, we're baking black-and-white brownies, an homage to the classic black-and-white cookies that have become synonymous with my home state of New York. As you heard from our little promo there—" she stepped to the side and gestured for Malcolm to stand next to her "—we're going to be showing you that the magic of baking is actually science."

Malcolm cleared his throat and started talking in what she assumed was the teacher version of her phone voice. It was smooth yet animated and ridiculously charming, like if Lin-Manuel Miranda was updating the Mr. Rogers show. "That's right. For example, you know how some brownies have that glossy, crackly top—"

"Oh, I love a good crackle top," Georgia interrupted him. "Sorry, go on."

"Well, that top is thanks to a chemical process similar to the way light refracts through crystal prisms to make rainbows," he explained. "When you use granulated sugar in a brownie recipe, the sucrose forms a smoother surface that reflects the light in a singular sheen, while the sugar molecules rise and dry during the baking to give the top layer that crisp effect we all love."

"That's interesting," Georgia said sincerely.

"That's science," he remarked wryly. "You know, the method for testing formulas and recipes until you're able to predict the outcome with reasonable certainty."

"I don't have a problem with science." She tossed a sideways glance at Caroline, the reason she was building up to a stress-induced migraine from working with this ridiculously opinionated man. “I’m just saying it’s not the only way to do things.”

“It is if you want things done correctly,” he insisted.

She pursed her lips to one side. It was one thing to joke around with him. It was quite another to let her daughter watch her back down when a man was challenging her baking authority in her *own* kitchen. “Of course, knowing the science behind the recipes is beneficial. But every mom out there knows thc rcal sccrct to making a recipe stand out is putting your heart in it.”

Malcolm stuck his tongue out and made a blech face. “I thought we were making brownies, not haggis.”

“I didn’t mean literally— You know what?” Georgia took a deep breath and reminded herself to smile. “Let’s get started on our recipe. So, I’ve lined up all our ingredients on the island here. I’ll mix them while Mr. G tells you a little bit about the science behind what the ingredients will do during the baking. After I put them in the oven, I’ll show you the finished product I made earlier today.”

She and Malcolm turned toward the island at the same time and performed the back-and-forth dance of trying to let the other person go first and stepping to the same side at the same time.

After the world's most embarrassing two-step, he stayed still and gave her a little nudge on the small of her back. His hands were warm and reassuring in a way she hadn't felt in a very long time. It almost made up for him undermining her in front of the camera.

"So I've got hot water here that we're going to use to bloom our Dutch-process cocoa powder," she said, holding up the glass pitcher of water she'd heated on the stove earlier. "By mixing the powder with boiling water, it thickens the liquid and intensifies the chocolate flavor, making your brownies extra rich and delicious."

"Fun fact—" Malcolm leaned in close enough for her to smell remnants of chalk mingling with his citrusy cologne. Who knew that was such an intriguing combination? "Cocoa powder is actually hydrophobic, because the fat molecules in the cocoa repel the water. You could dip a spoonful of cocoa powder in the water, and unless you stir it, you can pull the spoon out and it will stay dry."

Georgia turned her head to raise a skeptical eyebrow at him. "You're joking. I do not believe for a second that's true."

"Watch this." He swiped a spoon from the island and dipped it into the cocoa powder, then submerged the full spoon into the water.

Caroline hopped off the stool to bring the

phone in closer. Both she and Georgia gasped as the spoon of cocoa powder was completely dry when he pulled it out.

"That's amazing," Georgia breathed. Caroline didn't say anything, but her eyes were wide and impressed as she sat back down on the stool and put the phone back on the tripod.

"That's—"

"If you say 'that's science' again, I will dump this water on your head," she warned. "Our nicknames are cutesy enough without a catchphrase."

His full lips formed a mocking pout, but he raised his hands in defeat. "Fine. Carry on with your recipe, or lack thereof."

"I will," she huffed, then turned back to the camera. "So we're going to dump the cocoa powder in our hot water and stir until it's dissolved. If you really want to amp up the chocolatey flavor, you can use hot coffee or espresso instead of the water."

"Which one is better?" Malcolm asked. "Water or coffee?"

Georgia exhaled through her nose, still smiling. "It depends on your preference."

"But shouldn't the recipe specify?"

"Let's just say water for today," she said. "Moving on to our fats, I use a combination of butter and vegetable oil to produce a nice chewy mouthfeel."

"The different kinds of fat produce different results in baking, because while vegetable oil is an unsaturated fat, butter is primarily saturated fat," Malcolm explained before leaning over Georgia's shoulder as she mixed the ingredients. "What ratio of saturated versus unsaturated fats have you found produces the desired result, i.e. chewiness?"

She shrugged. "Um, I don't really know the exact ratio. It's at least double vegetable oil to butter, usually a little more. I go by the consistency of the batter as I'm mixing."

"Hmm."

She stopped mixing. "Hmm?"

"Well, it's just that the consistency of the batter while mixing isn't a constant variable." He straightened up and tilted his head. "You see, the thickness might feel different to you as opposed to someone like John Cena mixing brownies."

"I'm pretty sure John Cena pays someone else to mix his brownies for him," she muttered. "Next we add two cups of sugar."

"For all our metric system lovers across the pond and in Canada, that's five hundred grams," Malcolm chimed in.

"Ugh, I hate having to convert British recipes from the metric system to…whatever it is we use here," Georgia muttered. "Anyway, now we're going to, as the kids say, yeet in a good bit of vanilla. The recipe calls for two tablespoons, but I use vanilla in baking the same way I use garlic in cooking: Whatever the recipe calls for is merely a starting point for negotiations, so go ahead and pour, baby, pour." She didn't even have to look up to know that Malcolm was frowning again as she felt his entire body tense next to her. "Mr. G has something to say about that, I'm sure."

"It's just that without exact measurements, how can you duplicate the results?" His eyebrows knitted together over his nose, and genuine curiosity mixed with concern in his dark eyes. "The scientific method is all about repetition of experimentation to produce the same response between variables. 'Yeeting'—" he made air quotes with his fingers "—isn't a measurement you can accurately calculate and reproduce."

Georgia drew her breath to argue, then noticed how intently Caroline was watching them. Shoot. She'd lost sight of the whole reason she'd asked Malcolm to do this with her. Her daughter was missing out on not only an important part of the curriculum, but a subject that had been a passion of her dad's. Mike had loved science and would watch nature documentaries with the same fascination other men reserved for football games. He kept stacks of *National Geographic* magazines at the fire station to read during his downtime. This was about more than inspiring her own creativity or winning some competition. This was for Caroline.

"Mr. G is right," she said with a nod. "It's really important for all bakers to pay attention to their measurements and be accurate. As long as you remember that the creativity in cooking can go hand in hand with the science, because even great scientists like Albert Einstein questioned the accepted formulas from time to time, right?"

A grin spread across Malcolm's handsome features as he looked not at the camera, but right at her. "That's right. And keeping an open mind is how we learn more about the universe around us and how it works."

"Or how it doesn't work," Georgia said with a laugh. "I love brownies because you can mix in just about anything—one time I tried to mix hunks of rock candy into my brownie recipe, thinking it would be like adding sprinkles. I broke a tooth learning from that mistake." She dumped the flour in and added, "Oh, and here's a tip as we mix in the flour. If you overmix at this stage, your brownies will become chocolatey sinkholes. Lightly fold in the flour until it's barely visible."

"That's because air bubbles get trapped the more you mix," Malcolm said. "Then when you bake it, the air rises and collapses, causing your sinkage."

Georgia swiveled her head toward him. "'Sinkage' is a technical term, is it?"

"It is if you say it with enough authority," he countered, the grin taking on a satisfied smugness that would have been annoying without the teasing humor in his voice.

Georgia rolled her eyes. "So now we bake in a greased pan for twenty to thirty minutes, depending on your oven." Malcolm opened his mouth to object, and Georgia held up a hand. "Don't start with me on this—ovens have minds of their own, and I will not back down on this point."

Malcolm shook his head. "Wouldn't dream of it," he said soberly, although Georgia saw him wince as she closed the oven door without setting the timer. "How do you know when they're done?"

"My brownie senses start to tingle." She crossed her arms and lifted her chin defiantly, then tossed an oven mitt at him. "Just kidding. I'll set a timer and then go by the smell. Now, what makes our brownies black and white inspired is that when they're done, we cut them up and dip one half of each in melted white chocolate almond bark." She held up the platter with the finished result. "See how it looks like a black and white? You could use a ring mold if you wanted to mimic the authentic circle shape of the cookie."

"Fun fact," Malcolm said, dipping his finger in the melted white chocolate and inspecting it before licking it off. "White chocolate isn't actually chocolate. Not a single cacao bean was harmed in the making of this."

Fun fact: She would have strangled him with his apron strings if he hadn't made Caroline laugh for the second time in half an hour. That would have made the apron significantly less fun, but it also would have made her significantly less annoyed, so win some, lose some.

CHAPTER EIGHT

AFTER THEY HAD finished the live stream, Georgia took Caroline upstairs to get her ready for bed. When she came back down, Malcolm was elbow-deep in a sink full of bubbles.

"You don't have to do that," she said, punctuating the sentence with a jaw-splitting yawn.

Malcolm smiled. "I don't mind. My mom would be horrified if I went to someone's house, made a mess and didn't clean up afterward."

Georgia pulled a dish towel out of a drawer next to the oven and took a plate from his hand to dry it. "Was she single, your mom?" she asked with a sidelong glance at him after putting the plate in the cupboard.

"No," he replied. "But she was an engineer and my dad taught physics at the university. Dad was home much earlier in the day than she was, so he was the one who did most of the cooking, and I would help him clean up. Mom did all the maintenance on our cars and repaired anything in the house that was broken." He gave a small shake of his head. "Whenever they had to go to a dealership to buy a new car, all the salesmen would address my dad first, and he would point to my mom and say, 'I wouldn't know a carburetor from a carbon atom. Talk to her.'"

"They sound amazing." Georgia laughed as she took another dish from the sink. "But both of us made the mess tonight. Not that much will come from it, I'm afraid," she added ruefully. "You have to get a certain number of viewer likes on your live stream to continue in the competition. Most viewers tend to watch baking shows for comfort, not to listen to bickering and arguing. If they wanted that kind of content, they would have tuned in to cable news channels covering politics. This wasn't comfort, it was chaos."

"Chaos theory dipped in white chocolate," Malcolm mused. "Well, hopefully we were able to inspire some interest from Caroline. That was the main point of tonight's exercise, right?"

"Well—" Georgia slowed the pace of her drying. "It was. But I was also hoping to be able to keep going in the contest, at least a little longer. I'm in a bit of a—a creative dry spell with my recipes. Probably because I have a big job coming up and my timing is historically abysmal."

"Abysmal," he repeated. "That's a good vocabulary word there, Gigi."

"Thank you, Mr. G," she teased back. "Everyone in this town has nicknames. I don't know anyone who calls me Georgia anymore."

"So what's the big job coming up?" Malcolm handed her the last dish and pivoted to face her, leaning his hand on the sink.

She sighed. "I'm making my cousin BeeBee's wedding cake. It's a big deal because, A—" she ticked the letters off on her fingers "—BeeBee is one of my favorite humans, and the way she and her fiancé, Bill, got back together after years apart is nothing short of miraculous, and B, everyone in town is officially infected with wedding fever. It's all anyone is talking about, from wedding dresses to wedding plus-ones." She shook her head. "It's enough to put someone off the institution entirely, and it was already completely off my radar."

He frowned. Had her marriage to Caroline's father been that unhappy? It seemed too sensitive a subject to pry, especially with the parent of one of his students. He liked to keep his personal and professional lives in neat separate boxes. That question felt like opening a lid to a box labeled Property of Pandora.

"Well, I don't know much about baking wedding cakes, so unfortunately I'm no help there."

"You've used what little time off you have from teaching to come over here and do a cooking science demonstration for a less-than-enthusiastic nine-year-old and you're doing the dishes," Georgia said. "I should be asking what I can do to help you."

"Actually," Malcolm said. "I was wondering if you could tell me where you got that crystal on your necklace."

She lifted the pendant out from under her shirt. "This?"

"Yes."

"It's a kind of quartz, I think," she said. "My husband used to go for motorcycle rides into the woods around here, and every now and then he would find a really good one. This one was so perfectly clear and shaped just like a diamond, he had it made into a necklace for me."

The wistful note in her voice and the fact that she continued to wear a necklace from him caused Malcolm to rethink his hypothesis about her marriage being an unhappy one. There was definitely more to her story, and the longer he spent with her, the greater his interest in hearing it grew. "Do you think you could show me some of the areas where he— Where these crystals could be found?" It seemed better not to mention the husband too much until he had more information.

"I could look up some of his old maps," she replied. "He was always reading about the history of the region, like the lakes that covered this entire area millions of years ago. Apparently, they were so big that every now and then you can still find shark's teeth in the ground. I don't go back there much myself," she said, then, almost to herself, "Anymore."

"Would you mind if I borrowed the maps?" Malcolm asked cautiously, not knowing whether they might have some sort of sentimental value to her. "This is a great area for rockhounds, and since I'm kind of a geology nerd, I was hoping to do some exploring. If I can get a few of the kids interested enough, I'd love to start a rockhounds club someday where we go out for minor digs." It was a long cherished dream, but like so many of his goals, seemed mostly aspirational at the moment. Caroline's apathy towards science was, unfortunately, not uncommon, especially among girls.

"Mmm, I figured as much from the shirt." She pointed at his Geology Rocks T-shirt with a wry twist to her smile.

"Women who wear fun aprons shouldn't throw stones at men who wear fun T-shirts." He puffed out his chest indignantly. "Although if you did, I would be able to tell you where those stones came from and what type they were because..." Malcolm drew a hand below the lettering on his shirt as if to underline his point.

"Fair enough," she laughed. "Hold on. I'll go up to my closet and get them."

When she went around the corner, Malcolm rocked back on his heels and looked around. The kitchen and living room were separated by a partition topped with seasonal scented candles in burgundies and oranges. The walls were beige and the furniture and carpet white, but little pops of color were everywhere, like the rainbow of vintage glass in front of the window over the kitchen sink and the throw cushions embroidered with bright yellow sunflowers wedged next to the couch armrests. It was cozy and homey in a way that made him want to sit down with a cup of hot cider and a good geology book—except for one thing. The clutter. Shoes strewn across the floor, jackets on the back of the kitchen table chairs. The granite counters had a decent amount of space, but they were covered in wandering dishes and bright pink water bottles labeled with Caroline's name.

Glancing furtively around the corner of the staircase, Malcolm didn't see Georgia. Quickly, he rolled the vacuum into the foyer coat closet and placed the errant roller skates in a wicker basket next to the door. Moving efficiently from one space to the other, he put the cups and water bottles in the cupboards above the counter, hung the jackets in the closet and lined up the shoes on the rack next to the entryway. A neat fold of the blankets lying on the floor revealed another of Harley the cat's hiding spots. After being displaced from her cocoon, she gave Malcolm a piercing glare before stalking out of the room with her tail impressively perpendicular to her body.

"Did you clean up in here?"

Malcolm whirled around as Georgia returned to the kitchen with a thick binder under her arm.

"I, uh, well, yes, I just did a littlc pickup," he confessed, wrinkling his nose. "I'm sorry, I couldn't help myself. There's probably a self-help group somewhere for compulsive organizers. I just know how much parents have on their plates and wanted to do what I could."

Georgia surveyed the room and gave a nod of approval. "I'm impressed. Organization obviously isn't exactly my strong suit," she admitted, blowing a loose curl out of her face. "Usually, I start to pick up and then get so overwhelmed with how much there is to do, I get sidetracked and never finish the organizing I started." She held out the binder for him. "Here are the maps. Most of the land belongs to my aunt and uncle's dairy farm, although my cousin BeeBee has the run of it now. Some of the maps have old geological surveys from where there used to be mines and quarries centuries ago. The land is really beautiful, and there are some good walking trails the local wildlife associations keep clear."

"Thank you," he said, then gestured around the room. "Again, I'm sorry if I overstepped."

"Don't mention it," she said, followed by another large yawn. "I'm too exhausted to be mad about much of anything, let alone someone organizing my house for free. Next time you can tackle the laundry room if you want a real challenge."

"Don't threaten me with a good time," he joked. "Well, I should go and let you get some rest. Let me know if we make it to the next round of the competition."

"I'm not holding my breath, but I'll keep you posted." She pressed her lips together thoughtfully before continuing. "Caroline had a blast, though. Anyone that can make her laugh is always welcome in our home, no chore duty required. If you can get her interested in science, you'll be rolling in mini-muffins for life."

Back at his apartment, Malcolm put his shoes neatly away in the shoe caddy next to the door and set the binder on the work desk in his bedroom, which held only his laptop, a single sharpened pencil and a charging station for his phone, all lined up at precisely the same latitude. His bed was neatly made, and when he opened his drawers to get out his pajamas, everything in it was neatly folded to a military degree of precision. This was how he liked his life, how he functioned at his best, without extraneous decor or clutter weighing him down, holding him back. Life only moved forward, after all.

And yet, for the first time, when he climbed into his bed with its plain navy comforter tucked into tight hospital corners, everything felt almost sterile. Like it was missing something or someone.

Suddenly an alarm went off on his phonc and he sat upright, rubbing his eyes. When he picked up the phone, the notification read Call Mom and Dad.

It was September 17. Their fiftieth wedding anniversary. No matter where Malcolm was in the world or how busy his job got, he would always call his parents on their birthdays and anniversaries. The time difference between New York and Minnesota actually worked in his favor this time, because it meant his parents would be finishing dinner around the same time his day was finally winding down enough for him to talk to them without ungraded papers staring him in the face.

Setting it to FaceTime, he dialed, and they picked up on the second ring.

"Malcolm, sweetheart, it's so good to see you," his mom said, pushing her glasses up on her nose and yo-yoing the phone back and forth to allow her worsening eyesight to adjust. "There, now I can see you. How are you, dear?" Her voice was slightly hushed.

"I'm fine," he answered. "I'm calling to wish you and Dad a happy fiftieth. Where is Dad?"

"He's in bed," she answered, her brow creasing with concern. "He had a fall earlier today—He's fine," she added hastily. She opened the sliding door of Malcolm's childhood home and went out onto the back porch. It overlooked a beautiful lake that was frozen over for at least six months out of the year. Now he could see the fringe of trees behind her starting to change from green to yellow. Another summer officially gone in the blink of an eye. "But he was pretty bruised and sore, so I fed him an early supper and gave him a muscle relaxant. That knocked him right out. I was whispering before so I didn't wake him up. Of course, now that I'm out here, I can't ignore the leaves that need to be raked anymore." Back to normal volume, he could hear the concern in her words.

"You should hire one of the neighbor kids to take care of the lawn for you," Malcolm said worriedly. "And to snow blow the driveway this winter. I want you and Dad to be able to get out easily if he has another fall and you need to get him to the hospital."

"Oh, we're fine." She waved a hand in front of the camera, blocking herself from view momentarily. "Your dad just missed the last step going down to the cellar. He'll be back to his usual self in a few days. Plus, you know how he feels about hiring someone to do something if he can do it himself for free."

Malcolm rubbed the bridge of his nose with two fingers. "Let me pay for it then," he offered, although both he and his mom knew how tight his own funds were. Teachers' salaries, which had historically never pushed an educator onto the Forbes 400 list, were barely enough to cover his own living expenses, let alone save up for the future. He usually ended up doing private tutoring during the summer or writing freelance articles for scientific magazines and journals, which helped a little, but the reminder that his parents were in their mid-seventies and might require help to keep them at home as they wished added that much extra pressure to his financial crunch. "You guys can't be out there shoveling snow off the driveway when it's coated with an inch of ice. I want to help however I can, and this way I feel less guilty about being so far away from you guys."

Guilt had become a familiar companion over the last few years, ever since his stint teaching overseas in China seven years ago. It had been a great experience for him as a new teacher fresh out of college. But as he eyed a certain box at the bottom of the stack in the corner of his bedroom, he swallowed back the true reason he had agreed to go over there. At least this current source of guilt he could lessen by paying Ronnie, the teenager next door to them, a few bucks on Venmo once a month.

"Now, don't be silly," his mom chided. "We're so proud of where your career has taken you. I mean, you're in such a geologically unique part of the continent. Woods Hole did a recent study on the geological impacts of the Cambrian sea erosion in that area, and the findings were fascinating. So many wonderful places to explore with your students. I wish I'd had those resources when I was teaching." Her eyes misted over, even though as a scientist and a Midwestern mother, maudlin displays of emotion were extremely out of character for her. If Malcolm was someday half the dedicated teacher she was, he would count himself lucky. Her legacy of distinguished former students was a list as long as his arm.

"I was telling your father— Oh, speak of the devil, look who's up and about." She looked over the camera and motioned in the air. "Your son called to wish us a happy fiftieth wedding anniversary. Wasn't that nice of him? Here, you sit and chat with Malcolm, I'll go inside and get you an extra cushion for your back."

Malcolm's father's face filled the screen. His white hair still had streaks of coppery red around his ears, and his green eyes were as bright and alert as ever. That was a relief. But when he sat down on the Adirondack chair on the patio, a grimace of pain struck his expression and his posture seemed more bowed than it had the last time Malcolm had visited. "Well, thank you for the felicitations, son," hc said with a small smile.

Malcolm rolled his eyes. "Only you would still use a word like *felicitations*."

"If one has an advanced vocabulary, why not use it?" His dad chuckled, then coughed into his fist. "Pardon me. I had a cold last week, and this cough is dragging on longer than I'd like."

"You need to take care of yourself," Malcolm warned. "I already told Mom I'd pay Ronnie Jacobson to take care of the lawn and snow blow the driveway this winter. I want you guys to come out here to visit at Christmas. You can't do that if you're in the hospital."

"My father was out shoveling his own driveway when he was ninety-five years old," his dad shot back. "We Gullesons are hearty stock."

You Gullesons, Malcolm thought before instantly chastising himself. *You're a Gulleson, too, and nothing can take that away from you.*

If anything, this was a reminder that his parents weren't getting any younger. He didn't want to waste a single precious second with them feeling bitter about the inconsequential fact that they didn't share a genetic history.

"I'm back." His mom returned to tuck a pillow behind his dad's back. Draping her arms around Tim's neck, she leaned forward. In this position, they reminded Malcolm of the two-headed monster from *Sesame Street*. He supposed after fifty years of marriage, that was essentially what you became. Two different minds, one heart. "That's better."

"You take such good care of me." Malcolm's dad patted his mom on the hand. "Fifty years and it feels like yesterday I saw you walking down the aisle toward me. I couldn't believe that an awkward, gangly redhead like me could get so lucky as to marry the most beautiful woman in the world."

"Oh, stop," his mom giggled girlishly. "You were the most handsome man at Northwestern. I nearly pushed Susie Beckenridge into the pond to keep her from talking to you before I did."

Malcolm shook his head. "I hope I can find what you two have someday."

"You will," his mom assured him. "I have to admit, I don't envy you, though. Dating these days is so different. All the apps and algorithms.

You can't even meet someone in the workplace anymore without having to fill out fifteen different human resource forms. Well, of course you know better than to go down that road again." She lowered her glasses and gave him a stern look, having warned him against dating a fellow teacher and, as usual, having been right all along. "Used to be you could just ask your friends if they knew anyone available and could set you up."

Malcolm's chin shot up. "That's actually a great idea." His classroom motto was Teamwork Makes the Dream Work. Why not utilize it outside of the classroom as well? "You're a genius, Mom."

"As a matter of fact, her IQ does technically meet the qualifications," his dad said. "As does mine. Then again, I looked for my glasses for fifteen minutes this morning before realizing they were in my front pocket, so make of IQ what you will."

Malcolm sighed. His dad had always been the quintessential absentminded professor. Lately, though, he wondered if the forgetfulness was getting worse, and now there were falls. He wanted his children to know their grandparents, to have actual memories of them, not just pictures on a screen of a stranger with a kind smile.

Time was running out. If he was going to

find the right woman and start a family soon, he needed to assemble a group that was the romantic equivalent to the Royal Society of London in the eighteenth century. Surely that wasn't asking too much?

CHAPTER NINE

FOR MOST PEOPLE, an alarm going off at five on a Saturday morning would result in moaning, groaning and a subsequent smashing of the snooze button.

Georgia, on the other hand, almost always opened her eyes five minutes before her alarm went off anyway. Whether she was naturally a morning person or simply raised in a family of bakers would remain one of life's unknowable mysteries.

There was no question about Caroline, as getting her out of bed and ready to go with Georgia to her cousin Lucas's dairy shop for the morning pickup required threats and/or bribery. This morning both had been required, and Caroline rode with Georgia to Jane Street on the sole condition that they would get takeout from Mama Renata's for dinner that night. She perked up after they parked in front of the bakery and walked down to Crystal Hill Dairy Shop.

Chrysta, Lucas's wife, who ran a successful

cheese board–building party business from behind the shop, was out front with their seven-month-old daughter, Bell, in her stroller. She waved to Georgia as they approached.

"Good morning, girls," she said with a smile. "At least I think it's morning. The baby's going through a sleep regression phase, and the only way to get her back to sleep is pushing her in her stroller. I've seen more sunrises over the last month than I did working on charter yachts in the middle of the ocean."

"Mom, can I go see Bell?" Caroline tugged on Georgia's skirt. There was nothing in the world Caroline loved more than babies, whether it was the water buffalo calves on BeeBee's dairy farm or the ones lying in the bassinets at the church nursery.

"All right, but quietly," Georgia said with a gentle caress of Caroline's head. "Remember the number-one rule. Never wake a sleeping baby."

"Got it." Caroline grinned, then dashed down the sidewalk to stand beside the stroller and peer in. "She's so cute," she whispered to Chrysta. "Her hat has cat ears and whiskers."

"My mom knitted that for her," Chrysta whispered back. Looking over Caroline's head to Georgia, Chrysta inclined her head toward the shop. "Lucas is in there. He's just getting your order out of the fridge now."

"Thanks," Georgia replied. "And thanks for agreeing to watch Caroline for me today. She has a science project to work on, and there's not enough room in the back of the bakery for the supplies."

"I'm happy to do it," she said before bending down to ask Caroline, "What's your project about? I used to love science in school."

Caroline shrugged, hefting the pink unicorn backpack onto her shoulders. "I don't know. Something about the Earth."

"They're making a poster showing ways we can help keep the Earth healthy," Georgia said. "Mr. G said you can get as creative as you want with it."

"Mr. G?" Chrysta stood up and cocked her head to one side.

"He's a new teacher at the elementary school," Georgia said. "Caroline really likes him."

Chrysta arched an eyebrow and curved her lips in a sly smile. "Ooh, I bet that's who the moms were talking about at the back-to-school cheese board party I threw last week. It's not just the kids who like him, from what I'm hearing."

Georgia rolled her eyes. "That poor man. He's a really great teacher and all people see is a handsome face."

"So you agree that he's handsome?"

"I am going to choose not to answer that question," Georgia said, wagging her finger in response to Chrysta's teasing tone. "All I care about is that he's really invested in helping Caroline become more interested in science."

Caroline responded with a beleaguered sigh. "Can I go back to Lucas and Chrysta's now? I want to be ready to help feed Bell her breakfast when she wakes up."

"Only if you work on your project for a little while first," Georgia said, which resulted in her daughter producing an eye roll so like her own it was like looking at a mirror image, albeit a miniature one.

Georgia opened the door to the dairy shop for Chrysta to push the stroller through.

Inside, Lucas popped up from behind a giant wheel of cheese centered on a display table in the middle of the room. He was over six foot, with broad shoulders and a mass of dark hair that was perpetually sticking upright from him taking off the hair covering he used working in his cheese lab. He dropped a kiss on the top of his wife's head as she passed and gave Caroline a fist bump. "It's like a parade of beauty queens going by," he said quietly, leaning over the stroller and gazing at his daughter with an expression of pure adoration on his face.

"You're very sweet, cheese man," Chrysta said, rubbing his shoulder with one hand. "Now if you'll excuse us, the royal diaper needs to be changed. Onward, Princess Caroline—to the monarch's cheese chambers we go."

As they promenaded down the hallway that led back to Lucas and Chrysta's apartment, Lucas turned back to Georgia with a besotted smile lingering on his face. "I've got your order ready," he said, walking around the counter with the cash register to the fridge behind it. "Sixty-four ounces of cream cheese and thirty-two ounccs of sour cream. Any specials today?"

"Nothing new." Georgia couldn't help wincing. It used to be she came up with seasonal specials every week. Wild berry tarts in the summer, cupcakes infused with fresh herbs, tiramisu soaked in fresh ginseng tea instead of espresso. Now whenever she tried to find the same passion she once had for experimentation, she came up completely empty. "I put a container of my black-and-white brownies in Caroline's backpack for you and Chrysta as a thank-you for watching her this morning."

"The ones you made in your Food Network live stream last night," Lucas said. He hefted the brown paper bag onto the counter and tapped on the keys of the cash register.

"Ugh, you watched that?" She clapped a hand on her forehead. "It was a train wreck. I couldn't even bring myself to check the page today. I asked Caroline's teacher to do the presentation with me, thinking it would help get her excited about the science behind baking, and the two of us ended up bickering throughout the whole thing. I can't remember the last time I argued with someone like that. It was mortifying." Her cheeks flamed at the memory. How could she have let herself get sucked into going back and forth with Malcolm in such a childish way? The worst part wasn't even that it had probably ruined her chances of moving on in the contest.

The worst part was that she had actually enjoyed sparring with him. She and Silas bantered with each other, but it was a very different energy, more like brother and sister. Exchanging jokes and even attacks with Malcolm had felt intimate in a way she hadn't experienced in a long time. That had quickly been followed by a stomach-wrenching bout of guilt.

"Um, well, you might want to rethink that," Lucas said as she handed him her business credit card. "The online viewers loved you guys. I was up late with the baby and saw that you finished the night with the third most votes in the whole thing."

"You're joking." Georgia pulled her phone out of her bag and stared in disbelief. Lucas *wasn't* joking. They had over ten thousand likes and too many comments to read at once, but they appeared to be largely positive. "But—but how? We needled each other through the whole thing."

Lucas shrugged. "I thought that was on purpose." Handing the card back to her, he lowered his chin and looked at her with a mischievous twinkle in his blue eyes. "You guys reminded me of when Chrysta and I first got together. She used to call me Cheese Hermit and teased me about how seriously I took my work, but look who's living in the cheese cave with our Baby Bell now?"

Georgia took the bag from him with a stern furrowing of her brows. "Stop it right now or I'll tell BeeBee you got goat's milk from her ex-boyfriend's farm out in Bath."

"She doesn't have goats," Lucas muttered. "How else am I supposed to make goat cheese studded with pink peppercorns for Chrysta's breast cancer awareness month cheese board?"

"Anyway, it's not like that," Georgia replied, shifting the bag on her hip. Holding her phone in her left hand, she started to scroll through her texts with her right. "I guess I should text him and let him know we need to make plans for next Friday."

"I just saw him go into Big Joe's Diner," Lucas said absentmindedly, his right hand rising to stroke his beard. This was a clear sign he was drifting off into cheese-making mode at the mention of the goat cheese.

Georgia left the shop and made her way directly across the street. Big Joe's was the go-to breakfast spot in town, although it was usually fairly empty this time of the morning. If Malcolm was a morning person, at least they had that in common, if nothing else.

She crossed the street, holding the bag in front of her with goosebumps rising on her arms from the chilled contents. The sun still hadn't risen yet, although the sky was quickly lightening from a dark blue to the dove gray that preceded first light. Her favorite times of the day were these in between moments, just before sunrise and immediately following sunset. The world seemed to quiet, as if waiting for the bright splash of light or the soothing blanket of evening. She had always found a special thrill in that peace when nothing was happening. At least in the stillness of nothing, there wasn't anything to lose.

She moved the bag to her right hip to open the glass door to the diner, but the sudden weight shift sent a twinge of pain into her lower back—an occupational hazard of a job that kept her on her feet all day. As soon as she stepped into the small vestibule cornered off by a large cake stand and a Wait to Be Seated sign, she hefted the bag in front of her again, lifting it in front of her face as she arched her lower back to get the spasm to stop.

A familiar male voice reached her ears from a booth to her left. "Well, if you guys have any single lady friends or sisters you wouldn't mind fixing me up with, I'd really appreciate it," Malcolm was saying to someone she couldn't see from behind her brown paper shield. "It's hard to meet people outside of my job, but I really don't want to get involved with someone I know from work. I've learned from experience how awkward that can get when things don't work out. The problem is, between after-school tutoring, continuing education certificate requirements and all the extra stuff teachers are expected to do outside the classroom, it feels like the only women I see are fellow teachers or parents of students."

Parents like me? Georgia thought, instantly dismissing the pang of rejection as stupid vanity. And yet when Silas responded, "What are you looking for in a woman?" Georgia couldn't stop herself from inching a little closer, the bag still hiding her face from the direction of the voices.

"I mean, physically I don't really have a type if that's what you're asking," Malcolm said.

"I like tall women," Joe Kim, owner of the diner, called out from amid a clattering of pans.

"It'd be nice to have someone to reach the high shelves and change the smoke detectors for me. Plus, if we had kids, they'd have a fighting chance of making the basketball team."

"It's mostly about compatibility for me," Malcolm said. "I want to get married soon, before I get too set in my ways being single. Someone who sees the world in the same way that I do, you know?"

"But sometimes it's good to have someone who challenges you," Silas said. "That's what keeps things interesting when you've been married for decades. A little spice to go with the sweetness."

"You've been spending too much time in the bakery," Georgia's uncle and her cousin Bee-Bee's dad, Jack, chimed in. "I have a wife and four daughters. You don't need additional challenges. Every woman comes with her own spice blend."

"Are we talking matrimony or masala?" Joe joked. "You've lost the plot here. What kind of women have you dated in the past? Outdoorsy? Bookworms? Burning passion for salsa?"

"The dance or the condiment?" Silas teased in reply.

"Meh," Joe said. "Take your pick. I've had more than one relationship end over hot dog toppings."

"I really just want someone I can start my life with," Malcolm said. "A clean slate, without all the baggage that can weigh down a relationship. Being a teacher is hard enough, between making sure the kids' needs are met, making the parents feel heard, meeting the state requirements that seem to change with every budget meeting. I need someone who's on the same page with me so when we have kids they don't grow up to the soundtrack of their parents fighting all the time."

Georgia's heart sank at the same time the shaking muscles in her arms forced her to lower the bag. It wasn't like she had had any delusions about the time they had spent together being anything other than an unconventional tutoring session for Caroline. But for just a moment last night, between the verbal jabbing over the recipe and the brush of his hand on hers when he handed her the dishes to dry, she had remembered that heady feeling of attraction, the intoxicating swirl of romantic possibility. It was that glorious nothing just before the first rays of the sun burst over the monotonous shadows in her day-to-day life. There was nothing that compared to the feeling of being noticed by a handsome man, and she had fooled herself into thinking he had noticed her. Now all she felt was silly and embarrassed.

"Georgia," Silas called out, turning and draping one arm around the back of the booth. "It's nice to see you. Pull up a chair and join us."

"I can't," she said, wishing the paper bag was a magic one like Mary Poppins's, where she could jump inside and be transported to another world. "I just popped in to chat with Malc— Mr. Gulleson for a minute."

"Of course," Malcolm said as Jack slid out of the booth first to allow him to step out and make his way across the room to Georgia. "What can I do for you?"

She supposed asking him to stop smiling at her with a warm glow in his eyes that made her heart flutter with hope was a bridge too far. "I just wanted to tell you that our live stream made the cut for the next round in the contest."

"Really?" His smile brightened and widened, causing dimples to carve into his cheeks. When he reached out and touched her on the arm, her chest flooded with an unexpected rush of warmth, overtaking both her breath and her common sense. "That's amazing. I'm so glad I could help. Did you tell Caroline? Seeing her mom accomplish something like that has got to inspire her. You're giving her such a great model to follow."

The reminder that he was only doing this as her child's dedicated teacher somehow made him both more attractive and also amplified the sting of rejection. She was just another parent to him, with the baggage of being a widowed single mom in her thirties—exactly the kind of woman he was trying to avoid. Not to mention the way they had pecked at each other before the camera had even started rolling. She was everything he had said he didn't want.

"Say, Gigi." Joe leaned across the counter to hand a platter of waffles to his waiter and gave her a wink. "I'm still available if you're looking for a date to BeeBee and Bill's wedding."

"I thought you said you liked tall women," Silas interjected. "Gigi's tiny as a minute."

"*Gigi* doesn't want to have anything to do with this or any other wedding beyond making cakes for them," Georgia snapped. "But for the record, my great-grandfather was six foot four and descended from the warriors and hunters of Finland. You should be so lucky."

Backing away from the shocked faces around the table, she pushed the door open with her back before turning to face the sunshine beaming over the rooftops of town.

Georgia shook her head as she made her way across the street. She had always been one of those people others described as having a "sunshiny" personality. It was literally the word teachers used to use to describe her on report cards. But now, for the second time in two days, she might as well have been a roving storm cloud, zapping people with indiscriminate bursts of lightning. The one thing that was different was all the wedding talk she couldn't seem to escape no matter where she went. That had to be it. It was just as well she didn't ever see herself getting married again if she turned into the Hulk simply after being asked to make the cake.

Right before she turned to enter the bakery, Mrs. Van Ressler, who owned the bed-and-breakfast on the corner in front of the lake, stopped directly in front of her. She was in her mid-eighties and walked with a cane, although the assistive device did nothing to bow her ramrod-straight posture.

She glowered down at Georgia, but it wasn't an indication of a bad mood. Glower was Mrs. Van Ressler's default setting, just like sunshine had been Georgia's once upon a time.

Georgia took half a step back. "Oh my goodness, I didn't see you there," she said apologetically. "My head must have been somewhere else."

"Yes," Mrs. Van Ressler said dryly. "At least six inches lower than mine, I would think."

Georgia smiled. That was as close as her austere business neighbor got to a joke. "How are you today?"

"Near collision aside, I'm doing well enough,"

she replied, then squinted one eye at Georgia. "The real question is, how are you? You seem out of sorts."

Georgia sighed and leaned one hand on the lamppost to her right. "I just lost my temper with Joe back at the diner," she confessed. The sun was warm on the back of her neck, like a spotlight exacerbating the flush of shame. Aside from a familial tendency toward melanoma, the curse of having very fair skin meant every emotion showed in bright pink technicolor. "He asked me to go to BeeBee's wedding with him. I don't know why that ticked me off so much. Maybe because it's the fourth invitation I've had this week."

"Not usually something one gets upset about," Mrs. Van Ressler remarked. "Although I agree our town's tendency to celebrate absolutely everything under the sun does get rather old from time to time. But if I had to guess, I'd say that's not why you're upset."

"I guess." Georgia inhaled deeply and pushed herself off the lamppost. Fiddling with the chain on her neck, she looked down and then back up at the older woman. "It's hard, you know. Every time I think I've adjusted to the whole widowhood thing, it takes another hard left turn."

First it had been the influx of emails that had flooded her inbox after Mike had died. Within twenty-four hours of starting to plan the funeral, insurance companies, florists and people who turned the bodies of loved ones into compost for trees swarmed like flies on a dropped Oreo. Then, almost a year later, once she was starting to find her rhythm again, she had to go through the process of getting Caroline ready for school and filling out every form with only a single emergency contact. Well, apparently that wasn't okay. Every activity wanted two numbers. Two parents were the expected norm, and the rush of inadequacy both haunted her and fueled her to be the best parent in the world to make up for the one that was lost.

"It's a strange thing, losing a spouse." Mrs. Van Ressler nodded. "I understand. I certainly didn't lose my husband as young as you did, nor could I claim him as the great love of my life." If it had been anyone else, Georgia might have caught a note of sentimentality in the last few words. "But I do know what it feels like to have the way people see you and treat you change into something beyond your control."

"The town has supported me so much," Georgia said. "They gave me space when I needed it but never isolated me or treated me like I was made of glass." She shrugged. "Maybe I got used to being seen as a widow and a mom. It sort of threw me off when men started treating me like

I was available. I mean, I am, but I'm not sure I'm ready to be seen that way yet, you know?"

"Sometimes—" Mrs. Van Ressler started, then looked up at the sky as the sun hid briefly behind a cloud. "The people around us see changes we might not even recognize in ourselves. Or maybe society thinks that after a certain amount of time people simply 'move on'—" She rolled her eyes. "You don't move on from love. It doesn't go away, no matter how distant the love might be."

Georgia wiped her eyes with the back of her hand. "Thank you for understanding." Her voice came out wobbly and she swallowed. "Did you—do you think you might ever be ready to love again someday?"

Mrs. Van Ressler let out a laugh that sounded rusty, like hinges on a door that had been closed for years. "If there's one thing I've learned, it's that we're never ready for love." She arched an eyebrow. "It barrels at you, very much the way you barreled at me a few minutes ago."

"I am sorry about that," Georgia apologized. Crossing the sidewalk, she opened the door to the bakery. "Will a slice of Italian cream cake make it up to you? On the house?"

Mrs. Van Ressler sniffed as she walked past. "Now, that is something for which I'm always ready."

CHAPTER TEN

MALCOLM'S PHONE DINGED with yet another notification just as he was pulling his Easily Distracted by Shiny Rocks T-shirt over his head. He grabbed the phone and tossed it into his bag before reaching into the tank and booping Newton's scaly nose quickly on his way out the door.

As a rule, multitasking wasn't his superpower. He found it much more efficient to focus on one task at a time, yet walking to Georgia's house and checking his phone at the same time seemed like something he could manage. It was from the town librarian, Melissa, his upcoming blind date, whom he had rescheduled on twice already. Jack Long had set them up after their breakfast meeting at Big Joe's diner last weekend, and while Malcolm was looking forward to getting the romantic portion of his future up and running, the professional part of his present seemed determined to thwart him at every turn.

To be fair, he had volunteered to stay late and spearhead the third-grade teachers' after-school meeting to set up a better system for last-minute coverage of each other's classrooms due to the substitute shortage, but the other time he had a student with an IEP team conference that they had to do in the evening because of the parents' work schedule. All perfectly valid and part of his job. He wasn't sure whether Melissa or any woman would take to the constant extracurricular demands, though, so canceling on her a third time was not an option.

He pulled out his phone as he rounded the curve in front of the school. She had texted him to confirm their date for tomorrow afternoon, as she had a library fundraiser in the evening. The text ended with a smiley face emoji, which added a little bit of personality to their thread that had been otherwise somewhat bland exchanges of basic information and get-to-know-you chitchat. It was hard to tell someone's personality over text, however, and he was willing to give a lot of leeway in order to find the woman he was going to spend the rest of his life with—and hopefully soon.

Before Malcolm could put his phone back in his bag and enjoy the evening walk, it dinged again. He rolled his eyes. For a librarian, she was surprisingly chatty, at least via text. But this was from Georgia.

Georgia: ETA on Mr. G?
Georgia: Between the acronyms and initials, I feel like we're on some top-secret military baking operation. Operation Marshmallow Fluff ready to commence. Over.

Malcolm chuffed out a small laugh. Now there was a woman with personality that shone even through the phone. There was nothing cookie-cutter about Georgia, ironically given that tonight's challenge was a cookie recipe. She was witty, funny in unexpected ways and, despite looking as golden and sweet as a jar of fresh honey, there were depths of sobriety that made him want to sit with her and listen as she revealed them one slow drop at a time.

Since he was almost there anyway, he didn't respond, but as he put the phone back in his bag, the smile stayed on his face. *Danger, danger*, his footsteps seemed to say as he quickened his pace on the sidewalk. His focus needed to be on his student, not on her endearing and just-spicy-enough-for-his-taste mom. There would be no teasing shenanigans tonight, no matter how much he enjoyed the way her bottom lip pushed out slightly when he annoyed her. It was time to put his teacher hat on.

Metaphorically speaking, of course. His bright green You Can't Scare Me, I'm a Teacher hat was back at his apartment because it clashed with his red T-shirt.

He rang the doorbell, forcing all trace of his goofy smile off his face.

But when Georgia opened the door, the first thing out of his mouth was "Agent Gigi, I came ASAP from the PTA. Operation Marshmallow Fluff is a go. Do you copy?"

What was wrong with him? He'd done triathlons, for Pete's sake, yet he couldn't summon the strength to keep it professional with a parent? Fine, no more shenanigans, starting now.

The musical lilt of Georgia's resultant laugh did not help his resolve.

"Come on in." She beckoned him with a wave of her hand. "I've got everything set up and Caroline has promised to let us know *before* she starts filming this time."

He followed her into the kitchen, this time looking carefully enough to step over the soccer ball lying in wait next to a turned-over gym bag with cleats and shin guards spilling out of it. Harley the cat greeted him with a suspicious side-eye from her perch atop a stack of cardboard boxes marked "Books to Donate."

"If you want, I can drop those books off at the library for you," Malcolm said, jogging to catch up with Georgia and hooking his thumb over his shoulder toward the box. "I'm…meeting someone there tomorrow."

The guilty twinge at mentioning his upcoming date to Georgia was another warning sign. *Danger, danger, danger.*

"I heard," she said. Bending over to pull open a drawer, she looked back at him with raised eyebrows. "You'll like Melissa. She's very nice. Keeps the library super organized. You two should have a lot in common." Straightening up, she pulled two aprons out of the drawer and held them up with an apologetic grimace. "Cookie Monster or smiley face daisies?"

He pointed at her left hand. "Since they're the official flower of my birth month, April, I gotta go with the daisies."

She grinned. "I was hoping you'd say that. Cookie Monster is so my inner beast."

Malcolm threw his head back and started to laugh, then forced himself to cough into his hand instead. This was starting to feel almost like flirting, and if shenanigans were off-limits, flirting was completely out of the question. "I'll take that." He reached for the light blue apron with the flowers wearing sunglasses and turned to tie it. "Hi, Caroline," he said as he faced the little girl already perched on her stool in front of the tripod. "You did a great job on your poster. You were the only one who mentioned reducing food waste as a way to help the Earth."

She shrugged. "Mom's always talking about not wasting food. She drives half an hour every other day to donate unsold pastries to the nearest food pantry."

Of course she did, because Georgia being funny and gorgeous and a great mom wasn't tempting enough. She had to be caring and environmentally conscious to boot. "That's awesome," he said.

"It's not that big a deal," Georgia said as she turned on the faucet and began scrubbing her hands. "Anyway, let's go over the plan for this live stream so we don't have a repeat of last week's chaos."

Malcolm's face scrunched in confusion. Aside from the unscripted beginning, last week's live stream had been a success, judging by the numbers. If this was a science lab, they would run the experiment with exactly the same parameters to determine the validity of the conclusions. In layman's terms, if it ain't broke, why fix it?

"Um, okay," he said, standing next to her to run his own hands through with soap and water as she dried hers. "What's the plan?"

"We're making s'more cookies." She handed him the towel as he turned the water off. "It's a pretty basic cookie recipe, but I mix in graham cracker pieces, halved mini marshmallows and chocolate chips. So you can explain how things like baking soda and baking powder interact with the ingredients, why marshmallows expand when they're heated, why chopped chocolate doesn't melt in the cookies the way Ruth Wakefield thought it would when she invented the chocolate chip cookie by accident."

"Greatest accidental discovery since penicillin," he said. "Got it."

She nodded, then leaned back and looked at Caroline. "You're gonna give us a countdown, right?"

Caroline gave a thumbs-up, and Georgia took a step to the side, planting her hands on her hips.

"Caroline, we had a talk before this about not stuffing your cheeks with the mini marshmallows." Her voice had gone full Stern Mom, and Malcolm had to turn his face away from Caroline to keep from encouraging her with his grin. "I will pay you twenty bucks if you can say 'C is for cookie' right now without swallowing first."

Malcolm bit his lip and glanced back in time to see Caroline's eyes widen and her mouth open to reveal at least a half cup of partially chewed marshmallows. "She eish po cooco."

Georgia rolled her eyes. "I'm gonna hear it from the dentist at her next appointment," she muttered. "How about you just count down with your fingers?"

Caroline nodded and held up one hand, the other poised over the phone in the tripod. When she made it to one finger up, Georgia turned on a megawatt smile that Malcolm wished more than anything was directed at him.

"Hi, guys, it's Gigi and Mr. G here for another week of the regional cooking challenge," she said brightly. "Here in Crystal Hill, we get a yearly influx of tourists who come here every summer to get away from the city crowds for our beautiful, clear lake, fresh air and night skies filled with stars. What better way to enjoy your stargazing than with a delicious, gooey s'more, right, Mr. G?"

The image of sitting next to Georgia on a picnic blanket to watch meteors streak across the sky was more tempting than the bowl of chocolate chips sitting tantalizingly close to his hand as he leaned it on the island. Swallowing hard, he forced his teacher voice not to crack with longing. "Nothing better, Gigi."

"Today we're making s'more cookies. While I cream the half cup of softened butter with the cup of white sugar, how about Mr. G tells us what happens to marshmallows when you heat them up?"

"It's an interesting process, starting with molecules from the same kind of sugar Gigi is pouring into the mixer—how much in grams is that, for our British viewers?" he asked, hoping to spark a little of the banter they had enjoyed last week.

"That's two hundred and fifty grams, Mr. G," she replied in an even voice.

Hmm. Not exactly the same kind of fireworks he had expected given her previous annoyance with conversion rates. "Uh, thank you. So, those water molecules in the marshmallow's sugar actually do a little dance as they heat up, turning into steam and pressing gas bubbles outward, causing our fluffy friends to expand into puffy globs of white lava. You can watch this at home by putting the marshmallows into the microwave for a few seconds." He nodded encouragingly at Caroline, who returned the gesture with an unimpressed expression as she popped another forbidden marshmallow into her mouth.

"So we've creamed the sugar with the butter, and now we add one egg and a dash of vanilla."

Malcolm pounced on the opportunity. "I'm sorry, but there is no way a dash is an exact unit of measurement. I used to run track in college, so I know a little something about dashing." He held his breath, waiting for her eyes to narrow with adorable rage.

Instead, she smiled. "You're absolutely right."

"I'm what now?" He leaned in, putting a hand to his ear.

"Right," she repeated. "It's a teaspoon of vanilla. My bad, guys." She held up the measuring spoon before dumping it into the batter.

His shoulders slumped. Was she being deliberately compliant or was she trying to get him ready for a boring date with the librarian? Shaking his head to regain his composure, he watched as she added an egg and the dry ingredients.

"Is that baking soda or baking powder that you used?" he asked as she stirred with her big wooden spoon.

"Both, actually," she said. "Because these cookies have to hold up to the weight of the graham cracker pieces we'll add next, we need both. Can you tell the viewers why?"

"Well, they're both what we call leavening agents, meaning they release gas when mixed with something like acid or heat," he explained to Caroline and the camera. "While baking soda requires a liquid and an acid to activate it, baking powder doesn't and can be used to puff up recipes with fewer ingredients." He leaned over and whispered to Georgia, "I'm actually not sure why you would need both, though." Oh, he had some hypotheses, but perhaps he could elicit an exasperated exhale at his uselessness? Malcolm didn't know why he was so desperate to get a reaction out of her except that it felt more intimate somehow than her smiling vaguely at him the same way she would at any other of Caroline's teachers. Oh, this was more than dangerous—it was distracting from his teaching.

"That's okay," she said, her blithe tone unchanging. "In my experience, I've found that using both in a recipe with heavy ingredients can keep the cookie from getting too dense."

Malcolm resisted the urge to clap his hand on his forehead. He gave up and the rest of the video continued on the same monotonous route. They might as well have been strangers who were paired together at a cooking class. By the time they were finished and Caroline had started to look slightly green around the gills from eating too many marshmallows, he was certain that he had imagined the sparks between him and Georgia from last time. Which was a good thing, so why did it feel like he had as many lead weights sinking in his stomach as Caroline had marshmallows in hers?

Georgia took longer putting Caroline to bed this time, and when she came down, he had washed the dishes and put the ingredients away in the pantry, along with some light reorganization of her jumble of baking supplies. He would have offered to order her some labeled Tupperware containers to make things easier to identify, but that seemed like something friends would do, not cooking-station acquaintances.

"Everything okay?" he asked as she came back down the stairs.

"Oh, she's fine." Georgia twisted around to look back at the stairs before turning toward him again. "I gave her some gas pills to help with the tummy ache."

"No, I meant with you," he said. Perching back on Caroline's stool, he tapped the tripod. "While we were recording tonight, you seemed kind of, I don't know, acquiescent."

"Ooh, now that's a twenty-dollar vocab word," she said. With one hand propped on the island, she rubbed her eyes with the other. "Is that a fancy way of saying I wasn't arguing with you tonight? You make it sound like it's a bad thing."

"Well, our first live stream went over like gangbusters." He crossed his arms over his chest. "Why change it?"

"Because I felt embarrassed last time when we were supposed to be getting Caroline excited about science and I ended up bickering with you the whole time," she pointed out. "I didn't want her to see us fighting every Friday and think she had to choose sides. That's not how kids should grow up, right?"

She sounded like she was hinting at something familiar, and then his own words rang in his head. Last Saturday at the diner, Georgia had heard him talking to the guys about what he wanted—or rather, what he didn't want—and must have gotten the wrong idea. "You're talking about what I was saying at Big Joe's, about not wanting my kids to grow up thinking fighting is normal." He lowered himself off the stool and stood in front of her. "When I said that, I meant couples should be on the same page about the big stuff. Where to live, how to spend money, what shows to stream on a Saturday night after the kids are in bed."

"British period dramas on PBS, obviously," she said, smiling, but not meeting his eyes.

"Obviously," he agreed. "If *Downton Abbey* is wrong, I don't want to be right." He placed his own hand on the island, barely an inch from hers. A red light flashed somewhere deep in his brain. "Not to imply that we're a couple, of course. I mean, you clearly don't want anything to do with getting married again."

Her head snapped up and she frowned at him, her full lower lip doing that adorable pout he had been waiting to see all night. "And what's that supposed to mean? You don't know anything about me."

I desperately want to, he thought to himself. "For starters, the neck where Joe Kim's head used to be before you bit it clean off would like a word if it could still talk."

She snorted. "That reminds me, I have to apologize to Joe." Wrinkling her nose, she raised her shoulders and dropped them in a fatigued sigh that seemed to go all the way to her toes. "You're right about that. My cousin's wedding seems to have stirred up a lot of emotions for me. I'll be glad when it's all done and the whole town can just go back to normal—well, as normal as we get out here." She played abscntmindedly with the pendant around her neck, then her eyes widened. "Oh, how goes the crystal hunting? Did you get out on any of the trails yet?"

"I wanted to, but the main road is fenced off for the dairy farm, and the back roads looked pretty rough to take my bike on," he replied. "The quickest way to get back to where I think the best crystals would be is through the farm, but I feel weird going up and knocking on some stranger's door to ask if I can roam around their land to look for something sparkly." Plucking at his shirt, he got a laugh out of her that was more rewarding than the fresh-baked cookie he had helped himself to after organizing the pantry.

"Tell you what," she said, tapping her fingers on the island. "I'm bringing some wedding cake samples to BeeBee tomorrow afternoon. Why don't you come with me and I can introduce you? Fair warning—" She held up a finger, a dab of chocolate clinging to her elbow. "She's been super stressed with all the wedding plans. I've known BeeBee her whole life, and she has never been this crabby. Bringing food should help, but tread lightly. If you think I was mean to Joe, you won't want to see BeeBee when she's mad."

"Noted," he said. "That would be great, thanks. I mean, surely she won't object to just me walking back through the woods?" He would maybe wait and mention the whole Junior Rockhounds idea until their second meeting.

Georgia hesitated, then said, "I'll bring some doughnuts along with the cake."

As he walked back to his apartment, he realized that he had agreed to tomorrow without thinking about his date with Melissa. He would just have to risk angering the librarian, which was something he had learned as a teacher never to do. Librarians were well-read, organized and never forgot a debt owed. But it was worth it in pursuit of the shining treasure buried deep by relentless time, waiting for just the right person to catch a glimpse of its hidden sparkle.

He meant the quartz crystals, naturally.

CHAPTER ELEVEN

CAROLINE WAS PRACTICALLY bouncing off the walls that afternoon, and it had nothing to do with the sugar from last night's marshmallow fest or the small sips of coffee Silas let her have when he thought Georgia wasn't paying attention.

"I can't wait to see water buffalo calves," she exclaimed in between twirling and nearly knocking over two chairs in the process.

Georgia steadied her daughter with a hand on each shoulder. "Settle down. You can't go anywhere if you give yourself a concussion," she admonished gently. "Oh, I forgot the doughnuts. Can you run back and get them?" Her eyes followed Caroline into the bakery, then landed on the counter. "Silas, you okay to cover the shop for a while? I don't know how long we'll be."

"How long can a cake tasting last?" Silas asked.

"Usually not long, but Malc—Mr. Gulleson is coming with us to talk to BeeBee about doing some sort of dig in the woods on the edge of the property," she said, moving the box of cake samples to the side of her body and digging around in her purse for her keys. The fact that she could lose her keys in a small cross-body bag was a testament to her disorganization. Maybe she could let Malcolm take a crack at it. He had low-key tidied up the pantry last night at some point, and now it was so much easier to find what she needed to make breakfast.

"Oh reeeeeally?" Silas leaned an elbow on the counter and drummed his fingers on his chin. "You and Mr. G are spending an awful lot of time together lately. First the baking competition and now going off on afternoon walks in the forest together?"

Georgia let her bag fall back to her hip as she pointed her finger at him. "You have been watching too many rom-coms," she said. "Mr. Gulleson is Caroline's teacher, and he's a very committed educator. Neither of us would do anything that would compromise her learning. Trust me, nothing romantic happens in front of a nine-year-old."

"I'm just saying, you guys would make a cute little family." He held his hands up.

"Caroline and I are a family," Georgia shot back, not bothering to hide the defensive tone in her voice. "We have each other and that's all we need. It's this whole wedding hoopla making everyone think I need some handsome love interest to come and sweep me off my feet when in fact it's the last thing I need. My focus is on Caroline and my work. Is it so hard to believe I don't want anything more than that?"

"Not at all." Silas stood up straight as Caroline ran back with the box of doughnuts in her arms. "I just don't want you closing yourself off to the possibility of more than that. None of us know what the future holds, but we do know that time will keep moving forward with or without us. Don't let yourself get stuck, all right?"

"You're a good friend, Silas." Georgia smiled back at him, then bent down to take the doughnuts from Caroline. "All right, we're all set. Now I just need to find my keys."

"They're in your hand, Mommy." Caroline pointed to the hand resting on Georgia's hip beneath the cake box.

As she turned around, Georgia heard Silas mutter to himself, "I think I was giving coffee to the wrong Wright girl."

Georgia turned just as Malcolm strolled up the sidewalk toward them, eating out of a cup of yogurt from the dairy shop. He waved his spoon at them cheerily before dropping it and the container into a trash can as he passed.

"Mr. G!" Caroline ran up to him.

"Sweet Caroline," he sang in greeting, then

put his hands on his hips. "All right, what's today's selection?"

"Dance break!" she yelled, so loudly a bird fluttered out of the vintage bird feeder in front of the Stephenson's Antique Store.

He bowed. "Your wish is my command," he said, then clapped his hands to his side and broke into an Irish-inspired jig right there on the sidewalk. From across the street, the owner of the dance studio, Miss Marianne, nodded in approval before turning back to hang an autumnal wreath on the front door of the studio.

"Looks like someone else besides Caroline is caffeinated this morning," Georgia said, joining the two in front of her car.

"I've always been a morning person," he responded with a grin. "It's the best time of day to get out and enjoy the world around me while it's quiet enough to appreciate it. Helps with my job, too," he added, ruffling Caroline's hair.

"Same," Georgia replied. She unlocked her car with a click of the keys. "I got up early to help my mom at the bakery as a kid, but as an adult, I really appreciate having a few moments of peace before starting the nonstop rush of the day." She opened the back passenger door to let Caroline in first, then closed it. "I can't say the same for my daughter, though. She's only this perky because she's getting to see her favorite teacher on a Saturday."

It was chilly that morning, and Malcolm wore an emerald green Henley shirt with the sleeves rolled up to his elbows and dark jeans. She hadn't seen him in anything other than his geology T-shirts with one of her crazy aprons over it in a while, and she couldn't resist taking another peek at him as she walked around the car. Her heart jumped like it was doing a jig of its own.

They climbed in, and Malcolm sat in the front seat. Looking over at Georgia, he said, "I really hope this works and your cousin lets me do some digging on her land. Looking for these crystals was a big part of why I moved to this area."

"How'd you get into geology in the first place?" Georgia asked, pulling the car out and checking for traffic before turning around and making a right past the lake.

"I was that kid with a perpetual pocket full of rocks," he answered. "No matter where I went, I couldn't resist stopping to pick up anything that was shiny or a weird shape. My parents are both scientists, so instead of getting mad at me for leaving what was mostly gravel in small piles all over the house, they got me geology books and a rock polisher. One year we went to Crater of Diamonds Park out in Arkansas for our family vacation. I found a diamond that was probably about one one-thousandth of a carat, but that was enough for me. I was hooked."

"Sounds like you lucked out in the parent department." She smiled at Caroline in the rearview mirror. "Caroline wants to be a veterinarian, but if she started bringing snakes or lizards into the house, I'm afraid my first reaction wouldn't be to buy her reptile books."

"What would your reaction be?"

"Either screaming or fainting, but let's hope we never find out," Georgia said, adding a warning tone to the last few words.

"Well, you're right," Malcolm replied. "My parents were pretty great, although that wasn't so much luck as a really great social worker at the adoption agency."

"My dad was a social worker before he retired," Georgia said. "I think he started his career working in the foster care system, but he switched to hospice care after I was born. Social workers are definitely angels on earth."

"Mine definitely was," Malcolm agreed. "My parents used to send her Christmas cards every year. She passed away about six months ago, and at the funeral, there were dozens of families she had helped to create there to honor her."

"That's so nice," Georgia said. "When did you learn you were adopted?"

"I always knew," he said. "My parents talked openly with me about it. To be fair, they were both tall, fair-haired, blue-eyed Minnesotans who looked like they just got off a Viking ship, so I'm pretty sure they thought I would figure it out on my own eventually." He ran a hand through his jet-black hair. Peering out the window, he pointed at the thickly forested area on the right side of the road as they turned. "See, this is where I rode my bike out to after you gave me the maps, but the trails are pretty rough. It didn't seem safe, so I turned around before I got too far."

Georgia swallowed. "Your…bike? What, um, kind of bike?" She glanced back at Caroline again, but her daughter was deeply engrossed in a *Ranger Rick* magazine.

"It's a Schwinn full-suspension mountain bike," he said, swiveling his head back around as if noticing the way her voice had gone up an octave. "I had a different bike when I did triathlons, but with my job, I don't have time to train for those anymore, so I got something more suited for backwoods trails. Why?" Malcolm's eyes narrowed as if he could see the panic she was desperately fighting to hold back.

Georgia had never wanted Mike to get a motorcycle. It had been one of the only arguments they had had as a married couple…and the only time in her entire stubborn life she wished she hadn't been proven right.

"Just making conversation," she said lightly. Nodding at the windshield as the trees spaced out to reveal a large open field, Georgia pointed at a large sign at the side of the road that said Crystal Hill Dairy Farm. "Here we are. My cousin BeeBee's farm." She slowed the car as they approached the cluster of buildings at the end of the dirt road, then came to a stop. Malcolm reached for his seat belt, but Georgia put her hand on his to stop him from getting out. As if by instinct, her thumb curled briefly under his hand, touching his palm. The skin was rough and callused, not surprising given his hobbies involved gripping bike handles or digging rock faces. What caught her off guard was how comforting it felt. How long had it been since she had held hands with a man? Five years now, since her husband had died. The hands were different; Mike's hands had been thinner, his fingers longer. Yet the feeling of once again walking through this world joined even for a moment to another person was as familiar as the spicy-sweet smells of the bakery that always felt like home.

His eyes went to her hand, and she snatched it away, putting it to her hair to move a curl behind her ear. "I just wanted to give you a heads-up," she cautioned. "BeeBee's animals are basically like her children, so whatever you do, do not say anything that could possibly be construed as negative or making fun."

Malcolm shook his head. "This is a farm. Fuzzy goats, adorable lambs, some gentle dairy cows. What would there be to make fun of?"

Georgia pointed at the giant shaggy animals with large horns lumbering over to greet her. "Those." She turned to wink at Caroline, who loved seeing people's first reactions to the water buffaloes, but the back seat was empty. Georgia whipped her head back to see her daughter's curls flying behind her as she raced to the pen. Unbuckling her own seat belt frantically, she left the car and ran to catch up, chastising herself the entire time. How could she have gotten so distracted that she didn't even realize Caroline had gotten out of the car? True, there was no traffic or real danger to be concerned about here at the farm. BeeBee had given Caroline the safety-around-animals talk on her first of many visits. What sent alarm bells pealing in Georgia's head was how she had let her guard down as a mother so easily just because a handsome, charming man was sitting next to her.

She and Caroline were finally at a good place and acclimating to their reality as a family of two. They had gone through grief counseling, art therapy sessions and group meetings to get here. One of the things that had surprised Georgia the most about the mourning process was how much work was involved. On top of the monumental effort it took just to get through a normal day's routine as a single mother, there were appointments with therapists, journaling assignments, healing yoga poses that had rendered her incapable of lifting her arms above her head for a week. If it hadn't been for Caroline, she might not have had it in her to go through any of it, but that was part of being a mom. In good times and in bad, you did the work. There was no alternative.

The effort had paid off, though, and now she and Caroline could talk about their memories or look at old family photos without the sadness consuming them. It was still so fragile, however, and she kept watch vigilantly for any signs of the ebbing and flowing grief before it could become a tidal wave. Caroline's lack of interest in science worried her, especially for a kid who had been talking about being a vet from her first visit to the barn. Georgia refused to let anything get in the way of her child's dreams, not even a man who awakened feelings she thought were long ago petrified like a fossil in amber.

"Caroline, don't run off without asking me first." Georgia got to the fence seconds after

Caroline climbed onto the first horizontal beam. Clutching the cramp in her side with one hand, she checked the lock on the gate with the other. "You know what BeeBee says about safety."

"It's as important for the animals as it is for you." BeeBee trotted out of the barn, pulling her work gloves off one at a time as she approached them. "Remember, if you startle our nursing mamas, they won't produce as much milk, and their supplies are more limited than the cows' anyway." She nodded at Georgia. "Hey, Gigi. You're here with the wedding cake samples, right?"

Georgia looked down at her empty hands. "I left them in the car. Hang on—"

"I've got them," Malcolm said.

Georgia turned at the sound of his voice to see him coming up across the driveway with his arms full of the bakery boxes. With the clouds of dirt kicking up around his ankles, he might as well have been a mirage in the middle of the desert. A handsome man carrying delicious pastries. Her mouth went suddenly dry. If that wasn't an oasis, she didn't know what was.

"Thanks." Her voice squeaked like a gate in need of a good oiling and she coughed into her elbow. "Must be allergies or dust or…something."

"Something," BeeBee repeated with a wide

grin settling on her face. "Do you work for Gigi at the bakery? You must be new, since we've never met and I'm there nearly every other day, especially since Bill's foliage-viewing lunch cruises have been fully booked lately."

"Bill is BeeBee's fiancé," Georgia explained to Malcolm. "He's a former yacht chef who bought his own yacht to refurbish and use to take people out for seasonal cruises with gourmet meals he provides."

"When I entered the New York State Queen of the Dairy pageant, I asked Bill to help me learn to cook for the recipe portion of the competition," BeeBee chimed in. "I tanked the recipe but still won the crown *and* the man. I took that as a sign to leave the cooking and baking to the pros like Georgia."

"I couldn't agree more," Malcolm said. "My cooking skills are limited to ramen noodles and grilled cheese sandwiches."

BeeBee frowned and put her hands on her hips, the gloves still tucked in her left fist. "And Gigi hired you to work in the bakery? That's not reassuring." She turned her chin sharply in Georgia's direction. "Please don't make me go to Big Joe's for breakfast. I love the guy, but he takes forever because he's too busy chatting with everyone who comes through the door to cook."

"This is Malcolm Gulleson," Georgia answered. "He doesn't work in the bakery, so there's no need to defect to Joe's. Malcolm is Caroline's teacher. I've asked him to help me inspire her to get more interested in science by explaining the chemistry behind some of the recipes."

"Okay," BeeBee said with a suspicious lift of her eyebrow. "As long as he wasn't the one making the cake samples." She nodded at the boxes. "Is that all cake? Good gravy, that's a lot of different kinds of wedding cakc." Shc followed the statement with a groan, and one of the water buffaloes turned its head to regard her with concern in its dark eyes. "Look at what this wedding planning is doing to me. I'm complaining about having to try cake. Who am I?"

"I brought doughnuts for you, too," Georgia added, taking a step back to stand next to Malcolm and patting the top box with her hand. "Figured you might want a little something non-wedding-related for later."

"Are those water buffaloes?" Malcolm asked. He handed Georgia the boxes and walked to the gate where Caroline was sticking her hand between the wire and petting one on the nose. Crouching forward until he was eye level, he peered at them as if transfixed.

"Yes," BeeBee said protectively, walking between the two adult females gently snuffling in the grass sprouting up along the posts. "We're the only dairy farm in the region that offers fresh, premium water buffalo milk. It makes extremely high-quality dairy products. My water buffaloes are sired from an ancient Italian line."

"I remember seeing them when I taught in China." Malcolm stood up and crossed his arms over his chest. "They're different there, but just as beautiful. They were so gentle that my students often tended to the ones on the family farms there. Someone told me they're a traditional symbol of a contemplative and peaceful life." He gestured with one hand at the one nearest him, who raised her head tranquilly as if to demonstrate his point. "I can see why. They're beautiful."

BeeBee's cheeks flushed with pride. "Thank you for saying that." She opened the gate, and as she locked it, turned her head over her shoulder and muttered out of the side of her mouth, "I like your teacher, Gigi."

"He's not *my* teacher," Georgia whispered back hotly even as the sight of Malcolm kneeling next to Caroline and allowing her to show him how to pet the buffalo's nose made her knees wobble. "He's Caroline's teacher. Stop looking at me like that, *Beatrice*." Georgia hissed BeeBee's full name, which had the intended effect of stopping her cousin's absurd attempts at wiggling her eyebrows. "My daughter's been through enough the last few years. What kind of mother would add on to that by dating her third grader's teacher? It's out of the question."

BeeBee's face rearranged itself into a fake smile, which could only mean that Malcolm was standing right behind her. How loudly had she whispered that last part? Georgia pivoted slowly in the dirt, wishing she could just keep turning until she corkscrewed herself into the ground. "Why don't we go in and have some cake?"

"Great idea," Malcolm said. His face and tone were completely neutral, so there was a chance he hadn't heard her.

About as good a chance as BeeBee's water buffaloes spontaneously producing chocolate milk, but still. A chance.

CHAPTER TWELVE

"OUT OF THE QUESTION" was what she had said.

Georgia's words ran circles in his head with the same intensity he used to run the five-meter dash as he followed her and BeeBee up the driveway and into the white farmhouse. On the one hand, it meant she had at the very least entertained the idea and not found his special blend of nerd and outdoorsman wholly repellent. For Pete's sake, she had seen him do the greeting dance. That was usually the kiss of death for any illusions women might have had about his level of romantic game, yet she still seemed to enjoy his company. Malcolm liked that hand. He liked it a lot.

The other hand, the one that felt more like a hook slashing at his ballooning hope, was the part where she had said she couldn't date her child's teacher. He did *not* like that hand, most of all because it confirmed his own personal resolution not to date anyone connected to his work, teacher or parent. Things would get messy.

He didn't have time for messy in his life. Messy meant obstacles, and as a runner, Malcolm knew obstacles only slowed you down on the way to the finish line. His finish line—marriage, kids before he was too old to enjoy them—was there on the horizon. Catching feelings for the parent of a student was a rock that might snare his toe and sideline him until he was no longer Caroline's teacher. Catching feelings for someone who had no interest in getting married at all was a boulder directly in his path. Six tons of immovable granite that he had no chance of breaking through. Everything in him, the runner, the geologist, the dedicated teacher, knew the dangerous truth: The more time he spent with Georgia, the more deeply he would care for her and her daughter.

Sprint in the other direction! the runner yelled at him.

Look, a shiny rock! the geologist tried to distract him.

The child needs a focused educator more than you need a wife! the teacher scolded him.

"Malcolm, are you coming with me?" Georgia had paused in the doorway, holding the screen open for him. The wind ruffled the knee-length floral skirt she wore with a pink sweater that brought out the rose-quartz hues in her lips and cheeks.

"Of course," the man in him responded, taking the steps up to the porch two at a time.

They passed BeeBee's dad on their way in. "Well, hi there, Mr. G," Jack said warmly. "Good to see you again."

"You can just call me Malcolm, if you want," he said, stepping behind the tall man with the same sharp chin and dark eyes as BeeBee, to hold the door open for him.

"I forgot you're relatively new to our town." Jack chuckled. "Nicknames are a big part of the initiation here. Like Gigi and BeeBee back there."

BeeBee's voice echoed from somewhere in the kitchen to the right of the door. "Yeah, sure, blame it on the town and not you and Mom deciding to name me Beatrice."

Jack chuckled as he tipped his baseball cap. "That's the other thing you'll learn about Crystal Hill, Mr. G. The women outnumber us men, pretty much run the show around here and we're all the luckier for it. Have a good one."

"Is Caroline still out by the animals?" Georgia's signature scent, vanilla and cinnamon, reached him at the same time as her voice when she leaned a hand on the other side of the doorjamb. "Uncle Jack, can you tell my daughter to come inside, please?"

"It's all right." Jack stopped with one foot

on the top step and one on the step below it. "I'm heading out to check on the milking stand. I'll take her with me so you all can enjoy some grown-up time."

Malcolm let the screen fall closed, and Georgia moved in closer to him as she shut the door. They were only inches apart, close enough for him to reach out and smooth the haphazard curls the wind had blown around her face. Her eyes were cast down, but when they moved up to catch his gaze, he was sure she could see the longing he strained to control for both their sakes. They both knew a relationship between them was a recipe for disaster. But the searching way she looked at him made him think she was wishing for a magic ingredient that could make the impossible possible.

The rattling of silverware from the kitchen caught Georgia's attention. She whirled around, snapping into caretaker mode as smoothly as the gearshifts on his new bike. "BeeBee, let me help you with that," she said, her voice soothing and low.

"Thanks, Gigi." BeeBee collapsed into one of the chairs around a table in the kitchen as Georgia went to work setting out plates and forks. "You and Dad are the only ones in this whole town who understand how stressful the pressure of this wedding is on me. I feel like everyone expects me to suddenly turn into the frilly princess bride of their dreams, completely forgetting that I didn't even wear dresses until the pageant. Just because I'm getting married, I'm supposed to be someone else?"

"I know how that feels," Georgia said quietly. She pulled absently at her crystal pendant. "It's hard when you get comfortable with the way people see you, only to have it change all of a sudden. You start to wonder whether they're seeing you the way you are or the way they want you to be, and then you're not even sure what you want anymore."

Georgia seemed to be talking more to herself than anyone else, a mournful song sent into the void. Almost without thinking he started to reach for her hand, then BeeBee sniffed loudly. Going into comforting teacher mode, Malcolm grabbed a box of tissues from the end table next to the couch and rushed into the kitchen, only to see that the sniff wasn't so much the preamble to a sobbing fit, as it tended to be for his students, as it was BeeBee inhaling the top of the cake box.

"Bill is going to be sorry he missed this," she said, taking a break from leaning over the pink boxes to pull out the chair next to her for Malcolm. "He's running a cruise for a big group of tourists today. I was surprised since it's not quite peak season for the foliage yet. That's usually the first weekend in October, so about two more weeks still."

"Don't worry." Georgia settled herself into the chair on the opposite side of the round table from Malcolm. "I made plenty of samples."

"That's good, because I promised to save him some of everything for him to try." BeeBee opened the cake box and licked her lips, her eyes taking on a dangerous sheen. "Then again, I already promised to marry the man. That should be enough to satisfy him."

Georgia's laugh pealed through the kitchen with the echo of a church bell.

Malcolm felt a ridiculous smile stretch across his face at the sound, wiping it away when Georgia turned her head to look at him with a sudden sharpness. "Mr. Gulleson, you don't have any nut allergies, right?" Her voice was formal, polite. A warning. "One of them has a pistachio cream filling."

"No, no allergies." He shook his head. "BeeBee, if all this is too much, why not just have a small ceremony? Your farm would make a beautiful location for an intimate wedding, just close friends and family."

BeeBee already had a large mouthful of cake by the time he finished talking, and she swallowed it quickly before reaching for another.

"That would definitely be my preference. But between my friends from the dairy pageant and pretty much everyone in town asking me if they could come, there was no chance of this ever being anything but a circus." She angled the open box to Malcolm, and he considered the choices before selecting a small square of lemon cake with a raspberry filling. Georgia had taken the time to put removable white chocolate labels on each square, because of course she had. "This town is so special, and they've supported me so much over the years. I can't really say no when they asked me to have the ceremony at the gazebo on Jane Street, even if it means getting the opinions of every business in town over how to decorate their storefronts for the big day. Twinkle lights versus fake candles, hydrangeas versus peonies. Lace versus burlap for the folding chairs. It's too much." She pulled her fingers, her knuckles cracking rapid-fire with every word until Georgia put one hand over hers to still them and, with the other, put a piece of chocolate cake on the plate in front of her.

"You can do this," Georgia said. "Just let me know what you need and I'll help you take care of it, even if it means saying no to Mrs. Van Ressler when she asks to sing 'Ave Maria' as you walk down the aisle."

"She hasn't asked to— Oh, no, she's going to

ask to sing at the wedding." BeeBee shoved the entire piece of cake in her mouth with urgency.

"I'll take care of it." Georgia patted BeeBee's hand, then reached across the table to hand her a napkin. "Right now, all you have to do is eat cake."

BeeBee sat back in her chair and chewed quietly. "Thanks, Gigi," she said after she had somehow swallowed the entire thing without choking. "Such a mom, always knowing what to say. You makc cvcrything better for all of us."

Malcolm had no doubt that was true. But he wondered who made everything better for Georgia. Who in this whole town took care of her when she was afraid or upset or exhausted?

"How about I make some coffee to go with the cake?" Malcolm offered. Spying a coffee maker on the kitchen counter, he got up and started to fill the pot with water. "I'm going to need something to avoid a sugar crash."

"Coffee sounds amazing," Georgia said gratefully from the table, and Malcolm turned to hide his delighted grin at being able to do something for her. "Which kind do you like best so far, BeeBee?"

"I mean, they're all amazing," BeeBee said. "It's cake. Who doesn't like cake?"

"But…?" Georgia prompted.

"It's just that I feel like this is the one wedding

decision that I can make just for me and Bill," BeeBee said. "I know the cake is traditional, but neither of us are traditional types of people. I run a dairy farm with water buffaloes, and he's a dinner cruise pirate chef."

As he measured the coffee grounds carefully and poured them into the filter, Malcolm noticed BeeBee's voice had turned from brash and defiant to wistful and dreamy at the mention of her fiancé. He swallowed back the ache of wanting to have that with someone, to know that the most important things—family, forever—were finally yours. He was already thirty years old. He was ready for those things now.

Georgia sighed. "I know," she said, her voice uncharacteristically dejected. "These are my basic wedding cake samples. I've been trying to come up with something that really captures how unique you and Bill are together, but I keep coming up empty. I promise I'll keep working on it. In the meantime, have a doughnut."

"Didn't you have doughnuts at your wedding, Gigi?" BeeBee asked. "Instead of a cake, I mean?"

Malcolm peeked out of the corner of his eyes to see Georgia's reaction. She so rarely talked about Caroline's dad. Her face had gone as white as the sugar pearls on top of the cake samples, and her mouth opened and closed several times before she spoke.

"We...we did." She swallowed and closed her eyes, shaking her head. "We had a brunch reception. I can't believe I didn't remember the doughnut tower cake. I—I forgot."

She looked so shocked and sad at the same time. All of the joy from earlier felt like it had been sucked out of the room in a single inhale. Whatever had happened with her husband, it had not ended well. No wonder she never wanted to get married again.

Malcolm abandoned the coffeepot and rushed back to the table. He didn't have a plan, but letting Georgia suffer wasn't an option. Leaning forward, he moved the boxes to one side and interrupted BeeBee's squawk of protest.

"So, BeeBee, I came with Georgia today to ask a favor from you," he blurted. Georgia's chin jerked back in surprise, and her eyes darted to BeeBee as if in warning that this wasn't exactly the optimal moment for his proposal. He gave a quick nod to reassure her, then turned back to BeeBee. "One reason I accepted a job in Crystal Hill is that it's one of the few places in the world where you can find a specific kind of quartz. I'm kind of a geology buff," he added. "So these crystals are actually called Herkimer diamonds because they come out of the ground looking like perfectly faceted diamonds. Georgia gave me some old maps, and it looks like the woods on the far end of your property would be a great place to dig for these crystals."

He reached in his bag and pulled out the geological survey, unrolling it on top of the doughnut box. "See, all the way out here is the edge of what was once a giant lake millions of years ago. The crystals formed under the pressure of all the sediment as the waters eventually dried up and can be found in ridges just like these here." He dragged his finger along the far end of the paper.

BeeBee tipped her head to one side. "What would digging entail? Are you talking like with shovels or with heavy-duty equipment?"

"First I'd have to walk back and explore the land to see if there are any exposed cliff faces available," he said, rolling up the map and nudging the doughnut box closer to BeeBee. Georgia had told him last night she was much more amenable when she was well fed. "If it were just me digging, I could make do with a jackhammer to break up some of the larger rocks. But if I'm right and the area is a prime spot for mining, I'd love to bring a group of kids from my class back there to see if I can drum up enough interest for a junior rockhounding club. To do that, it would be really helpful to clear the area with a small excavator or a tractor with a digger attachment.

That way we can make it easier for the kids to find small crystals that have been dislodged."

BeeBee grimaced. "I don't like the sound of that," she said. Leaning back in her chair, she turned her head to look out the bay window in the living room, which provided a view of the barn and the grazing fields beyond. "My water buffaloes are very sensitive to changes in their environment, especially loud noises. I don't want to do anything that could upset them or their milk supply."

"BeeBee, you haven't had a doughnut yet." Georgia opened the box and put one on BeeBee's plate. "I brought the doughnut holes with the Bavarian cream inside. Your favorite."

"Mmm." BeeBee's spine straightened. She leaned over the box and plucked out a doughnut hole, popping it in her mouth and chewing it thoughtfully. After she swallowed, she narrowed her eyes at him before looking at Georgia. "What do you think, Gigi?"

Georgia inhaled deeply, looking at her hands folded on the table. "I think that anything that gets kids excited about the science of this region is a good thing, right?" She got up and walked over to the cabinet, taking out three mugs and setting them on the counter before turning back around. "I mean, you're always talking about how special our town is," she said, gesturing a hand to BeeBee. "Bingleyton has a big commercial mining operation there, and it doesn't seem to impact their dairy farms."

"Bingleyton," BeeBee muttered without any attempts to veil the obvious animosity in her voice. She took another doughnut hole out of the box and shook her fist at the sky, heedless of the powdered sugar raining down on her. "They think they're so cool over there. Well, if Bingleyton can do it, so can we. Besides, that spot looked pretty far away from any of our typical grazing areas. There's a chance the animals might not even hear the machines."

The front door opened and Caroline burst through, followed by Jack. "Mom, I got to bottle-feed one of the calves," she squealed. "It was so cute." Her eyes zeroed in on the open boxes. "Ooh, can I have a doughnut?"

"Go wash your hands in the bathroom first," Georgia said with a smile. She started to pour coffee into the mugs and set one in front of BeeBee and the other in front of Malcolm. The soft brush of her hand against his shoulder as she reached past him lingered even after she sat back down in her seat.

"Dad, we have a digging attachment for the tractors, right?" BeeBee called across the room.

"Sure do," he answered after closing the door and lifting his feet out of his work boots. "Used it to clear some of the new grazing grounds after BeeBee and Bill brought Fernando home from Italy." He nodded at Malcolm. "This area is great for farming, but you wouldn't believe the size of the boulders we have back there. Gnarly-looking things, too."

"That's a great sign for potential mining." Malcolm couldn't contain his excitement. "Believe it or not, we say that the uglier the rock is, the more likely it is to contain some great crystals on the inside."

BeeBee dunked her doughnut hole in her coffee and ate it over her plate. "Tell you what," she said through a mouthful of pastry in one cheek. "If you wanna take the tractor out to where you want to dig, I'll stay here and monitor my animals. We can do a baseline check of their milk supply before and after the dig, and if it's not affected, you can go rock hunting to your heart's content."

Caroline reentered the room as BeeBee finished talking. "How do you hunt rocks?" she asked, climbing on BeeBee's lap and reaching for a doughnut hole.

"Well, you dig for them," Malcolm explained. "There's a kind of shiny quartz crystal I think can be found in large quantities in the woods around here. BeeBee's going to let me use some of the farm equipment to move some of the big rocks and dirt and see what I can find."

"Wow." She looked at Georgia. "Mom, can we go with Mr. G to find the shiny rocks? Please, please, please?"

Georgia had been looking at her phone, and her daughter's voice seemed to startle her out of her reverie. "I'm sorry, I didn't hear what you were saying, sweetie." The corners of her mouth turned down, and her eyes flicked back to her phone as she spoke.

"Everything okay?" Malcolm asked.

"Not really." Georgia handed him her phone. "Take a look at the votes from our last live stream. We barely made it to the next round. A lot of people were commenting that this video didn't have the same 'spice' as our first one."

Malcolm looked at the numbers. She was right. They had barely squeaked past a baker from Louisiana who had made crawfish cutout cookies. "I guess some people like a little sugar and spice," he said, handing the phone back to Georgia. Their fingertips touched in the exchange, and Malcolm's heart went to his throat.

As painful as it would be, after this baking contest was done, he needed to take some space from Georgia. He had so little free time outside of his job. It wouldn't make sense to spend his precious evenings with a woman who could barely talk about the subject of marriage. If they made it through the last round, they would have one final baking challenge and then he could go back to just being Caroline's teacher. That was the reason for all of this anyway. The goal had been to win his student over to the appeal of science, not to win her mother's unavailable heart. Some distance would really be best for all of them.

"So can we go with Mr. G when he digs for the crystals?" Caroline repeated, tugging on Georgia's sleeve with jelly-stained fingers.

Georgia looked over at Malcolm and shrugged. She didn't look at all happy about the prospect. "I mean, if it's okay with Mr. G."

Caroline turned pleading blue eyes to him, and Malcolm caved like a glacier exposed to warming temperatures and a constant eroding water flow. "Sure. Why not?"

So much for not spending any more of his free time with the Wright girls.

BeeBee looked over Caroline's head at Georgia's phone and made a dismissive *pfft* sound. "I don't know what these people are talking about," she said. "Who needs spice with a baking show? Personally, the only thing I need with my sugar is more sugar." She raised her chin and eyed the dwindling contents of the boxes. "I wonder if anyone has ever filled a cake with a doughnut hole."

Malcolm and Caroline laughed, but Georgia's eyes shifted to one side and her mouth opened slightly. She pulled her phone back toward her and started tapping out a rapid-fire text.

The faraway look on her face combined with the sudden intensity of the message sent a streak of jealousy through him, white-hot and admittedly untethered to the reality of their situation. Their relationship couldn't be a romantic one. He knew it, she knew it. Heck, even the water buffaloes out in the field would advise against it.

So Malcolm took out his phone and sent a text of his own. If he really wanted to start his family, then spending all his free time with an unavailable woman was a terribly inefficient way to do it. But there was someone he knew who wanted to settle down and settle down now. He knew, because he'd already dated her once before.

CHAPTER THIRTEEN

It was only Wednesday, but it felt like it had been an entire month made of nothing but Wednesdays.

Georgia swiped her forehead with the back of her arm, probably leaving a smear of melted chocolate on her face, but she didn't have time to look in the mirror. It was the last week in September, so the fall tourists had arrived in town for the beautiful kaleidoscope of leaves ringing the lake in fiery reds and golds. That meant double and even triple her usual orders of pumpkin muffins, apple hand pies and crullers dusted in cinnamon sugar.

As she boxed up the last maple scone in the case and handed it to a customer, Silas looked up curiously from the table he was in the process of wiping down. "Are you feeling okay?"

Georgia waved at the customer as they left, then put her hands on her hips and tipped her head to one side. "I'm fine. Why do you ask?"

"It's just that normally by this time in the season you're so tired I'm tempted to put sunglasses on you and pull a *Weekend at Bernie's*, baking edition," he commented, picking up the sugar dispenser to wipe underneath it. "But this whole week you've been positively perky."

"I'm always perky," Georgia said indignantly. "Ask anyone. Comes with the blond curls and high-pitched voice. I tried to go goth in high school once, and it lasted less than a day because my friend said goths didn't giggle."

"No, this is different." Silas shook his head. "You're, like, radiating excitement. And I bet I know what it is."

Georgia knew, and her cheeks flushed at the fact that she had been so obvious that Silas had guessed at it. This week she was getting to see Malcolm two extra times in addition to their usual Friday night baking live streams. She had stopped by the school yesterday for the PTA bake sale, and he had graciously given up his whole lunch break to staff the table with her. He made her laugh so hard with his list of kid expressions that milk she had been drinking from one of the little cartons had almost come out of her nose. Friday they would be baking, and then the following Monday he had off for Columbus Day, so the three of them—Malcolm, Georgia and Caroline—had made plans to go to BeeBee's farm and dig for the crystals Malcolm hoped lay under the rocks and brush.

"I—uh—I can't imagine what you're talking about." Georgia busied herself dusting her hands on her bluebird-printed apron. She turned and caught a glimpse of her reflection in the gleaming napkin dispenser behind the counter. Silas was right. She was positively beaming simply at the thought of seeing Malcolm. And if Silas knew about her crush on the teacher, which was becoming harder to deny, who else knew? Caroline? Or, worse, Malcolm himself? That would be the most embarrassing of all, as she knew from the whisper network that he had been seen walking around the lake with Ada Brunner, one of the prettiest single women in town. She had already spent years being pitied as the town's widowed single mother The last thing she wanted was another thing for people—especially Malcolm—to feel sorry for her over.

"The Food Network competition, obviously." Silas rolled his eyes. "This week is the semifinal, and if you get enough votes, you'll be one of the final three bakers in the running to be on TV! I'm giddy for you and I'm not even competing!"

"Oh." Georgia whirled around. "You're right. The competition." Even though it was ostensibly the reason she and Malcolm were still spending every Friday evening together, it had somehow gotten pushed into a corner of her mind like a laundry basket full of clothes that needed to be folded but would have to wait. This was a feeling she knew very well, because there was always a basket of laundry that needed to be folded. "Yeah, I mean, it's still not a done deal. I don't want to get my hopes up. But at least Caroline seems to be doing better in science class, so no matter what, it wasn't a waste of time."

At the bake sale, Malcolm had made a point of telling her that Caroline had actually raised her hand to answer one of the questions about different kinds of rocks.

"She even laughed at one of my stupid jokes," he had leaned over to confide, the feel of his arm against hers thrillingly firm and inviting.

"What was the joke?" she had asked.

"I can't tell you," Malcolm had responded with an adorably self-deprecating wrinkle of his nose. "It's too embarrassing."

"Please?"

"I said, 'Sedimentary, my dear Watson.'" He had buried his head in his arms on the table, which was just as well, because it was a stupid joke and the only reason any adult would laugh at it would be if they had a ridiculous, impossible crush on the person telling it.

And she had grinned and giggled like a Cheshire cat that had been fed too much catnip.

"I figured," Silas said as he opened the door to flip the sign in front to Closed, the ring of the bell bringing Georgia back from her reverie. "At the very least, I knew it wasn't because you decided to bring that gorgeous teacher of yours as a date to BeeBee's wedding. Julio at the barbershop was asking if I'd put in a good word for him, by the way."

"Again, he's not *my* teacher." Georgia untied her apron and flung it over her head and onto the hook with a little more force than she had intended. "Why does everyone keep saying that? And for the last time, I'm not bringing a date. At this point, I might not even be bringing a cake. BeeBee wasn't happy with any of the samples I brought, and I thought I had an idea, but I can't get it to work." She had been so sure the cakenut would be a winner that she had texted the idea to herself while at BeeBee's so it didn't fly out of her head. But the results, while delicious, still hadn't been what she wanted for the perfect wedding cake.

"I liked the cakenut," Caroline said from behind her. She had been in the back of the bakery since getting out of school, helping to frost the leaf-shaped sugar cookies. "A doughnut hole inside a cake? Yum."

"Thanks, kiddo," Georgia said, frowning. "But the texture wasn't right. I need something inside the cake that contrasts with it. Something sweet, maybe a little tart, but with a crunch."

Silas shrugged. "Those decisions are above my pay grade, sweetie."

"I pay you in baked goods," Georgia pointed out as she grabbed her purse and offered her other hand to Caroline.

"Exactly," he replied with a wink. Opening the door, they stepped into the cool air of early evening. The streetlamps were just turning on, and a breeze hurried the dry leaves along the sidewalk with a pleasant rustling noise. The sun had begun to melt into the lake behind them on the other side of the street. It was the perfect time of day to stroll with a special someone's arm around your shoulders as you both sipped on cups of hot apple cider and waited for the first star to appear so you could wish for this moment to last forever.

"Mom, can we get pizza for dinner?" Caroline asked, pointing down the sidewalk at Mama Renata's.

The thought of adding to the dishes already forming a leaning tower in the sink was enough to make her say yes. "Sounds good to me. Silas, wanna walk down to the restaurant with us?"

"I think I will," he answered, zipping his jacket all the way up. "Ed is doing inventory of an estate sale collection he picked up recently, so he won't be done until late."

They walked down the sidewalk, raising their hands in greeting to Lucas as he arranged a display of cave cheeses under a sign that read, "September Special: Buy one cheese, get a Genoese salami half off."

Silas opened the door to Mama Renata's and indicated with a sweepingly gallant move of his hand for the ladies to go first.

Georgia and Caroline walked into the dimly lit restaurant, breathing deeply to gather the smell of roasted garlic that hung in the air. The contentment the smell brought faded as she looked around at all the couples clustered over the tables covered in red checkered cloths, the light of the tea candles reflected in their adoring gazes. If Big Joe's was the town hub for gossip, then Mama Renata's had the market cornered for romance. It was the premiere spot for date night, and suddenly Georgia wished Caroline had asked for Chinese from the takeout place in Bingleyton.

Especially when she saw Malcolm cozied up in a corner booth with a tall brunette she didn't recognize.

The woman suddenly reached forward and grabbed Malcolm's arm with long scarlet fingernails, her voice loud enough to carry over the low hum of acoustic guitar playing on the loudspeaker. "Oh my gosh, you would be perfect for the biodome project. Me and a bunch of my coworkers at the museum are applying. Can you imagine spending a year in a simulation of a colony on Mars together?" She leaned forward and batted her eyes. "I wouldn't mind being stuck on a desolate planet with you."

"Is that Mr. G?" Caroline asked. "I want to say hi to him."

"I don't think we should interrupt his dinner, sweetheart," Georgia said, watching as the woman released Malcolm's arm, blowing him a kiss as she stood up from the table and made her way to the bathroom. "We'll see him Friday for the baking semifinals."

"Caroline, let's go order." Silas bent down next to Caroline and nodded at the counter at the back of the room. "We can raid Mama Renata's peppermint dish while we're there." He looked over Caroline's head at Georgia and gave a meaningful dart of his eyes in Malcolm's direction.

Georgia looked across the room again to see Malcolm already standing up and taking a step in her direction. She shook her head and wove between the tables, motioning for him to sit back down.

"Fancy seeing you here," he said, settling once

more into the black leather booth and putting the napkin back in his lap.

"We're just stopping by to pick up a pizza for dinner," she explained. "We're going soon. I don't want to interrupt your date."

He raised his eyebrows. "How did you know I was on a date?"

Georgia's heart breathed a sigh of relief. "Well, this is the most romantic place in town, and you and that woman certainly looked…familiar."

He looked down with a wry twist of his full lips, then back up at her. "Well, we are. Felicia and I used to go out in college. We broke up before graduation, but we've kept in touch over the years. I knew she lived in New York, so I sent out a text to let her know that I was living here and we should get together sometime if she was ever in the area." Malcolm raised his eyes back to hers. "I, uh, didn't think she would respond so quickly."

"Have you run out of single women in Crystal Hill already?" Georgia teased. "Goodness, that was fast."

He laughed. "No, although I do think the librarian officially gave up on me after I canceled for a third time." Malcolm leaned over to peer in the direction of the bathroom, then sat back in his seat. "It's just that dating is so hard when you're new in town. Especially when the only people I have time to meet are other teachers, who I don't like to date because if it doesn't work out, I have to see them all the time, and parents who—"

"You can't date because it could interfere with the student's education," she finished softly.

"That is my usual rule of thumb." His gaze deepened, and he looked at her as if seeking the answer to an ancient riddle. "That would mostly depend on the parent's point of view, though," he said softly.

The back of Georgia's neck grew hot, as if someone was holding one of the candles right behind her. "I thought following rules and methods was very important to scientists like you," she murmured.

"It is," he said. "But some rules are more like guidelines. And some people..." He trailed off, reaching his hand toward where hers rested on the top of the table. "Are worth it."

She tucked a strand of hair behind her ear, studying the tile on the floor. Was he saying he was interested in her? But then why was he on a date with an ex-girlfriend? She cleared her throat pointedly. "I, um, I really should let you get back to your date," she said. "I wouldn't want to face the wrath of those talons if she thought I was hitting on you or something."

He grimaced. "It had been a long time," Malcolm said. "I'd forgotten about how sharp those nails were. Truth is—" He straightened the silverware on the table until it was perfectly lined up with the placemat. "I'd forgotten why we broke up in the first place and figured it was worth trying again. Back then I was young and thought I had plenty of time to find a wife."

"You're still young," Georgia scoffed. "And it's not like there's a deadline on marriage. What's the rush?"

"Because I'm tired of waiting," he said loudly, then, looking around and lowering his voice, he went on. "I want a family of my own. I come home every day to an empty apartment. It's neat and tidy, but it's not the home I thought I would be in at this age. I'm not some playboy going out on dates every week for fun, if that's what you were thinking."

"It wasn't," Georgia reassured him, placing her hand on his, then just as quickly removing it. "But it does seem like asking out an ex-girlfriend because you're tired of dating is a shortcut that won't end well."

The grief that came without warning or welcome sent prickling tears behind her eyes. It was a shortcut on a dark, icy road that sent her husband's motorcycle careening into a ditch. Her breath caught in her chest, and she moved her hand away quickly.

"I know," he admitted with a mournful shake of his head. "And I've heard it a thousand times—the right one will come along when you're not looking for her. But I'm never not looking for her," he said. "It's like when I see a glint of druzy on a boulder, that means there could be a perfect crystal hidden inside. I can't stop digging until I find it. All I want is to find the woman of my dreams so the best parts of my life can begin. I—I'm sorry," he said, looking up at her with remorse cutting across his features. "I know marriage isn't a happy topic for you."

She drew a deep breath. "My marriage was a very happy one," she said, hearing the defensiveness in her own voice and softening it as she continued. "It just wasn't long enough."

His mouth fell open as if surprised. "I guess I misunderstood," he said. His brows furrowed. "The way you talk about weddings, I just assumed—" He held up a hand. "You don't have to talk about anything you don't want to with me. But I'm happy to listen when and if you're ready."

"Thank you," she swallowed back the tears to say. "And for what it's worth, I think any woman would be lucky to share her life with a man like you. You shouldn't settle for fool's gold. Trust me, the real thing is worth the wait."

She nodded and turned to walk away. As she

joined Caroline and Silas at the counter, she could hear the woman's high-pitched laughter back at Malcolm's table.

"You're so funny," she was saying to him. "You have to come give a lecture for the geological society gala. They'd love you."

How could anyone not love him? The thought appeared in Georgia's head before she could stop it, accompanied with an uneasy feeling of disloyalty.

Uneasiness of an altogether different variety struck her when Marco, Renata's son, appeared behind the counter with their order in a white to-go box. He looked her up and down and lifted his salt-and-pepper eyebrows. "Miss Gigi. You're looking lovely as usual."

Marco was a handsome man at least a decade her senior with dark hair that was silver just at his temples and a distinguished Roman nose. He was also highly aware of his looks and had been divorced twice thanks to not only eyes that wandered.

Georgia pulled the collar of her dress together with one hand and took the box with her other. "That's kind of you to say, Marco," she replied.

He nodded back in the direction of Malcolm's table. "Your teacher isn't stepping out on you with some other lady, is he?" Marco cracked his knuckles, a layer of dark hair on his wrist showing as his sleeve cuff lifted. "You know, if you wanted to make him jealous by, say, looking amorous with another man, I'd be more than happy to volunteer. It's a thing I saw in the movies, you know, where the girl and guy pretend to go out to make someone else jealous and then oops, they fall in love for real." He leaned an elbow on the counter and winked at her suggestively. "BeeBee's wedding's coming up. It's a nice public place to be seen on the arm of a handsome gentleman such as myself."

He pulled a card out of the breast pocket of his pin-striped suit and handed it to her.

Georgia reached out and pinched it gingerly between her thumb and pointer finger. "That's a very…generous offer, Marco, but Malcolm and I are just friends. No need for pretend romances."

Standing next to her, Caroline looked up at Silas and asked, "What does 'amorous' mean?"

Georgia put the card on top of the to-go box and pulled on Caroline's shirt, backing away. "See you, Marco." She forced herself not to look back at Malcolm's table one more time before they moved quickly out the door.

As they walked back to the car, Caroline leaped ahead of them and hopped over cracks in the sidewalk. An owl hooted overhead from the trees around the lake, and Georgia slowed her pace slightly.

"Silas," she said carefully. "What do you think is the cause of the recent uptick in romantic propositions I've received lately? Do you really think it's just everyone getting excited for Bee-Bee's wedding, or is it something else?"

Silas came to a stop in front of the antiques store and glanced up at the lighted window in his home above it before leveling Georgia with a sober look. "You want the friendly patter or the nebulous truth?"

"Truth," she answered, even though no one ever really *wanted* to hear the truth. They simply needed to hear it, and she was starting to run out of ways to avoid it.

"I think—" he started and stopped himself with a thoughtful purse of his lips. "You are a beautiful young—yes, young, I'm twenty years older than you and I'm not old, so hush—woman with a lot to offer. It's not that you're putting out some sort of festive plumage signaling your readiness to mate or anything. But in the past two years, you've been reaching out to others more than you did in the beginning after Mike passed. You helped BeeBee with her pageant preparations, you did a few catering gigs with Chrysta when she started her cheese board business and you've completely revitalized the PTA. Plus, Caroline is older now, so it's not like you're chasing around this tiny whirlwind who more than once darted into traffic to save a rogue caterpillar."

Georgia shuddered at the memory. "She has always taken her love of animals to an extreme."

"My point is that you've shown so much love to the people around you," Silas said, placing a hand on her shoulder. "I think that some may interpret that as an openness to the idea that you might want to receive love from someone else. Or maybe most men are just pigs." He rolled his eyes skyward and shrugged, then smiled down at her. "You don't have a blinking 'open for business' sign over your head, if that's what you're asking. But you have the biggest heart of anyone I know. There's room in there for as much love as you want, and the best part is that you get to decide whether or not you want it."

"Hmm." Georgia breathed out a sigh that felt like floodwaters rushing out of a dam. "I'm not sure whether it being something I can decide makes all this easier or harder. I kind of figured there would be like a light-bulb moment when I would just know I was ready." She shook her head sadly. "I'm starting to think that's not how any of this works."

Later that night, after she had put Caroline to bed, Georgia walked down the stairs as she always did, stepping over the piles of shoes and books that she placed there meaning to put them away in the evening and finding herself too tired in the evening to move anywhere. She stopped to lovingly trace one of the pictures on the wall above the handrail. There were so many that the wallpaper was barely visible, from her and Mike's wedding pictures to their honeymoon trip to New Orleans and the Mediterranean cruise they had taken right before she had gotten pregnant with Caroline. Their first family vacation to Disney World, when Caroline was only three, which they had no way of knowing would also be their last trip as a family of three. So many wonderful memories placed in a haphazard array of different-shaped and -colored frames.

Georgia smiled, thinking about Malcolm's penchant for arranging things in neat columns and perfect angles. He seemed to get such enjoyment out of transforming chaos into order. Every Friday after he left, it felt like her kitchen grew in size because of the way he organized things and removed unnecessary clutter. The only problem was now she had grown used to it. What would happen when he found that wife he wanted so badly? When the contest was over and they went back to the way things should be between them, teacher and parent?

Her hand fell slowly away from the photo of Mike holding Caroline up on his shoulders on one of their family nature walks. Those used to be her favorite part of the weekend, when they would all get up early on a Sunday morning and find new paths to explore together. Mike loved being outdoors, loved learning about plants and taking pictures of trees to look up on the computer when they returned home so he could teach Caroline all about them. It was so important to him that she appreciated the natural world and how it worked. Georgia would listen from the kitchen as she made dinner while he and Caroline looked over their collcctions of leaves and flowers each had picked up on the trail. She always suspected he timed this so she could cook dinner without having to worry about a toddler underfoot. He had always been intuitive about her needs that way, the perfect partner.

Georgia's reflection frowned at her from the glass covering the photo. Shouldn't that be enough? She had meant what she said to Malcolm. It had been a wonderful marriage. She had gotten a beautiful, smart, kind daughter out of it, and the memories they had made would be with her forever, even if they were starting to seem distant, as if they had happened in another lifetime. That chapter of her life felt closed and complete. Yet Malcolm's words tonight stirred more than just the memories of what she once had with Mike. He reminded her of the tomorrows she had once assumed were guaranteed, a whole future with the person she loved. At the restaurant, her typical resistance to all the marriage talk had crumbled because she knew he was right. The best things in life were only made better with the right person by your side.

She couldn't blame him for wanting it as soon as possible.

But now she was left wondering if the reason she had been so hostile about the wedding fever sweeping through town was because she wanted it for herself with someone new.

CHAPTER FOURTEEN

"This week is bread week." Georgia smiled for the camera. Malcolm noticed that she had on deep red lipstick this week instead of her usual natural pink look, and it brightened her whole face in a way that made his words jumble and stick in his head. "It's fall, so I love to use all the seasonal spices, like cinnamon and cloves. But the unsung hero of your spice rack that in my opinion doesn't get nearly enough attention is cardamom. Today's recipe is a nod to my dad's Finnish heritage, korvapuusti."

"Gesundheit," Malcolm joked and was rewarded with a laugh in Georgia's real voice, not her "Mom on camera" voice.

"Korvapuusti means 'slapped ear' in Finnish," she explained. "I don't know where the name comes from, but my friend Mr. G should be warned not to push my buttons too much during tonight's challenge or the dough won't be the only ear that gets slapped."

"Which ear?"

"Whichever one you like the best," she quipped, reaching up to give his left earlobe a little tug. The intimacy of the gesture made his heart swell like the dough she had prepared last night and left to rise in the fridge. "I joke, of course. We'll leave the violence to the actual Vikings."

"A shout-out to my home team, the Minnesota Vikings." Malcolm pounded his chest and kissed his fingers to the camera. "Go Vikes!"

"Watch it, bud." Georgia wagged her finger at him. "You're in Buffalo Bills country now. But back to our recipe. Make sure when you're using yeast that you proof it first. Add your active dry yeast to the lukewarm milk."

"And by lukewarm, Gigi means one hundred and eight degrees Fahrenheit milk," Malcolm added. "Too warm and you'll kill the fungus in the yeast that is responsible for the rising action we want in the bread."

"One hundred and eight, give or take," Georgia stepped in front of him to clarify, following with a stage whisper closer to the phone. "But really, as long as it's not boiling you'll be okay—I can see you making the numbers with your fingers in the camera, Mr. G," she said in a louder, still on-camera, but definitely more stern Mom voice. Rolling her eyes at their audience, she hooked a thumb over her shoulder. "This guy is going to end up with a sore left ear before we're done, mark my words."

"How did you know the left one was my favorite?" he said in a pretend shocked whisper, covering his left ear with one hand, then tossing a wink over the phone at Caroline. "So what do we do after our yeast is proofed?"

"We add our sugar," she said, reaching for the ingredient and pouring it into the stand mixer on the counter. "Now, you can vary the sugar based on how sweet you like your cinnamon rolls."

Malcolm shook his head. "But what does the recipe call for?"

She turned her head and pretended to glare at him. "My recipe calls for three-quarters cup, but remember we'll be adding sugar pearls at the end, so that will increase the sweetness. Recipes are important, but especially with family dishes passed down from generation to generation, adjustments get made due to personal preference."

He shrugged. "I don't have a lot of experience with intergenerational cooking, but I do know that sugar is an essential part of baking because not only does it attract water molecules, keeping our cakes nice and moist—"

Georgia made a face. "Ugh. I hate that word."

"Good to know," Malcolm said with a mischievous smile. "Now I know how to get even after you slap my favorite ear. Sugar also inhibits gluten development, so too much of it isn't great for our breads, because gluten is a protein that gives bread the nice chewy texture we want."

"After the flour, we're going to add the cardamom straight to the dough," Georgia said as she poured the prepared ingredient cups into the mixer. "This is what makes this dough different from the gigantic mall cinnamon buns we had as kids."

"What's a mall?" Caroline asked.

Malcolm and Georgia exchanged looks. "Kids," they said in unison. He had to hold back a sigh that might give away how much he loved moments like these with her. This was what he wanted, the joking back and forth as a family, having a kid of his own to tease with another adult instead of always having to be the lone disciplinarian in his classroom.

Being with Georgia and Caroline every Friday evening made it even more clear that he was ready for this season of life to begin. When they were together, they slipped into the roles so naturally that he almost couldn't remember what his Fridays were like before them.

The dough thumped loudly against the side of the mixer, and Malcolm raised his voice to be heard over it. "Did you know that the reason yeast causes bread to rise is because it's actually a microorganism that produces CO_2 gas after it consumes the sugars in the recipe?"

Georgia stopped the mixer and turned around, leaning against the counter with her arms dropped to her sides. "I'm sorry, what?"

"Yeast," he said matter-of-factly. "It's a tiny critter that loves sugar and produces copious amounts of gas. Basically all of the boys in my third-grade class, am I right, Caroline?"

Caroline clutched the stool for dear life as she dissolved into a fit of giggles.

Georgia, meanwhile, continued to look at him with a mixture of horror and disbelief. "I—I did not need to know this," she said, then leaned her left elbow on the edge of the counter and addressed the camera. "See, this is the problem with scientists, folks. Sometimes it's better to believe things happen by magic."

"Magic doesn't just happen on its own," Malcolm pointed out. "If you want something, you have to do the work and make it happen."

Georgia turned, and he held her stare meaningfully as long as he could before turning back to the camera. "So here's another interesting thing about yeast..."

By the time he had finished his lecture, Georgia had sworn off bread entirely. "Good going, Professor," she said sarcastically, pushing the plate of cinnamon buns fresh out of the oven away from her. "You ruined one of my favorite foods for me. Are you done, or is there some sordid story you want to share about a beloved cartoon character from my childhood?"

He grinned. "More slapped ears for me, then." Grabbing one of the buns off the plate, he blew on it before taking a large bite. "Mmm." Malcolm sighed contentedly as he took it into the living room and collapsed on the couch. "Microorganismy goodness. Only one cell, but ten out of ten for taste."

She shook her head, but relented and took a bun, placing it on a paper towel before joining him on the couch. "You've spent too much time in elementary school," she said. "Your sense of humor is on par with Caroline's."

"I happen to think your daughter has an extremely sophisticated sense of humor," he rebutted, finishing the last bite of his cinnamon bun and dusting the crumbs off his hands.

"Either way, it was good to hear her laughing so much. That's a sound I'll never take for granted."

"She's a great kid." He bent one knee up on the couch and twisted to face Georgia. "You're doing an amazing job. I hope you know that."

"Thank you," Georgia said, ducking her head and catching him in one of her sideways glances that made him want to pull her in close and never let go. "It's taken a lot of work to get to a place where we're okay just the two of us. Even now, I still feel like I'm treading water to get through one day at a time."

Malcolm pulled his arm back from resting on the edge of the couch behind Georgia. "I'd like to help if I can," he offered sincerely, placing his hand on her knee. "I mean, I know that's why I'm here, to help get Caroline more enthusiastic about science, but I'm also here if you need to talk or vent or just sit and take a breath. I don't know exactly what you've been through in the past, but I know there are amazing things in your future."

Georgia let out a bark of a laugh. "My future." She put her bun down on the end table to the left of the couch armrest and faced him. "What is it with you and the future?"

He tugged at the bottom of his apron decorated with tiny pink cupcakes and martini glasses. "Because time only moves forward, Georgia. What good does it do to dwell on the past? It's over. There's nothing we can do to change it."

"Because our past makes up who we are," Georgia said. "It's what life is all about, the stories we accumulate and pass down to our children and our children's children. Tomorrow is never promised to any of us. But the memories of the ones we loved, the ones who came before us, the ones who made us…" Georgia put her hand over his and this time not only let it remain but squeezed with what seemed like everything she had. "That's what life is all about. We won't last forever, but our stories live on."

A part of him wanted to let her keep holding on to his hand and stay in the warmth of her grasp regardless of her words that stuck in him like barbed arrows. But it wasn't in his training as a scientist to deny a fundamental truth. "So, what about the people who don't have anyone to pass their stories to?" He moved his hand away, running it through his hair. "What about people whose stories get lost? Do their lives not have meaning?" He stood up and took his plate to the sink, rinsing it off as he tried to breathe through the sadness he'd thought he had outrun. After he put the plate in the drying rack, he took his apron off, balling it in both his hands as Georgia walked slowly into the kitchen after him.

"I'm sorry," Georgia said quietly. "I didn't mean to upset you. I'm a good listener, too, you know."

He gripped the fabric tighter, then released it with a sigh and looked back at her. "It's nothing. I'm fine." Handing Georgia the apron, he forced a copy of his usual smile. "I'm just tired, that's all."

She arched an eyebrow at him, folding the

apron over her arm. "Wife hunting is exhausting business, huh?"

"Make fun, but I stand by what I said earlier." He placed his hand on top of the mixer. "Magic doesn't just happen. You have to go after the things you want or you spend your life waiting for them."

"There's a difference between working toward a goal and forcing things to happen before you're ready," Georgia pointed out. "Marriage is hard enough without a solid foundation to stand on. You should already feel complete as a person before you meet your partner, not expect them to fill in the gaps left by trauma or hurt in your past."

Malcolm's mouth fell open at the direct hit. "Wow. That's—"

"Hang on." Georgia's eyes had taken on that same shine he had glimpsed weeks earlier at BeeBee's. "I've got an idea."

"About my love life?" Malcolm crossed his arms. "If there's a single woman left in town who isn't a fellow teacher, I've already been set up with her."

Georgia waved a hand distractedly at him and paced around the island, weaving the apron through her hands. "I've seen it done before, but it would have to be just right," she muttered to herself. "Not a geode, but not a bomb, either."

"All right, now I'm starting to get worried," Malcolm said. "Should I start hiding the sharp objects or are you going to explain what's going on here?"

"Where's my phone?" Georgia searched the pockets of her pink gingham apron, preoccupied.

Malcolm crossed the room and picked the phone up off the kitchen table. "I'm getting you a charging station," he said. "Did you know that your phone can accumulate more bacteria than a toilet seat?"

"Shh." Georgia held a finger up to him as she took the phone from his hands and scrolled through before raising her fist in triumph. "Yes! I knew I'd seen it before. This is BeeBee's wedding cake." She held the phone up in front of his face.

On the screen was a picture of a pristine white cake that had been sliced open, and inside was a core of glittering rock candy. He raised his eyes to see Georgia riffling in her pantry, filling her arms with boxes and sacks of sugar.

"How do you make this?" he asked. "Please tell me you have an actual recipe, because this looks really difficult."

"Well, I have a recipe for a geode cake." She looked over her shoulder at him, and the rising tower of baking materials in her arms swayed precariously. "But this is different. See—" Georgia added, turning around and leaning back slightly to peer over a box of kosher salt. "Instead of the rock candy placed on the outside, we'll put it inside the cake. If I do it after baking, we'll avoid the brownie landslide from the first time I tried this. Sugar in sugar, that's what BeeBee wanted." She staggered to the table and Malcolm rushed to steady her with a hand under her elbow, another on her lower back. "Thank you."

"I love it," he said, unloading the boxes from her arms and placing them on the table. "It's unexpected and fun, just like BeeBee."

"Exactly," Georgia said, letting out an exhausted breath and putting her hands on her hips. "I've been stuck for ages trying to figure out what her perfect wedding cake would be, and this is it." She sank into the chair at the table as if someone had suddenly deflated her. "Finally, I broke my slump." She tipped her head back and her eyes found his. "I had hoped baking for this competition would inspire me, but it turns out I just needed you."

Malcolm swallowed hard. The excited flush in her cheeks and the brightness in her eyes, tired as they were, were the most beautiful thing he'd seen since his trip to see the Hope Diamond at the Smithsonian. If only she needed him as more than a baking assistant, as more than Caroline's teacher. After the struggles she'd alluded to earlier, he knew more than ever he couldn't do anything that would impact her progress. But in nine months, he wouldn't be Caroline's teacher anymore…

He looked at Georgia again, fighting the urge to kiss the victorious smile turning the corners of her lips upward.

Would waiting nine months really be so bad if that was the reward at the end?

CHAPTER FIFTEEN

WHEN GEORGIA AND Caroline arrived at BeeBee's farm that Monday, they were already twenty minutes latc. What was unusual about it was that she had actually slept in until six thirty this morning. She assumed Malcolm would forgive the tardiness as he was, if not partially at fault, complicit in the cause for her fatigue.

Malcolm had come over again on Sunday night and they had stayed up until almost midnight sketching out plans for BeeBee's wedding cake. The high school industrial science class had a 3-D printer he said he could use to make a special heatproof cake pan that would allow her to insert the rock candy cylinder in a perfect fit into the cake using different size layers. The rock candy would go through the core and onto the silicone circles where the cakes would sit, giving the impression of a layer of crystals underneath the buttercream frosting and the cake itself. He had explained it in excited geologist terms of which she understood possibly ten percent. The important thing was that it would work. That particular problem might have taken her weeks of trial and error to solve, yet with his help it had only taken hours.

She had forgotten how much easier it was to solve problems when the burden wasn't completely on her to solve them.

"Move with purpose, sweetie," she told Caroline as they parked the car in front of the house. "Mr. G's car is already here."

Caroline threw open the passenger side door and was already halfway up the driveway by the time Georgia unbuckled her seat belt. Caroline had been looking forward to this all week, poring over the geology books Malcolm had sent home with her with the same enthusiasm Georgia used to reserve for the Pioneer Woman's monthly recipe magazine. Georgia shook her head as she got out and followed her daughter up the steps. She'd gone through this whole cooking demonstration thing to get Caroline into science and to fire up her own inspiration, yet it wasn't the competition or the fact that they had made it into the final round that had done it.

It had simply been Malcolm.

BeeBee greeted them on the front porch with her work boots and gloves already on. "Hey, ladies." She waved as she closed the door behind her. "My dad and Mr. G are already out there. They took the tractor out a while ago. Your teacher said he wanted to get some of the rocks broken up before you guys got here."

"He's not my— Oh, you're talking to Caroline." Georgia bit her lip after realizing BeeBee had been looking down at her daughter.

"Mmm-hmm." BeeBee raised her eyebrows but thankfully didn't say any more about Georgia's telling reaction and the blush that seemed to rise on her cheeks whenever Malcolm's name came up. "I'll take you guys down in our riding mower. It's almost time for the buffaloes to come back from their morning wallow in the creek. I want to observe their behavior while you guys are out there doing your mining stuff to make sure it doesn't affect my babies."

"Mr. G taught us about how observing things is part of the scientific method," Caroline said, beaming up at BeeBee. "After that, you form a hypothesis and then conduct experiments."

BeeBee nodded and bent down, putting her hands on her knees. "Well, my hypothesis is that you are going to be a wonderful veterinarian someday if you listen to Mr. G." She stood back up and cracked her back. "Oof, although if you wanted to become a chiropractor, I would let you practice on me. I had to stand still for over an hour yesterday for a wedding gown fitting. I'm having my grandmother's wedding dress remade—" She stopped herself, cringing. "Sorry, Gigi. I know you don't like to talk about wedding stuff."

"It's all right." Georgia shook her head. "I had a revelation last night about your cake—I'll bring over some new samples next week, by the way—and now I'm actually really looking forward to it." She looked down and ruffled Caroline's hair. "Caroline is so excited to be your flower girl, too. Your wedding is going to be perfect, we'll make sure of that."

BeeBee heaved her shoulders in a sigh. "Perfect would have been having Fernando the water buffalo as the ring bearer, but we couldn't get the permits for that, no matter how many town committees my mom heads up. Anyway—" She gestured with her chin toward the equipment shed next to the silo. "Let's head on out before the guys get too far ahead without you."

They rode out on the large mower with Caroline seated in the small attached cart behind it. It was a beautiful autumn day, the tall grasses rippling like water in the wind as they drove through the fields. They turned in to the wooded area past the grazing fields, and the trees overhead formed a canopy of oranges, reds and earthy browns. As they ventured into the woods, the sounds of rocks tumbling and crashing grew louder, interspersed with the mechanical whirring of the digger.

BeeBee slowed the mower to a stop, concern wrinkling her forehead. "Gosh, that's loud. Still, we're pretty far back from the farm," she said, looking over her shoulder in the direction they had just traveled. "I'd better get back to keep an eye on my herds. Happy digging," she said with a wave of her gloved hand.

Georgia helped Carolinc out of the back trailer and they waved as BeeBee carefully backed the mower into the field. The trail from the digger was visible in the partially cleared woods, so they followed the tire tracks and the sound until they reached an opening in the tree line where a small stream cut through and led to a rocky outcropping.

"Careful where you step," Georgia cautioned Caroline, grabbing her hand as they navigated around the large upturned boulders in their path. She held the other hand over her eyes and followed a clanking sound to where Malcolm was in the middle of whacking the side of the gray cliff with a large hammer. She swallowed hard at the sight of him with his sleeves rolled up enough to show the defined muscles in his forearms as he worked, his jawline tight with intense focus on the task at hand. He wore safety glasses over his dark eyes, and his usually neat hair was tousled from a morning of effort. But what was most attractive was the satisfied expression on his face. He was so clearly in his element, and when he turned his head and smiled at them, it was like the sun finally bursting through what felt like years of storm clouds over her skies.

"Come on over." He gestured to them, setting down the hammer. "I can't wait to show you what I've found."

"Is it safe?" Georgia called back.

"I won't break any more rocks until you both have eye coverings on," he called back. "Hurry up, this is amazing."

Georgia rolled her eyes. The man had absolutely zero patience, but his enthusiasm was so infectious it was almost endearing. "Hold your horses. We're on our way."

They stepped carefully over the small field of broken-up boulders to where he stood next to the digger with his gloved hands on his hips. When they made their way to the side of the cliff, he pointed to what looked like a small hole in the rough face of the rock.

"Look in there," he said, crouching down and reaching an arm out to steady Caroline as she peered inside. "What do you see?"

Caroline gasped. "It's—it's a crystal. I can see the points, just like in the books."

He turned his head to give Georgia a proud

grin. "That's right. That's what we rockhounds call a goonie right there. It's probably the size of my fist," he said, balling his hand up to show Caroline. "Wanna help me dig it out?"

She squealed so loud, Georgia was surprised it didn't start an avalanche.

Malcolm handed them both plastic safety glasses and had them stand back as he chiseled around the edges of the hole. Once the sides of the rock had fallen away, he and Caroline worked together to carefully extricate the crystal from its cavern. Even covered in dirt, it glinted in the sunshine as Caroline held it aloft.

"Mommy, look," she said, her voice now hushed with awe. "It's beautiful."

Georgia took the rock from her hand and gazed into the smoky depths before handing it back to Malcolm. "I can't believe you pulled it out like that. It looks like someone already hand-cut it into a perfect diamond."

"That's why they call them Herkimer diamonds," he said. Picking up a satchel from by his feet, he carefully set the crystal inside, then dug around and pulled out a closed hand. "I picked these up off the ground after we broke off a couple of those big rocks from over where you were a few feet away."

He uncurled his fingers to show smaller crystals around the size of her fingertips, but while the larger one had been darker with clear edges around the tip, these were perfectly clear and sparkled brilliantly as Malcolm held them between his fingers one at a time for them to see.

"That looks just like the stone in my necklace," Georgia said, taking one out of his hand to hold up in the light. "I thought Mike had taken it somewhere to cut it and polish it, but they really do come out of the ground looking just like that, don't they?"

"It's because of the pressure from what used to be deep sea waters covering the land millions of years ago," Malcolm said. "I bet there's all kinds of fossils around here, maybe even sharks' teeth, too."

"Wow," Caroline said. "That's so cool. My dad said he found a shark's tooth on a beach in North Carolina once that was as long as his finger."

Malcolm sat back on his haunches and put his hand on Caroline's shoulder. "Your dad was really into science, wasn't he?"

"Yeah," Caroline said, turning one of the small clear crystals over in her palm. "He knew all about plants, like what kind of plants could be medicines and which ones were safe to eat. We used to go on long walks in the woods as a family, and he would pick plants and wild blueberries and things for Mommy to use in her recipes."

Georgia's throat tightened. She used to experiment all the time with the local herbs, like using wild ginseng to make tea and putting that flavor in her cupcakes or making tarts out of the blackberries that grew in thick clusters along their favorite walking paths. Mike loved exploring and finding new discoveries for her to use in her baking. He called them his treasure quests and never went out for a motorcycle ride without a gallon Ziploc bag in the pocket of his leather jacket to collect his bounty for her.

"You know," Malcolm said quietly, "sometimes when things go away, like how the water here dried up, it feels like they're lost to us forever. But nature has this trick where it shows us that the things we miss the most can come back in different ways. The water isn't here anymore, but instead we have these beautiful crystals to remind us of it. Look—" He held one of the crystals up to the perfectly blue sky. "Doesn't that look like a big blue sea to you?"

"Yeah, it does," Caroline said excitedly. "I see it."

"I bet if you go look over in that pile of rocks I broke up, you'll find more tiny pieces of the ocean," he said, inclining his head to his left. "You have to look really carefully to see something shiny."

Caroline trotted off to search among the rocks,

and Malcolm pressed his hands on his knees to stand, then walked over to Georgia. "How long has it been since your husband passed?" he murmured at her side, his arm brushing gently against hers.

"Almost five years," Georgia said. She could scarcely breathe, too many conflicting feelings pressing against her at once. The reassuring warmth of Malcolm's nearness fought against the familiar tide of sadness and loss. She inhaled deeply and, strangely, found that the conflicting emotions could coexist without pulling her under the tides. "Caroline was only four years old."

"It's nice that she can remember so much about him."

"At first I couldn't even talk about him," Georgia said, turning to face Malcolm. "But after the first year of just surviving, we started to see a counselor and found a really great support group. They helped me get to a point where I could tell her stories about him and the memories were… well, they were still painful, but the more we talked about them, the more it helped us adjust to the loss. Now I try to share as much with her as I can so she feels like she still has a connection to him. I'm afraid…" Georgia inhaled deeply. "I'm afraid of him becoming less real to her. Already sometimes it feels like the memories are pictures that fell out of a photo album, and it's getting harder to remember what order they were in to begin with. As hard as it has been for both of us, we've gotten to a really stable place, and I'm so afraid of anything that could disrupt our progress."

"It makes sense now, why she was so reticent about our first science classes." Malcolm looked over at Caroline then back at Georgia. "I started the earth science unit by talking about how important trees and plants are and asked them to find a leaf to bring in from their yards or the park. I'm so sorry if that triggered the grief for either of you."

Georgia put her hand on his chest. "You've been a wonderful teacher for her," she said, focusing on the soft feel of the fabric, the way the light gray collar was darker around the neck from the sweat of his exertions. Anything but the feel of his eyes trained directly on her, seeing through her. "With the crystal digs and the geology, you've helped her find a connection to her dad's love of science in a way that isn't tied to the loss. This— You," she corrected herself, finally daring to lift her eyes to his face and feeling her breath still at his gaze. "You are exactly what she needed."

"If you'll let me—" He lowered his head toward hers, the husky whisper sending shivers down her spine. "I want to be what you need.

Like last night with the wedding cake. Georgia, there's something here, isn't there? Please tell me it isn't just in my head."

Everything about this moment felt perfect: the soft autumn light bathing them in gold, the quiet trills of the birds overhead, the crunch of the leaves underfoot as he took another step toward her. It was all of her favorite things about the season making her senses come alive and cry out for a new beginning, for adventure, for love. But then Caroline's joyful exclamation from behind a boulder brought her back to the sobering reality. There was already love in her life that needed her utmost attention and care. This gorgeous, funny, too-intelligent-for-his-own-good man was her child's teacher. She couldn't do this, not with him. Mike might be gone, but his child was still here, and she owed it to him to be the world's best mother.

No matter the cost.

Dropping her hand from his shirt, she stepped back and shook her head, keeping her eyes on her daughter's blond ponytail bobbing just beyond the ridge. "Mr. Gulleson—"

The hopeful expression on his face cracked sorrowfully at the formality. Pain and regret tore at her even as she continued to talk.

"I can't thank you enough for everything you're doing for my daughter," she said, forcing strength into her voice even as she had to wrap her hands behind her back to keep from embracing him. "And for me. I know you've made huge sacrifices of your time with this whole baking contest, and it's certainly paid off." Georgia looked into his eyes only long enough to paste a casual smile on her face before glancing down at the ground. "But you want a wife and a family, so much so that I think you're confusing friendship with romance. We're friends and you're Caroline's teacher. That's it." She inhaled a shaky breath. "Now, why don't you take this Friday off from our baking shenanigans and go out on a real date?"

He ran a hand through his hair and looked over his shoulder, blinking. "I—I guess that's… logical."

Caroline emerged from behind the rocks holding up a hand in triumph. "Look what I found, Mr. G!"

He held up a hand to her, then faced Georgia with a smile that didn't light up his eyes the way it usually did. "Looks like my student needs me," he said, a small note of bitterness in his voice.

"Malcol— Mr. Gulleson," Georgia started, but he shook his head and held up a hand.

"It's fine." He shrugged. "Not the first time I've read a situation completely wrong. Last time

I did this, I ended up leaving the school and moving because the fellow teacher I had been dating and had actually proposed to was still in love with someone else."

"Oh, no," Georgia breathed softly. "That must have been awful."

He cleared his throat. "It was." Malcolm bent down and picked up his rock-collecting sack off the ground. "That's why I made my rule about not getting involved with people related to my work. I guess I just needed a reminder."

He walked over to Caroline, leaving Georgia wondering why something they'd both agreed was the right thing to do suddenly felt so wrong.

CHAPTER SIXTEEN

NORMALLY COMING BACK to school on Tuesday after a three-day weekend was even harder than returning on a normal Monday. The kids were off their routine just enough to be extra wired and yet somehow simultaneously more tired than usual despite having an additional day to sleep in.

This Tuesday morning, however, Malcolm couldn't wait to see his students and show them all the incredible finds after just a few hours of excavating and light digging yesterday. He gathered them around his desk and spread out the best crystals on a brown leather backing.

The reaction was worth it.

"So cool," Riley Brewster shouted. To be fair, he was one of those kids who shouted everything, but the grin on his freckled face was one of pure exhilaration.

"I bet you could sell those for a lot of money," Jeremy Binkus said, his fingers creeping surreptitiously close to the largest crystal in the corner. "Like a thousand dollars each."

"Even though they're called Herkimer diamonds, they're not worth as much as real diamonds," Malcolm explained. "They're actually quartz crystals. Remember how we talked about how diamonds are carbon atoms that are stacked by the pressure from deep within the earth and lined up in a certain way that makes them true diamonds? Herkimer diamonds are formed by silica deposits and pyrite inside gaps in the dolomite that was underwater millions of years ago. As the water dried and the sediments piling up added both pressure and heat, these certain types of quartz crystals formed slowly inside the cavities."

"My dentist said cavities were bad," Hanna Dettweiler said.

"A cavity is just a hole or an opening," Malcolm offered. "Your dentist is right, cavities in your teeth are bad. But a cavity in a rock means there's space for something beautiful to form under the right conditions."

"Mr. G found holes in almost all of the rocks we dug up yesterday," Caroline chimed in from the back of the group, and the semicircle of kids turned to face her. "He and my great-uncle Jack used a big digger to smash up a big rock wall, and all these boulders came falling down. You could see the holes inside the rock, and Mr. G hit them with a hammer to find the biggest crystal I ever saw."

It was the longest she had ever spoke during a science unit, and Malcolm had to restrain himself from doing his morning greeting gallop out of sheer pride. Now that he knew why she had been holding back her interest in the subject, he didn't want to push her into anything that would make the grief fresh again. Yet here she was acting as a peer leader in discussion time all on her own. If only Georgia was here to see this, she would be thrilled.

"You got to go with Mr. G to dig up crystals?" Riley turned back to face the desk. "I want to go next time."

"My mom went, too," Caroline said, smiling up at Malcolm. "She and Mr. G are doing the baking competition for the Food Network. He's over at our house all the time."

"Can we do a field trip to dig up crystals?" Owen Kent asked. "Please, Mr. G?"

All twenty-one kids turned into a harmonized chorus of pleading.

Malcolm stood up straight and crossed his arms, both pleased and a little overwhelmed. His initial plan had been to try to form an extracurricular club for the five to maybe ten kids he thought would show an interest. But this response was more than he had bargained for. A class field trip would be a totally different ball game, though.

"Just so we're clear—" Malcolm held out a hand to quell the noise. "You *all* think it would be fun to go back into the woods and spend the day picking through dirt and rocks to try to find crystals? There's nothing else there, no rides or games or toys. Raise your hand if that's something you would be interested in doing."

Every single hand shot up and waved frenetically in the air. He rubbed his chin with one hand, the plans aligning in his head like carbon atoms stacking on top of each other. This could be so much bigger than just a junior rockhounding club. If he developed the site to make it an educational experience, it could inspire kids to a new appreciation for the science of geology, not to mention teach them more about the unique geographical history of this region. Look at what it had done for Caroline in such a short amount of time. How many more budding scientists could he inspire with a place like this? He would be able to run it during the summertime when he wasn't teaching, and the weather would force it to remain closed for November through April up here anyway. Plus, having a seasonal business like this would add to the income he needed to help his parents as they aged, not to mention save for the family he hoped to build here.

But creating something like the site he was envisioning would take time, patience and money, three resources he had in very short supply. Waiting for something else he really wanted might just cause his head to explode.

He looked over the small heads milling around Caroline. She was officially the class star of the moment, her cheeks rosy with excitement as she told the other children all about their adventures yesterday. She was such a resilient little girl, mature beyond her years after all that she'd gone through. Clearly having him around her mom didn't bother her; on the contrary, the association seemed to be helping her come out of her shell even more. But it didn't matter unless Georgia felt the same way. Did she really mean it when she said they were just friends or was she pushing him away for Caroline's sake? He knew her well enough by now that she would do anything for her daughter, even deny her own heart. Respecting her wishes and maintaining the appearance of friendship he could do. Shutting down the feelings growing stronger every time he saw her was going to be a lot harder.

The alarm on his watch signaled it was time for lunch and as the children dispersed to gather their lunch boxes, Malcolm put his hand on Caroline's shoulder and took her aside by his desk.

"Hey, kiddo," he said quietly. "Is your mom working at the bakery after school today?"

"Yup," Caroline responded quickly. "She's there almost every day. I won't be there because I'm going home with Olivia H after school this week."

"Awesome." He gave her a thumbs-up, then nodded at the line of kids by the door. "Go grab your lunch and get in line. Oh, and great job in class today. You were a super helper."

"Thanks Mr. G." She rocked back on her heels and beamed before dashing to the back of the room to grab her lunch from her backpack hook.

Malcolm's cheeks started to burn from the grin he hadn't even realized was practically splitting his face in two. She was such a sweet kid. He cared about all his students and their progress as learners, but watching Caroline's interest in science blossom during their time together had meant more to him than he could have ever thought possible.

After school, he had a quick faculty meeting with the vice principal, then he went straight to his car and drove into town to the bakery. Practically leaping out of the car, he sprinted through the door and leaned heavily on the front counter where Georgia's friend Silas jumped back in alarm.

"Whoa there, Mr. G, where's the fire?" Silas clutched a hand to his heart, then shook his head. "Don't tell Gigi I said that. She gets superstitious about making fire jokes in a building filled with ovens. What's up?"

Seemed like it was true that his official name to everyone was Mr. G. He supposed there were worse nicknames. "I was hoping to chat with Georgia for a bit. Is she around?"

Silas jerked his head toward the back. "She's in there. Normally, I'm not supposed to let anyone back there, but I think she'll make an exception for you."

Malcolm could have sworn the man winked at the last word. "Thanks."

Making his way around the counter, he pushed the double doors to the back of the bakery open and looked around before spotting her golden hair gleaming under the fluorescent lights as she bent over a tray of cupcakes. She squinted in deep concentration, and her pursed lips looked as if they were made for him to kiss. Malcolm took a deep breath and slowed his pace as he crossed the room.

"Need a hand?"

Georgia blinked as her back straightened abruptly. "Malcolm, what are you doing here?"

Her mouth formed an O as a hand shot out and gripped the gleaming countertop. "Is Caroline okay?"

"She's fine," he reassured her with a smile. "She told me she was going to a friend's house after school."

"Yeah, Olivia Hamilton's mom picked her up." Georgia smiled. "She lives in our neighborhood. The girls have been friends since they were toddlers. So, what's going on?"

"Well, I, uh, wanted to see how things were going," he said, suddenly very aware that barging in, in the middle of her work, wasn't exactly the best timing, especially when she had told him to let her do this on her own. "The baking show finals are less than two weeks away, right? I—I just wanted to let you know that I'm here if you need anything. As a friend, of course." That was his working hypothesis: she really did just want to be friends as she had stated. But the scientist in him needed to eliminate all the other possible outcomes, including the tiny chance she shared his feelings, before giving up hope entirely. If he sat and talked to her long enough, the answer would hopefully become clear as a perfect crystal with zero occlusions.

A cloud of flour bloomed as she dusted her hands off on her apron. Malcolm wondered if she was trying to give him the brush off as well or merely taking the time to think over his offer. Reaching under the counter, she dragged out a stool, wincing at the loud scraping sound. "Friends are always welcome at my table," she said with a tight smile. "I was just finishing these cupcakes with apple pie filling if you want to perform a little quality control." She grabbed a paper towel off the end of the counter and placed a cupcake on it, sliding it over to him as he sat on the stool. "Honestly, I've barely had time to think about what I'm going to bake in the final. The show sent over a contract this morning. They're going to send a film crew to the bakery next week to do some shots of me preparing and edit them into the episode if we win."

"When you win," he corrected her, peeling the wrapper off the side of the cupcake. "You've got this in the bag."

She looked up from piping caramel-colored frosting on the cupcakes with a barely suppressed smile. "You know I entered this contest to try and shake myself out of the doldrums I'd been in, but now it's actually starting to feel real. I shouldn't get ahead of myself, though. I mean, there's no point in getting ahead of myself when I don't even know what I'm going to do for the final bake."

"What are the parameters?"

She raised her eyes at him and quirked an eyebrow sarcastically. “Leave it to you to make it sound like an experiment,” she joked, bending her head down to finish the last row of cupcakes. “It can be anything, but it has to be inspired by autumn.”

“Autumn.” He took a bite of the cupcake and chewed thoughtfully. “Well, this apple cinnamon cupcake is very autumn…y.” He swallowed and shook his head. “My dad would be making a face if he heard me say that. He’s a stickler for exact vocabulary.”

“The word you’re looking for is *autumnal*,” Georgia said, blowing the hair out of her face as she shook a kink out of her hand. “It’s so basic, though.” She frowned as she gestured with her icing bag. “I really want to do something that represents how special our town is, but something totally out of the box. Nailing BeeBee’s wedding cake idea has my creative spark back in full force. I really want to create something special that no one else has done before, not just the same old autumn spice profile of cinnamon and ginger, you know?”

An idea was rolling around in his head. More like a memory, even though it was one he tried not to dwell on too much. “You know, in Chinese culture, there’s a harvest festival celebrated in autumn that honors the moon. A big part of the festival is eating what they call mooncakes, this round pastry with a sweet filling."

Her eyes lit up. "I've heard of them but never had one. I like the idea," she said, pulling up another stool and settling herself in it. "But I would also like to tie it in to something special about Crystal Hill. You know, the way I'm doing with BeeBee's wedding cake and the crystal rock candy inside."

"Well, you couldn't do rock candy inside these." He wrinkled his nose. "The pastry is really delicate and flaky—it would fall apart." More memories from the festival came flooding back, the sweet red bean paste mingling with the bitterness of disappointment, the full moon overhead seeming to feel as solitary as he had in that moment despite being surrounded by hundreds of people in the square. That had been the night he'd learned what had happened to his birth mother. It had been that night that he'd closed up the one box he wouldn't unpack until his future was happy enough to erase the pain of the past.

"You taught in China, right?" she asked. "Do you have family back there who might have a recipe? I would need to know the authentic way to make one before I could play around with a different interpretation of it."

Malcolm stiffened. "No. No family there." He

set the rest of the cupcake down, his mouth suddenly dry as if the cupcake was filled with sawdust. "Um, hey, changing the subject, did you hear from BeeBee about how her animals reacted to all our digging?"

"No." Georgia tipped her head, looking confused at the abrupt segue. "Malcolm, are you all right? You got pale all of a sudden."

"It's just, um, a sugar rush," he said, standing up suddenly. "I think I might head over to the farm tonight to check with BeeBee about an idea I had for the dig site. You wanna come with me?"

"That would be fun, but I've got to pick up Caroline, then work some more on the homemade rock candy for BeeBee's cake samples. I'm hoping to get those done and bring them over to the farm on Friday. Since we're not baking this week, I have that evening free." She glanced down at her fingers drumming on the counter before looking back up at him. "So, uh, you probably have a hot date all lined up for your night off from being my baking assistant? You know, wives aren't like quartz crystals. You won't find one just walking around looking at the ground."

Well, Malcolm guessed that was his answer. This was the second time she had encouraged him to date other women. The experiment had been repeated and now there was only one conclusion: She simply wasn't interested in being anything other than friends and baking partners. His heart sank all the way down to his toes.

"Caroline did great in class today," he said, changing the subject to the one thing they agreed on. "I think the dig really inspired her. It inspired me, too, actually. That's why I want to go talk to BeeBee as soon as possible. I had an idea today, but I'm going to need her permission before I can go any farther with it."

Georgia paused with a handful of sprinkles poised over the cupcakes. "Good luck." She tossed him a nod over her shoulder. "I don't think you'll need it, though. She said you really seemed to fit in with the town, and from Bee-Bee, praise doesn't get much higher than that."

He took a step next to her, close enough to pull her in for an embrace if she happened to turn around. "I really feel like Crystal Hill is where I'm meant to be," he said in a low voice.

She turned, and for a moment, it seemed like she was leaning in toward him for the kiss he had longed for since the first moment they met. Then her eyes widened and she looked over his shoulder. "Silas, hi."

Malcolm whirled around, then stepped away. No need to get the gossip mill whirring over a romance that would only exist in his dreams. "I was just, um, helping Georgia with the cupcakes," he said, going behind her to adjust the rows whose asymmetry had been bothering him since she had removed one to give to him. "That's all."

"Mmm-hmm," Silas said, tapping the toes of one foot in front of the other. "Gigi, Ms. Hooker from the paper is here. She wanted to see if you had time to do a quick interview about the Food Network contest."

"Sure," she said. Swiveling her head around, she elbowed Malcolm in the ribs. "You want to do this with me? We're a pretty good team."

Forever, he wanted to say, but instead he shook his head. "I've really got to talk to Bee-Bee about the site as soon as possible," he said, nodding at the cupcakes as he brushed past her. "They're delicious, by the way. You should keep that recipe in mind for the final. The mooncake thing was just a suggestion. I'm sure there are way better options. So, I'll, uh, see you around."

"See you," she called after him, her tone breezy and distracted.

Malcolm got back into his car, having gotten an answer to his question about Georgia's feelings. It hadn't been the answer he had hoped for, even if it was the right one. Being a good teacher was important to him, but the longer he spent in Crystal Hill, the more he wanted to make it his forever home with a forever family.

As he squinted away from the sun setting over the lake, he found himself for once out of hypotheses as to what was wrong with him. Why was this so hard?

Maybe it was time to face the uncomfortable truth that the confounding variable in his experiment…was him. He picked up the phone and made a call to the number he'd almost deleted a year ago when she called off their engagement.

Lisette agreed to meet him in Bingleyton, at a small Chincsc rcstaurant insidc a quaint brick shopping center. He hadn't seen her since the end of the last school year, when the other teachers had thrown a going-away event for him. He wouldn't call it a party because of how awkward it had been. Everyone in the room knew what had happened between them and why he was leaving. But looking back, there was more to the story. There had to be, and if he didn't find the answer, he might spend the rest of his life alone because of it.

They sat at a small table and ordered hot tea and soup. Lisette nervously twisted the ring on her right hand. It wasn't the one he had given her. She had insisted he take that one back after he had found her kissing the gym teacher in the supply closet.

"How have you been?" he asked politely, trying to break the tension.

She sipped her tea and made a face. Taking an ice cube out of her water glass, she slipped it in and Malcolm grimaced. Watering down perfectly good oolong. She had always been less adventurous than him when it came to food, ordering chicken tenders and fries at Middle Eastern restaurants and refusing to try anything new. "I'm all right," she said. "My class this year is good. A couple of my old students' younger siblings in the mix, so it's nice to already know the parents."

"That's good," he said. Straightening his collar, Malcolm ran his finger down the laminated menu. "I think I might try something a little spicier this time—"

"Malcolm, why did you ask me to meet you here?" she asked bluntly. Her brown hair hung over one eye like a curtain, and she pushed it anxiously out of the way. "If you are trying to get back together with me, you should know that Jason and I moved in together. You and I are not going to happen," she enunciated clearly, moving her finger back and forth between them.

"No, that's not why I wanted to see you," Malcolm clarified, setting the menu down on the table and leaning forward. "I'm glad you're happy. I just want some information. That's all."

Her shoulders slumped with relief. "Of course. Leave it to you to leave no stone unturned when it comes to research." She smiled. "What great problem of the universe are you trying to solve now that you need my help?"

"It's me, actually." He took a deep breath and looked directly at her. Funny how this had been the woman he was sure he was meant to spend his life with, and now less than a year after he had proposed to her, the butterflies were completely gone. She might as well have been a stranger. "Why do I go after unavailable women? Is there something wrong with me?"

Her eyes widened behind her red-rimmed glasses, and her chin jutted forward. "So this is what we're doing? Okay." She pushed the tea out of the way and put her hand on his arm. "Malcolm, you proposed to me after we had only been dating three months."

"So?" He shrugged. "Some women find spontaneity romantic."

"But you're not a spontaneous person," she said. "You're methodical when it comes to every aspect of your life except love."

"That's not…entirely true," he argued. "I wear fun T-shirts."

"Science-themed T-shirts, but that's not my point," she said. "You wanted to get married so badly, it didn't matter to whom. When I got the ring cleaned at the jewelry store, they said you got it years before you proposed to me, when you were dating Felicia and she was clearly not right for you."

The back of his neck got hot and Malcolm tried to sputter a defense, but none came. "I—I thought maybe she could be, you know, the one," he stammered before throwing his hands up. "Why do I do that?"

She shook her head and pulled her hand back. "Only you can answer that. But I'm guessing it has something to do with that box you refuse to unpack. Whatever you found out in China, you've never dealt with it. Until you do, you're always going to be looking for answers in the wrong places."

He swirled his spoon through his soup, focusing on the steam rising from the liquid. "Huh."

Lisette sat back and crossed her arms. "Speaking of Felicia, I heard she was looking for speakers at a big geology convention at Cornell next week. It's a little last-minute, but I'm sure she would put your name in. It would be a great opportunity for you, especially if you're looking to branch out of elementary education anytime."

His chin shot up indignantly. "And what's wrong with elementary ed?" Malcolm asked. "I love teaching at this level. This is where we can make a difference, where we shape the kinds of learners they're going to be."

"Let's see." She blew a strand of hair out of

her face. "The money's barely enough to raise a family on, for one thing. Jason and I had a really hard time finding a place on both of our salaries. You keep talking about wanting a family, but I think teaching is holding you back from that goal."

He shook his head. "You're wrong. Teaching is what led me to..." Georgia's smile filled his mind and brightened his heart. How could he have ever thought Lisette was the one? Now that he had met Georgia, it was like night and day. She knew who he was, how important teaching could be. Sure, Lisette had a point about their salary, but if he could get his mining business up and running in the offseason, it would more than make up for it.

"Never mind. Anyway, I'm working on a side hustle that I think could be really big." A light bulb went off inside his head. "A side hustle that would actually benefit from some sponsors in the geology community." A grin started to spread across his face. "You know what? I think I will call Felicia about that conference. Do you know when it is?"

"Next Friday," she said. "Glad I could help."

"In more ways than one," he said, leaning back in the chair.

Back at his apartment, Malcolm didn't even greet Newton. Instead, he went straight to his room and pulled out the box Lisette had talked about, the one thing he owned that didn't have its own designated spot on a shelf.

It was a small box with only a few items in it. A few pictures, a broken teacup and a corkscrew press mold with stamps that looked like flowers, but it was old and worn, so that the flowers looked as though they had been dropped on the floor and trampled. He picked up the picture first. A young Chinese woman standing in front of the window of a bakery and a tall white man in a tailored suit with his arm around her. The branches of some kind of flowering tree reached over them with white blossoms that brushed the top of the man's head.

Malcolm traced the edge of the photograph with one finger, then set it back down. His last name was Gulleson and he was proud of his parents, of their accomplishments and of the way they had raised him. They had never shied away from the truth about his unique cultural heritage and had encouraged him to be just as proud of the country where he had been born as the one where he had been raised. But even the best parenting couldn't shield a child from the inevitable sadness of growing up and learning that nothing was as simple as one plus two equals three.

Next, he picked up the mold. The rust could be cleaned off and the stamps easily dinged back into shape. He was sure she could order some online, but they wouldn't be authentic mooncake molds, used for generations of bakers in a tiny shop in the Guangdong Province. This mold was special because of the wear and tear, because of its history. It had been saved all those years for him and him alone.

Just like Georgia.

Were there other women here in Crystal Hill he could date, marry, have a family with? Absolutely. The men at Big Joe's hadn't been kidding about the ratio. But there was only one woman who felt like she had been made just for him, one woman whose history and the bruised corners of her heart made her even more precious to him. Even if he had completely blown his chances with her and she never married him, this time he wasn't just picking up a box and moving on to the next one.

This time, he would settle in, get comfortable and wait for her to realize, as he had, that the only future worth having was one they spent together. But first, he was going to have to tell her the full story of his own past, one he didn't like to revisit because it too was messy and complicated.

CHAPTER SEVENTEEN

IN ALL HER years at the bakery, Georgia had never thought she would get sick of the smell of cinnamon, sugar and vanilla.

But here she was, thirty-two years old and it finally happened.

She was sick of every single autumn spice in her cupboard. Cloves, ginger, nutmeg, all of it made her gag after days of doing nothing but baking autumnal sweets, none of which seemed special enough. She had four days before the Food Network crew came to film her for the final bake, and she had no idea what she was going to make. She buried her head in her hands, not caring that she was going to leave white streaks of flour in her hair. So what if she ended up looking like the witch from Hansel and Gretel? Cannibalism aside, that woman baked an entire house. *She* clearly had no issues with being creatively blocked.

A knock sounded at the doorway of the bakery.

"I'm in no mood for another inspirational pep

talk, Silas," she groaned with her forehead still resting on the counter. "And as much as I love musicals, if you break into another Rodgers and Hammerstein medley, you may never walk alone again, but you will be limping."

"Wow," a deep voice that definitely did not belong to Silas said, punctuated with a whistle. "Is this a bad time?"

"Malcolm," she breathed, lifting her head. "What are you doing here?"

And why do you look so good on a Saturday morning? Georgia thought. He had on a navy blue suit over a white button-down in place of his usual silly geology T-shirts. His hair was combed off his face, and he held something behind his back.

He took a tentative step inside the bakery kitchen, leaning forward and lifting his eyebrows. "I came to see you, but I can come back another time, when you're not choosing violence at the sound of beloved Broadway standards."

She tried to smile, but the corners of her mouth were too tired, frustrated and sad, along with every other part of her. "You're safe," she said, then held up one finger. "But one lonely goatherd yodel and you're out."

"Understood." He bobbed his head. "I, uh, I know you're busy, and I know I'm not your favorite person right now, but I brought you something." From behind his back, he withdrew a metal pastry mold and stamps. "If you're still thinking about doing mooncakes for your final bake, you can use this. It was my birth mother's."

Georgia stared at him for a moment, shocked and confused. "I—I hadn't realized you had met your birth parents."

"I didn't," he explained, setting the mold on the counter and pulling up a stool to sit on. "After college, I took the job teaching overseas with the intent of tracking down my birth family. My parents knew the province where I was born and the orphanage. Once there, I was able to find out my birth mother's name and the family bakery where she had worked." He nodded at the mold. "I visited the bakery, and the lady who worked there had known her. She was able to tell me about her—her and my birth father," he added as he leaned his elbows on the counter.

"Malcolm, you don't have to talk about this if you don't want to," Georgia said quickly, reaching out and putting her hand over his.

"I want to." He looked at her hand, then back up at her. "Because I think you're the only person who might really understand what it felt like. My adoptive parents are incredible, warm, loving people who gave me an amazing childhood. They were one thousand percent devoted to being the best parents they could be. And even though they encouraged me to look up any genetic family I had in China, a part of me felt like I was betraying them. Like, how could I possibly want any more than the love they had showered on me my entire life? And when I found out that my birth mother had died from breast cancer a few months after I was born, the grief made the guilt worse somehow. Like how could I mourn the loss of a mom, when I still had one that was very much alive?" He shook his head. "Does that make sense?"

"It does, actually." Georgia felt the tears track down her cheeks through the coating of flour left on them from hours of baking. "I mean, I can't imagine what you went through because it's not the same, but I understand the feelings. How grief and guilt can get all twisted up together. You want to stay connected to the people you lost, but you also feel this pressure not to take time for granted because you know better than anyone how uncertain it all is. It's a lot, especially if you're trying to protect someone you love at the same time." She squeezed his hand. "What about your birth father?"

"He was actually an American, the woman at the bakery told me," Malcolm said. "He and my mom dated when he was overseas on a business trip to the China Import and Export Fair held in Guondong where she lived. Apparently, he told her he would come back and they would get married, but he never did. I did a genetic search online when I got back to the States. He died about twenty years ago in his fifties. Never married, no kids except for me." He let out a sigh. "Anyway, I had thought finding out about my birth parents would give me some closure, but it left me feeling untethered. I think that's why I started to have this urgency about having a family of my own. Like you said, when you know how easily it can all slip away, there's a pressure not to waste any time."

Georgia nodded. "Even now, I feel guilty whenever I lose my patience with Caroline or grumble about having to go to another parent-teacher conference, because I know Mike would have given anything for just one more mundane day of being a parent. He loved her so much." At last she gave Malcolm a weak smile. "He would have really appreciated the way you've taken so much time to get her invested in science, not to mention the way you've inspired me. Baking-wise, that is."

She couldn't tell him the other feelings he inspired in her, feelings she'd thought she might never experience again. The way her heart fluttered when she hadn't seen him in a few days. The way she found herself reaching for his hand whenever he was near. If she told him any of this, she would have to admit to herself that this friendship was turning into something more, and that was the last thing Caroline needed right now. They were so close to turning the page on this new chapter, just the two of them. There was no room in their tiny, cluttered kitchen for her feelings right now.

"At the bakery, I did get to see how they made the mooncakes for the festival," he said, picking up the mold and turning it over in his hands before offering it to her. "I could help you, if you wanted. We started this whole thing together after all. I understand you don't want anyone to get the wrong idea about us." He dipped his chin down and gave her a significant look as if to say he knew she didn't want to lead *him* on. "I'm glad to continue on as a scientific consultant as I recall an earlier offer of mini-muffin compensation being bandied about."

Georgia's heart suddenly lightened as if someone had taken a weight off it and allowed it to stir once again. "I would love that. I played around with some recipes I found online," she said. "But when I tried to bake the rock candy inside the pastry, it melted. I love the idea of using the crystals around here as inspiration combined with the mooncake for the lunar festival in autumn."

Malcolm scratched his chin. "Traditional mooncakes sometimes have an egg yolk inside the sweet filling, usually sesame paste or lotus seed." His eyes narrowed and his face took on that scrunched-up expression of deep contemplation that Georgia found so irresistible. Suddenly his features opened with an internal light. "Kohatkutou."

"What?" Georgia wasn't sure whether he was sneezing or having a stroke.

"It's a candy that looks like a gem or a crystal," he explained. "It's made with this kind of jelly that hardens on the outside but stays chewy on the inside. It uses agar-agar for the stabilizer and probably wouldn't melt the same way rock candy did. I had some when I flew out to Japan on holiday while I was over there. The name literally translates to 'amber candy,' because it resembles the gem."

Georgia shot to her feet. "Well, what are we waiting for?" Grabbing her phone in one hand and the mold in the other, she started typing with her thumb. "We've got a lot to do before the final bake on Friday. How do you spell *kohatkutou*?"

Instead of looking excited, he clapped his hand over his forehead. "Friday. That's what I forgot. The final bake is this Friday."

"You got a hot date you can't miss?" Georgia joked, but her insides twisted at the thought.

"Not exactly." He stood and brushed off his pants. "But my ex Felicia told me about an opportunity in the geology community that I can't pass up. I leave this Friday."

Georgia's phone fell out of her hand and onto the counter with a clatter as the memory of his conversation she had overhead echoed in her head. "Is it—it's not the Mars simulation thing, right?" She picked up her phone and studied it for cracks, unable to look at him. "I couldn't help overhearing you talking with her at Mama Renata's. I mean, it's a great opportunity for a scientist, but—but you'd be gone a long time, wouldn't you? You can't leave us— I mean, your students for that long. Especially since Caroline is doing so much better in class." She knew she was rambling, but she couldn't stop herself.

Malcolm took both her elbows in his hands, keeping the distance between them she said she wanted despite the overwhelming urge to pull her close. "I'm not going anywhere for six months. There's an opening to speak at a geology convention at Cornell on Friday. Felicia, who is dating someone else, by the way—" A mischievous twinkle in his dark eyes told her he knew exactly how jealous she had been. "She put my name in for it because we're friends. That's it. Friends like you and me. Right?" he asked pointedly, the intensity in his eyes belying the casual statement.

"Oh." Georgia blinked, embarrassment flooding her cheeks with heat. "I—I see."

His eyebrows knit together, pushing a crease over his nose. "I feel terrible that I can't be there. Who's going to be the science nerd to your free-spirited creative chef?"

"I will," Caroline's voice piped up from behind the doorway. She poked her head around one side of the doorway, followed by the appearance of Silas's head on the other side. "I can do the science part. Mr. G can help me know what to say, right?" She stepped all the way into the doorway and grabbed his hand, jumping up and down. "Please, please, please."

"I don't have to be at the event until the evening, so I can help you prepare right up until just before filming." Malcolm looked down at her with a look of pure affection, then back at Georgia with a shrug. "What do you say? Are we a team of three?"

"Team." Georgia beamed back at him, then leaned over to point at Silas. "Don't even think about singing right now."

Silas pouted and disappeared back behind the counter.

"Caroline, he said yes," Georgia exclaimed, tugging her daughter away from Malcolm by the hook on her backpack. "You're going to get his nice suit all messy." She looked him up and down appraisingly. "Why do you look so nice, by the way?"

"I had a meeting at the bank this morning," he said, straightening his jacket. "Hoping to get a loan to develop the dig site. They're looking over the proposal and calling me back tomorrow." As he rubbed a hand through his hair, his mouth turned down in a concerned grimace. "I'm not optimistic. It's a big loan, and a teacher's salary isn't exactly the best collateral."

"Well, I hope you get it," Georgia said. "It's a great idea. I know you're eager to move forward."

"I am," he agreed, then reached forward to tousle Caroline's hair before staring at Georgia meaningfully. "But some things, the best things, are worth waiting to do them right."

She gripped the mold still in her left hand even tighter, knowing what his words and that look meant. But how long would it take for the guilt to release its hold on her heart? Almost on its own volition, her hand moved to the pendant around her neck, and Georgia swallowed a lump in her throat that felt just as hard as the stone itself.

CHAPTER EIGHTEEN

FOR ONCE, MALCOLM WASN'T using his free period while the kids were at recess to volunteer in another classroom or help the art teacher clean up the aftermath of the lesson on Jackson Pollock.

In fact, what he was working on wasn't related to teaching at all. He felt almost rebellious, like he could get away with anything. Caught up with the spirit of defiance, he moved his Marie Curie bobblehead haphazardly askew from its traditional place of honor directly in line with his periodic tables mousepad. He instantly regretted it and moved her back.

"Je suis désolé, Madame," he muttered. Shifting his focus back to his laptop, he scratched his chin. A new layer of stubble had formed, courtesy of not shaving last night like usual. He had spent the evening experimenting with different formulas—recipes, that was—for the kohatkutou candy for Georgia. Using agar-agar would give them a hard enough exterior both for the crystalline appearance and hopefully to allow them not to melt during the baking process. He had sent pictures of his results to Georgia. Each text had ended with the phrase I'll bring them over to you before he immediately deleted it.

She had feelings for him. That was as clear as the small faceted crystal on his desk he kept as a reminder of the glorious plans soon to come to fruition for his mining operation. But every time it seemed like she was ready to take that next step with him, she pulled back, not just physically, but emotionally, back into the past.

His cell rang, and for an absurdly hopeful moment, he thought he might actually have manifested Georgia calling him and asking him to meet her after school like a movie from the 1950s. Instead, it was the bank representative he had spoken to yesterday about the loan.

"Hello," he answered. "Uh-huh. Yes. I see." He listened as the man went on for several minutes about things like sufficient collateral and financial risk assessments before hanging up once he had finished. Setting the phone down, he went back to his laptop, but instead of typing, he simply stared at the opening paragraph he had written for his speech at the geology convention at Cornell this Friday.

> In a way, the science of geology is a lot like falling in love. It's a chain of chemical re-

actions whose true beauty is revealed only after the passage of time.

A bitter taste like pennies soaked in vinegar filled his mouth as he highlighted the entire sentence and deleted it, just like he deleted the only thing in the texts to Georgia that really mattered. If they knew the truth, the smart people at Cornell would laugh him off the stage at those words. His credibility in both fields, geology and love, was laughable at best. He was a third-grade teacher whose only rock-related comment today was asking Riley Brewster if he needed a “bless you” (tissue) for his “nose boulders” (self-explanatory). And love…

He was almost thirty-one years old and only now starting to understand what true love felt and looked like, and it wasn’t because he was on the receiving end of it. Georgia’s love for her late husband was so powerful it froze her in the past. The chemistry between her and Malcolm was so potent that the air felt electrified when she so much as brushed his hand, they made each other laugh, and he balanced her beautiful mess with a structure and organization that allowed her the freedom to create. And yet it still wasn’t enough to get her to move forward with him.

“Mr. G?” The school physical therapist, who was very clearly pregnant, interrupted his pity party by knocking on the door with one hand while stabilizing the handles of a student's wheelchair with the other. "I'm sorry to do this on your break time, but would you mind hanging out with Kieran for just a moment? I need to run to the bathroom quickly, but he gets anxious when he's alone."

"No problem." Malcolm waved a hand down the hallway in the direction of the bathrooms. "I always enjoy hanging with my buddy Kieran."

Kieran had a spinal cord injury that had left him paralyzed from the waist down. He wasn't in Malcolm's class, but occasionally Malcolm was a volunteer with the local Move United Junior Olympics chapter, and he had helped Kieran train for the mini javelin throw.

"Hi, Mr. G," Kieran said after rolling the wheelchair through the door with his hands. "What are you doing?"

"Well, I was working on a speech to promote this idea I had to a big group of geologists at Cornell," he said, closing his laptop and swiveling his chair around to face Kieran. "But it looks like my idea isn't going to be as big as I'd hoped."

"What's this?" Kieran asked, leaning forward to pick up the crystal off his desk.

Malcolm smiled. "That is a Herkimer diamond quartz crystal," he replied. Leaning his elbows on his knees, he pointed at the tiny imperfections inside. "See those little black dots? Those are tiny bits of sediment preserved in the crystal from millions of years ago. Dirt that existed at the same time as the dinosaurs."

"Cool." Kieran turned the rock over in his hands, then held it up to the light. "Where did you find it?"

"Here in Crystal Hill," Malcolm replied. "There's a great mineral pocket on the outskirts of the Long family's dairy farm. I was hoping to get enough money to turn it into a big mining and educational center where school-aged kids could come from all around to excavate these."

"That would be such a great field trip." Kieran handed the crystal back to him. "We just go to the Bingleyton Zoo every year." He shrugged. "It's all right. I think they have a hard time finding places with ramps and stuff. I think it would be so cool to find things like this."

Malcolm nodded. Kieran was right. It was really hard to find places to take children that were accessible to special needs of different varieties, whether it was ramps to allow wheelchair mobility or sensory-safe options for students on the autism spectrum. "It's a nice zoo, from what I've heard," he offered feebly, taking the crystal and setting it back on his desk. "I think they're getting a pair of red pandas this year."

As adorable as red pandas were—and they were adorable—Malcolm understood Kieran's lack of enthusiasm, especially when they went to the same zoo every year. One of the things he loved about digs was that you never knew what you might find. The Herkimer diamond quartz crystals came in different colors ranging from smoky gray to rich amber in addition to the perfectly clear ones. Sometimes you even found ancient sharks' teeth buried in rock that was once covered by an ancient sea.

"How much money would you need to build somewhere with ramps that I could go to?" Kieran's face looked so hopeful, and it destroyed Malcolm's heart. "We do fundraisers all the time. Maybe you could do something like that."

"It's a lot of money, bud." Malcolm scrunched up one side of his face and sat back in his chair, folding his hands over his stomach. "Normally grown-ups try to get money from the bank for a loan for something this big, so that's what I did. Unfortunately…" He trailed off. Unfortunately, while the bank was willing to lend him enough for the very discounted lease BeeBee had offered, the costs of his proposal were wildly out of reach for a teacher's salary without so much as a mortgage to offer as collateral. These were adult problems, though, and adult feelings and problems were never okay to dump onto a child.

"Sometimes things just don't work out the way you want them to. Sometimes you just have to accept the next best thing."

Like taking small groups of kids for limited digs at little more than a dug-out cliff face instead of an incredible geological experience that they would want to come back to every year.

Like being Georgia's friend/baking assistant/daughter's teacher so he could at least stay in her life, even though it tore him apart not to shout to the world that she and Caroline had his whole heart.

The physical therapist showed up back at the door, a hand on her belly. "I'm back," she said cheerfully to Kieran. "Did you have a nice visit with Mr. G?"

"Yeah," Kieran said, holding his knuckles up for a fist bump, which Malcolm reciprocated. "He showed me this really cool crystal that you can find around here." The boy's wistful tone as he pushed his wheelchair out of the door stayed with Malcolm even after he had disappeared down the hallway. "I wish I could do that."

Staring at the doorway, Malcolm rubbed his chin again. The spiky stubble wasn't comfortable, but the stimulation seemed to wake him from his stupor.

He was doing it again. Refusing to wait, refusing to take the slow, steady steps of kneading the dough and waiting for it to rise, pretending that store-bought bread would taste just as good. Rushing to accept good enough because it was there instead of being patient enough for just right.

Waiting for Mrs. Just Wright.

Well, this time was different. This time he wasn't just some guy who wanted to get married and have kids right away. He was a teacher, a good teacher, darn it, and good teachers didn't let kids like Kieran have wishes that went unfulfilled. There had to be a way to make this happen, even if it right now it seemed like it might take another million years for the seas to recede.

CHAPTER NINETEEN

IT WAS ONLY after Georgia pulled up to the Hamiltons' house to pick Caroline up that she realized she still had her apron on. But for once she was not just on time, she was early enough to wrestle Caroline's curls into a proper bun for dance class rather than just throwing it into the usual unbrushed ponytail with a hair tie she found at the bottom of her purse.

With four days before the filmed finale of the baking competition, Georgia was literally eating, sleeping and dreaming mooncakes. Occasionally Malcolm made his way into those dreams, and when she woke up, it was always with a smile on her face. There was no way she would have gotten this far without him. In fact, she had a hard time picturing her life without him anymore. That was a sobering reality that woke her up from the fantasy every time, the idea that once this contest was over, they would go back to simply him being Caroline's teacher and her being the parent. Which was as things should be, of course. She wasn't ready to think about anything more than that just yet.

Relishing the sound of crunching dried leaves under her feet on the sidewalk, she straightened her apron as if she had intentionally left it on and rang the doorbell.

Jessica Hamilton opened it and smiled. "Hey, Gigi, the girls are just cleaning up. Wanna come in for a cup of coffee?"

"I'll take a rain check," Georgia replied, checking the time on the wall clock over Jessica's shoulder. "I've got to get Caroline to dance class."

"No problem." Jessica held the door open and called behind her, "Caroline, your mom's here to pick you up."

The sound of high-pitched little girl squeals and stampeding feet immediately followed, and Georgia shook her head. "It's amazing how much energy they have even after a full day of school."

"Speaking of school—" Jessica glanced side to side, then craned her head forward to whisper to Georgia. "I hear this year is going especially well for you so far."

"Well, it was kind of a rough start," Georgia said. "Caroline was having a really hard time connecting with the material for the science unit. She seems to be doing better with it now, although we'll see how the first quarter report card turns out."

Jessica made a tsking noise with her teeth. "No, silly. I mean, with you and Mr. G." She wiggled her eyebrows salaciously. "Word on the street is that you two are getting awfully cozy. Who knows? Maybe by next year, instead of Gigi, I'll be calling you Mrs. G."

It felt like someone had taken the apron loop around Georgia's neck and pulled it so tight she could barely speak or breathe. "I—I don't know what you're talking about. Malcolm—Mr. G, I mean, is Caroline's teacher. That's it. We're not dating."

"Could have fooled me." Jessica crossed her arms. "I watched your last live stream for the baking contest. You two have real chemistry, and I'm not talking about the class both of us nearly flunked in high school. Oh well." She shrugged a shoulder and put her hand on her daughter's head as the girls rushed up to the door, still giggling. "Just say the word if you want me to run interference with the other single women at Bee-Bee's wedding for the bouquet toss. It's about time you got back out there, and he is easy on the eyes, that's for sure."

"If you say so," Georgia mumbled. "Anyway, thanks for having Caroline over this afternoon."

"Anytime, hon," Jessica said, waving as Georgia put her hand on Caroline's back and steered her to the car.

As she drove back toward Jane Street, Georgia looked at Caroline in the rearview mirror. She was still grinning happily as she sipped on her school water bottle and gazed out the window. But if rumors about Georgia and Malcolm were spreading among the moms, it was only a matter of time before the kids heard and inevitably repeated them to Caroline. These were the times when parenting felt like high-key international diplomacy.

"So how was school today?" Georgia tossed back, trying to sound casual. "Anyone say anything…interesting? Nobody picked on you, did they?"

If this was a courtroom, she was sure the judge would rap the gavel and reprimand her for leading the witness. Fortunately, nine-year-olds weren't familiar with judicial etiquette.

"It was fun," she said, slurping the last of her water through the attached straw. "Mr. G brought in the rocks we dug up at the woods behind BeeBee's dairy farm. I told everybody that we were there with him and now all the other kids want to go digging for crystals, too."

"And did anyone say anything about, oh, I don't know, me and Mr. G?" The imaginary judge would absolutely hold her in contempt for that one.

"Not really," Caroline said. "I told them you and Mr. G made it into the final baking contest. Jeremy wants you to bring cupcakes into class if you win."

"Sure, as long as we do a check for any classroom allergies first," Georgia said, glancing in her side mirror as she turned right. "We're almost there. Get your dance bag ready."

Georgia's anxiety settled into a dull roar, and she released the invisible jury. Caroline's friend Olivia must have gotten the wrong idea about their relationship with Mr. G from the way Caroline had been talking about spending time with him. That would explain it. Hopefully it was only Jessica who had been mistaken about the whole thing, because once the rumors started flying around Crystal Hill, it was like trying to catch all the fireflies around Crystal Hill Lake and put them in a single jar. If these rumors got back to Malcolm, he might think that she was the one who wanted them to be more, derailing all the progress they had made with Caroline's interest in science. Plus, it would make things incredibly awkward since they still had to bake together in the final round of the contest. It was a good thing she'd squashed this romantic nonsense with Jessica early, before it got to Malcolm—or, even worse, Caroline.

"All right, go right in and get changed, then I'll do your hair," Georgia said after she parked the car on the street in front of the dance studio.

As they walked in the door and past the line of moms getting their children's dance shoes on in the hallway, the stares and whispers made Georgia's stomach plummet. All of them had seen her wearing funny aprons around town before, so she was pretty sure they weren't staring at the witch flying on a spoon instead of a broom on her front. Her face heated and she ducked her head, keeping one hand protectively on Caroline's shoulder as she walked down the light pink corridor decorated with ballerina stencils. By the time they got to the changing room, Georgia felt like her apron might as well have had a scarlet letter on it.

"Okay." She forced a breezy tone to the word. "Put your leotard and tights on. I'll put your hair in a bun today."

"Yay," Caroline cheered before disappearing behind the door.

Georgia sat on a chair beside the door and ignored the continued hum of whispers, occupying herself by searching in Caroline's dance bag for a hairbrush and bobby pins. It was hard to hear exactly what they were saying, but it definitely seemed that the attention was directed at her. But before she could stand up and declare to the entire room once and for all that Malcolm was just Caroline's teacher, her daughter burst through the door in her lavender leotard.

"I'm ready," she said, twirling in place excitedly.

"You have to stand still," Georgia muttered, putting the bobby pins between her lips as she stroked the brush through Caroline's hair. Twisting it into a cinnamon-bun shape at the back of her head, she couldn't help overhearing one of the moms next to her mention the dairy farm.

"Was it from one of the animals?" the woman in the chair next to Georgia leaned forward to ask the woman sitting across the corridor. "Those water buffaloes are enormous. I know BeeBee says they're gentle as kittens, but I still wouldn't want one of those things chasing a ball of yarn in my living room."

"I don't think the accident was actually on the farm." The other woman shook her head. "When I drove past, the ambulance looked like it had stopped on the road beside the woods."

Georgia's mouth dropped open, sending the last bobby pin pinging to the floor. *No. No, no, no.* Please say it wasn't Malcolm. *Not again.* She picked up her phone and called him. Straight to voicemail. His phone was never off. She felt suddenly dizzy with fear, her ears blocked to everything except the continued conversation of the women next to her.

"All I know is my husband's a volunteer with EMS, and judging from the call over his radio, it sounds like the guy's in pretty rough shape," the first woman said in a serious voice. "I've heard crush injuries can be really bad."

"I just hope it wasn't his face," the other one replied. "He's so hot. And nice, too. Hard to believe he's still single."

Georgia's hands shook as she bent over to get Caroline's ballet shoes out of her dance bag. An accident on the property by BeeBee's farm, right where Malcolm said he was going tonight. It had to be him—who else would it be? The only other guys that would be there were BeeBee's dad or her fiancé, Bill. In a female-dominated town like Crystal Hill, there was a dearth of single, good-looking men, so as much as she wished they were talking about anyone else, there could only be one possibility: Malcolm had been in an accident at the dig site, and it sounded serious.

"Hey, sweetie." Georgia straightened up and handed Caroline her dance slippers. "I'm going to text Uncle Lucas or Silas and see if one of them can pick you up from dance tonight, okay? I have a quick errand to run that I—I forgot about until just now."

"Okay." Caroline bobbed her head, then waved

to her friends as they lined up outside the studio. "I'm going in so I can get the spot next to Charlotte at the barre. 'Bye, Mom!"

She dashed over to the line of little girls filing into the mirrored studio, and Georgia picked up her phone again. Forcing her hands to steady themselves, she sent Chrysta a text, and fortunately she replied instantly that she could pick Caroline up since the cheese shop was just across the street. Her chair fell over as she leaped up, but she didn't stop to set it upright as she ran out of the door and straight to her car.

She gripped the steering wheel all the way to the dairy farm, leaning forward because for some reason if she relaxed back into the seat, it felt like she was giving up on him. His car was still parked in BeeBee's driveway when she got there, but that didn't make the panic dissipate. If anything, it confirmed the fear that he was where the women said there had been a terrible accident. Sprinting down the driveway, all Georgia could think of was that she should have gone with him when he asked, that she could have done something. Just like the night that Mike left for his motorcycle ride. He had asked if she wanted to take Caroline and go for a walk that evening and she had said no. She couldn't even remember why she had said no, another memory that felt fuzzy and displaced. Time and grief had a way of blurring the edges of memories so that they slipped too easily from her grasp.

She didn't know what she expected when she burst through the front door of the farmhouse—a triage situation, maybe—but it certainly wasn't the sight of Malcolm and BeeBee sitting at the table laughing as if they didn't have so much as a paper cut.

"Are—are you okay?" She bent over with her hands on her knees. Relief hadn't fully penetrated the fear yet, but it was beginning to prickle through at the edges enough so that she didn't feel the terrifying numbness anymore. She did, however, feel like she needed to join a gym or something if running this short a distance left her so out of breath.

Malcolm's forehead wrinkled as he looked at her with furrowed eyebrows. "Um, yeah. I'm fine." He stood and crossed the room. "Are you okay?" He put a steadying hand on her back as she straightened up.

"I just—" Georgia swallowed, her mouth dry as if it was coated in sawdust. "I just heard there was an accident on the property and that—that someone got hurt." She reached for his arm to reassure herself that it was true, that he was here, that he was okay.

"It was Law." BeeBee raised her voice from where she sat at the table. "Lucas the cheesemaker's brother," she clarified for Malcolm. "He was in his woodshop on the plot of land next to ours, the one his folks gave him, and a piece of equipment fell on his arm. Thank goodness my mom was over there picking up an order for the town and she called the ambulance right away. They said if they hadn't gotten there that quickly, he might have lost his arm."

"I hope he's all right," Georgia said as she walked to the table and collapsed in a chair. Even though it was BeeBee she was talking to, she kept her eyes on Malcolm the entire time. He did the same to her, his gaze seeming to repeat "I'm fine."

"Yeah, me, too," BeeBee said, taking a sip from the mug in front of her. "Want a cup of hot apple cider? Malcolm brought some over and I heated it up."

"No, thanks." Georgia sniffed the air. "Is the stove still on? Something smells like it's burning."

BeeBee cringed. "I might have gotten distracted while I was heating the cider and it boiled over," she confessed, leaning forward on her elbows. "Don't tell Bill. It's been a week since I burned anything." She jerked her thumb over her shoulder to the small chalkboard hanging up on the wall with a big number seven circled on it.

"It's my fault," Malcolm interjected, turning his head from Georgia to BeeBee then back again as if it was hard to tear his eyes from her.

"I was talking to BeeBee about my idea while she was doing it."

"What is this big idea?" Georgia settled back in her seat, suddenly feeling exhausted by the shift in emotions. "You said it had something to do with the dig site."

"So, I was showing the crystals to my students, and I thought maybe a few would be interested in doing something like a recreational club where we went out for nature walks and did some light digging," he explained, gesturing with one hand and picking up his mug with the other. "But every single student in my class was asking to go for a dig. I couldn't believe how excited they all were, especially when Caroline started talking about it. She was a real discussion leader," he said to Georgia, the mug unable to conceal his proud grin as he took a sip.

"I wish you had been there. She basically took over the lecture for me. So I thought that maybe this could be more than just a place where we did occasional digs. Maybe it could be an actual educational site with a kid-friendly mining area, a learning center where we had showcases on the geology of the region. I made up a brief sketch of what it might look like and a mini proposal."

"I was very impressed." BeeBee nodded at him. "He knows what he's talking about. Plus, none of the activity last week seemed to bother my animals at all, and it's in the wooded area where they don't graze or wallow. We don't really use the land for anything, and leasing it to him would be money we can use to add to our herd. Malcolm came over to tell me that the bank denied his loan, so it might take a while for all this to get funded, even with the family discount I offered him." She threw him a conspiratorial wink before toasting her mug in Georgia's direction.

That brought Georgia back to what had gotten her upset even before the misunderstanding over the accident. Jessica's insinuation, the whispers and stares at the dance studio. Now BeeBee was talking as if he was a member of the family. She had to put a stop to this now. "Malcolm, can I talk to you in private outside for a moment?"

"Sure." He set his mug down and stood, looking down at BeeBee. "I'll call you and set up a time to meet with a lawyer about a contract after I figure out if I can get a big enough loan for the first few payments."

Georgia waited for him to make his way around the table, then led him to the door and ushered him out to the porch.

Malcolm leaned with one hand on the railing next to the steps in that casually confident way that most men had no idea was so appealing to women. "What's up, doc?"

A small flicker of anger shot through her at how he could be so free and easy after everything she'd been through. Anger was a feeling she found much easier to deal with than the complicated tangle of fear, panic, concern and inconvenient attraction to him she had been fighting all day. So she leaned into it. "We have a problem."

"Is Caroline all right?" He pushed off the railing and stepped in closer to her.

The fact that her daughter was his first priority made him even more endearing and attractive, which in turn made her angrier. "She's fine. I wanted to warn you, though. For some reason, her friends and their moms all have the impression that you and I are an official couple. As in the romantically attached, his and hers matching towel sets kind of couple."

"Oh, that's all?" He chuckled and shook his head. "I guess I'm not surprised. We have been spending a lot of time together, and Caroline told the other kids that the two of you went with me. Between that and our baking together for the contest, it's understandable people might get that idea."

"How are you so cavalier about this?" Georgia said, throwing her hands in the air. "I thought you were on the hunt for a wife. Won't it be harder for you to find the right woman if they think you're already taken?"

Malcolm reached for her hands and took them in his, catching her so off guard that she let him. "What if I've already found the right woman?"

Georgia couldn't take her eyes off the way his hands covered hers entirely. It seemed like they no longer belonged to her, like she was looking at a picture of someone else who was being taken care of and adored by this unbelievably handsome man. "I—I don't understand. I thought we had an understanding." Finally she looked up at his face and willed him to have some common sense, as hers was faltering by the second. "You're Caroline's teacher. If we dated, it might open her up to teasing or distract her from learning. You said she's doing well and participating in the science lecture. That was the reason behind us spending time together."

"And spending time with you and Caroline has only made it more clear to me how much I feel about both of you," he said in a tone so earnest she could barely stay upright. "Why else would I cancel dates with other perfectly nice women on my one free night each week?"

"Because—because you're a good teacher," she insisted. "And good teachers don't date their students' moms."

"Georgia, I was worried about the possible ramifications, too. In the past, dating someone involved with my work ended up with things getting messy. That's not what I want, especially given everything Caroline has been through. But after this year, I won't be Caroline's teacher anymore. That's only eight months away. I can wait eight months if it means on the other end, I get to be with you and Caroline. We can go camping, take trips, do whatever we want without worrying about what other people might think."

"Go on trips together?" Georgia put a hand to her forehead to make the world stop spinning. "Where are we going?"

"Anywhere." He smiled, his eyes sparkling as he looked over her head as if seeing something beautiful in the distance. "We can go for bike rides around the lake, walks in the woods. Without funding from the bank, I won't be able to get the dig site ready by this vacation season, so we can use this summer to just spend time together like a family."

Like the family she had. Like the family and the life and the future she lost that night her husband went out for a motorcycle ride alone and never came back. She felt like she was on a ride of her own right now, one that was careening out of control. "Malcolm, we need to pump the brakes."

"On what?" he asked.

"On everything." Georgia pulled her hand away and swept it in front of her as if wiping away whatever vision had captivated him a moment ago. “On rides and walks and trips. Things a family does together. It’s too soon.”

Malcolm’s face paled, and the hurt was visible in his eyes as if she had struck him. “Georgia, what are you waiting for?” He put a hand over his mouth, then let it fall and his words flowed out, rapid and unhindered. “Caroline is doing great, in school and at home. She likes spending time with me and I like being around to take care of you both. I’m ready for this, for a real family. I’m not going anywhere, if you’re worried about her getting attached to someone who isn’t serious. My feelings for you are real. I’m in this for real. So I want to know, what are *you* waiting for?”

“I’m not waiting for anything,” she argued. “I’m afraid. What if this is moving too fast and Caroline has a setback in her recovery? We’re finally okay, and pushing her forward if she’s not ready isn’t something I’m willing to risk as a mom.”

“Being a mom is an important part of you,” he pushed back softly. Raising his finger to her cheek, he brushed a curl behind her ear and yearning sang through her entire body. “But you’re not just a single crystal. You’ve got more facets than the Hope Diamond, for crying out loud. You’re beautiful, caring—everyone here talks about how much you do for them. You're smart, funny, an incredibly talented baker."

She chuffed a small laugh, giving in to the comforting warmth of him with a lean in. "Well, now that I'm finally unstuck with my creations," she said with a sigh.

He cupped her chin with his other hand and lifted her face up to his. "Georgia, you're not stuck creatively." His dark eyes penetrated into hers like he was trying to bore into the rock wall protecting her memories. "You're stuck in the past. I would never want you to forget the love you had for your husband or push you to move on from what you shared. But if you let me, I can help you store the memories where they belong so they don't hold you back from the beautiful future waiting for you."

There was that terrifying word again. *Future.* Terrifying because she wanted it so badly. That was the worst part of it, that she could want to move on from another life and another person that she had loved so deeply. It wasn't fair, any of it. It wasn't fair that she had to raise Caroline alone, it wasn't fair that she had finally managed to feel like she could and now this man showed up making her feel things she'd thought she would never feel again. It wasn't fair to drag his neatly arranged plans and perfectly aligned future into her mess.

"Malcolm, you're wonderful," she said slowly, carefully. "And you deserve only the best things for your future. But I don't know if I can give those things to you. My life is so—" She turned and walked down one of the steps toward the driveway, glancing at the forest that held the worst memory of her life. Looking over her shoulder, she shrugged. "It's messy. It's complicated. And you're clearly not a guy who does messy and complicated."

Georgia sighed. It would be easier, kinder to lie. But he deserved the truth even if just saying the words made her squirm with guilt.

"I know Caroline really likes you." She swallowed hard and closed her eyes, unable to say out loud that Caroline wasn't the only one. "But our grief and recovery and everything we've put into it still feels underdone in the middle, like a cake that falls apart if you try to cut it. If I've baked something once, I can do it again just by feeling it out, but walking through this kind of grief is something I've never done before. There's no step-by-step recipe, no scientific method for this. It's this crazy mixture of guilt for wanting more than the beautiful life we had with Mike and fear of what a different life looks like. You can't possibly understand how torn I feel."

Malcolm stepped down beside her. He stood quietly for a moment, the sound of the animals gently shuffling around inside the pen to their right the only thing interrupting the evening stillness. "Is there anything I can do or say to help?" He faced her, pleading striking his features with such openness it was all she could do not to fall in his arms.

She forced herself to untie her apron so that she didn't do just that. "I don't think so," she said, pulling it over her head and balling it in her hands. "In fact, I think it's best if I prepare for this final bake on my own. I can figure the mooncakes out by myself from here." Georgia took the steps down the rest of the way to the driveway, then turned and faced him. "You need your nights free if you're going to find the perfect woman to take to BeeBee's wedding as your date."

"And what about you?" Malcolm asked, ringing one hand around the post behind him and leaning forward like a siren perched on a rock. "What do you need?"

You, her heart whispered as it broke all the way into two pieces, one for the man she'd lost and the other for the one she was letting go. "I just need to get through today," she said right before walking straight to her car without looking back.

CHAPTER TWENTY

Growing up, one of Georgia's favorite cookies to make had been the holiday spritz cookies that used her grandmother's cookie mold to form the sweet sugar cookie dough into flowered shapes.

If possible, she loved the mooncakes even more.

The delicate pastry, the rich, almost savory sesame-paste filling and then when you cut into it, the surprise of the beautiful kohatkutou crystal candy. She had made so many mooncakes she had a circle from pressing the mold permanently indented into the palm of her hand, but the end result was worth it. The people in town seemed to agree. Georgia had put only the best mooncakes out in the display case this week as what Caroline described as the data-collection step of the process. They had flown off the shelves faster than the black and whites, an unprecedented occurrence. Of course, not many of her customers had ever had a mooncake before, so this data set could only speak to the taste and not necessarily the authenticity.

The only person who could do that hadn't spoken to her since Monday at BeeBee's farm, and it was already Thursday.

That was how it should be. Teacher and parent with a side of baking consultant. Some other time they could have been more. Georgia wasn't sure whether that other time was in some alternate reality past, where she never met Mike, or in some distant tomorrow she couldn't bring herself to envision. But here, today, it didn't matter that he was handsome and smart and funny and amazing with her daughter.

Did it?

A knock sounded at the door. Georgia's heart leaped for a moment even though she knew it wasn't him. BeeBee and Bill were coming to take Caroline for a final fitting for her flower girl dress for the wedding.

Standing up wearily, Georgia walked to the door with her hands on her lower back. In addition to the usual regimen of being on her feet for her job, she had spent the off hours cleaning the bakery until it shone in preparation for the film crew to come tomorrow. It was so beautiful now, she was almost afraid to bake in it. For the first time since Mike's funeral, she would close the bakery on a nonholiday. This was a big deal. Her work and her town were going to be showcased on national television, and everyone who came into the bakery couldn't stop talking about and asking if she was over the moon to have an opportunity like this. She should be over the moon and yet, she felt like she had fallen into one of its craters, unable to claw her way out to see the vast splendor of the view ahead.

She opened the door and simultaneously Bill and BeeBee said loudly, "Happy bake-off eve!"

Georgia rolled her eyes at the ridiculous two-headed monster they had become. "How long did you guys rehearse that?"

Bill promptly replied, "An hour" at the same time BeeBee said, "Rehearse what? That was totally unplanned." She shot an elbow into his ribs and glared over her shoulder at where he stood. "You'll walk the plank for that treachery, Cappy."

Bill grinned back at her. "Worth it," he replied, taking her hand in his and kissing it.

"You lovebirds want to come in for a bit before you take Caroline?" Georgia gestured inside the house. "It's even more of a mess than usual, but I used up all my cleaning energy at the bakery, so it's going to stay that way for at least another day." God, she missed those Friday nights with Malcolm when she'd came down from putting Caroline to bed to find him efficiently tidying up her home. She loved that he did it in a way that didn't feel like he was judging her lack of organization and that was easy for her to maintain when he wasn't there. It was the same way he operated even setting up a bake sale and arranging the cupcakes in pleasing geometric shapes. It was him that she missed, which was silly because he hadn't gone anywhere other than back to the appropriate role he should always have played in her life.

"Thanks, but we'd better get going." BeeBee checked her watch. "The tailor gets cranky with me when I'm late. Would you believe she didn't even accept manure recycling in our fields as an acceptable excuse to miss a wedding dress fitting?" She shook her head in obvious disbelief. "It's better for the herds and the soil. What could be more important?"

"Some people." Georgia shrugged, then called up the stairs behind her. "Caroline, BeeBee and Bill are here to take you to the dress shop." Turning around, she asked, "BeeBee, are you sure you don't want me to come along? She's already wound for sound over the big bake tomorrow, and I haven't even given her any sugar yet today."

"So you won't mind if we stop for milkshakes at Big Joe's after the fitting?" Bill asked, smiling over Georgia's head as Caroline leaped down the last two stairs. "If I don't feed BeeBee every two hours, it's like watching a Mogwai take a shower after midnight."

"I'd get offended at being called a gremlin by my fiancé, but honestly he's not wrong," BeeBee said, reaching out to Caroline and gathering her in a big hug. She picked her up, then set her down and nodded at Georgia. "You take the night off, Mama. If anyone has earned it, it's you."

Georgia made a *pssht* sound and waved her hand. "Please. If you're talking about the bake tomorrow, it was truly a team effort. Besides, I haven't earned anything yet. The votes will decide the winner by midnight tomorrow."

"I wasn't talking about the baking contest," BeeBee said. "You work so hard baking for special events for the town like my wedding, school events, all the festivals and holidays, but it's more than that. You're always there to listen when any of us need a shoulder to cry on or sage advice on a problem. It's like you're the mom for the entire town on top of being an amazing single mom to Caroline. We see you taking care of everyone else's needs all the time. Don't forget to take a moment for yourself here and there, okay?"

BeeBee was known throughout town for saying exactly what she felt at all times, which occasionally ended with unfortunate consequences. This time, however, it was exactly what Georgia needed to hear. She hadn't even realized how much until the tears clutched at the back of her throat. "Wow," she said, her voice thick and almost unrecognizable. "I guess I raised you right, huh?"

"You sure did." BeeBee smiled and put a hand on Caroline's head, then slid her eyes to Bill. "Now this time, what are you going to say if the tailor gives me a hard time about wearing sneakers under my wedding dress?"

"The bride gets what the bride wants," Bill repeated dutifully as they waved to Georgia and headed down the walkway. "But to be fair, I think it was what your sneakers had stepped on before you got to the shop, not the actual shoes that she found objectionable."

Georgia chuckled as she closed the door behind them. Turning her back to lean heavily against it, she stared at the trail of clutter leading from Caroline's shoes and dance bag in the hallway to the reusable grocery bags scattered around the island. She should do what Malcolm did, pick one section of the house at a time to clean and organize rather than looking at the whole thing and getting completely overwhelmed. But just the thought of it hit her with fatigue so powerful it sank into her bones. Plus, the light streaming in from the glass panel in the door meant that it was almost sunset. There would always be more time for cleaning, but sunsets? Those only lasted for a few precious minutes, and she knew better than anyone else not to take those minutes for granted.

Wiggling her feet into her sneakers, Georgia refilled Harley's food so she wouldn't destroy her curtains while she was gone, as the cat tended to respond to hunger with the same equanimity as BeeBee. She grabbed her keys off the table by the door and went out to the car. It wasn't a long drive from her house to the lake, less than ten minutes, and she was able to park in front of the shore right as the sun had begun its descent. She had planned to sit in one of the Adirondack chairs on the sandy area next to the dock to rest her back, but suddenly a restlessness gripped her, urging her to walk the path through the pine trees between the lake and the road. Well, sticking to plans and recipes was for scientists like Malcolm. Following her intuition was her own way of doing things. Tonight, she was on her own path again.

The trees on this side of the lake were sparse, and a small trail wound through them in a circle to the other side of the lake, where the foliage thickened and overtook the light from above. It would be too dark by the time she finished to make the whole loop, so Georgia walked until she was about a quarter of the way through the trail. There was a large boulder next to an ancient maple tree where tourists had been carving their names into the rock with pocket knives for decades. Georgia sat on the rock and drew her knees up to her chest, her midi-length skirt draping over the tops of her feet.

As the sun went down, the light struck the opening between the trees and illuminated the ground in front of her. It was beautiful, the way the beam shone on the different-colored leaves on the ground and made them shine with vibrancy and life. She rested her chin on her knees and concentrated on the lovely scene in front of her. Fall was, after all, her favorite time of year, in large part because of moments just like this one. Yet the unsettled feeling in her stomach didn't evaporate in the stillness as she had expected. It was a feeling of unfulfilled wanting, of searching for something. Suddenly, she realized what had drawn her on this walk.

She was looking for a sign from him.

"Mike?" Georgia looked up to the fading light and whispered in a choked voice. "Please. I need to hear from you. Before I can move on, before I can let myself have a life with anyone else, I just want one more clue that you'll always be with me. I—I can't do any of this without your blessing. Please," she repeated desperately. "It doesn't mean that I didn't love you with all of my heart while you were here. And I'll talk about you with Caroline while there's still breath in my lungs. She won't forget you. I won't forget you. I may not feel ready—I may never feel ready to get married again. But I'm tired of taking care of everything and everyone on my own. If I've found someone who understands me, who cares about me and Caroline, who makes life feel less heavy, you would want that for me, wouldn't you?"

Before losing her husband, she'd been skeptical at best about this kind of thing. Then, only a few days after his passing, Georgia had been on her way home from meeting the pastor at the church when an eagle flew overhead, its white head distinctive in the early morning sun. This wasn't uncommon, especially on the other side of the lake where the woods were at their most dense. But this had been out of sight of the lake and the bird had flown low, so unusually low that she could see its gnarled talons tucked below its tail as it soared in front of her and then disappeared. Mike was originally from Philadelphia, and even though he had moved to Crystal Hill in ninth grade, his loyalty to the professional football team of his hometown remained stalwart his entire life. She had known, instantly and without a doubt, it had been a message from him.

There had been other instances in the first year or two. Little things that could only have come from him. The power flickering when she turned on her straightening iron to get ready to go out (he had loved her naturally curly hair), an inexplicable stain on a white shirt coming out of the dryer in his favorite shade of green despite there being no evidence of anything in that color in the machine. But it had been a long time since she had received any of these, a long time since she had experienced dreams so realistic she had woken herself up talking to him. She had assumed that was normal. Mike had always been an extrovert in this life, stopping to talk to people wherever they went. It made sense he would stay just as busy greeting newcomers to the next life. Georgia laughed softly to herself thinking of him standing at the entrance to heaven with his barbecue tongs in hand, gathering people to his eternal tailgate even if they happened to be Giants fans.

Now, when she needed to hear from him most, however, there was nothing. Not a speck of Philadelphia Eagles green in all the scarlets and burnt oranges carpeting the ground. She scanned the trail for some of the plants he brought back for her flavors, but there was nothing except for the occasional bit of everyday grass. Not even so much as a chipmunk (the only Christmas song he liked being the one sung by Alvin and the Chipmunks) scampering past her feet. Georgia's eyes filled, but she swallowed the tears back, despite her therapist telling her never to hold back the feelings when they came. She was so tired of feeling sad, lonely, so tired of how much work it took to get back to being just okay.

She turned around and trudged back the way she had come, the restless searching replaced by unsatisfied resignation. It had been too much to hope that an otherworldly message would appear on demand. Life didn't work that way, and apparently neither did the afterlife. Sometimes cakes fell even when you had measured the ingredients perfectly; sometimes people left when you needed them to stay by your side. Sometimes the only thing you could do was go home and curl up under the covers with a large cat on top of your feet and try not to think about the fact that tomorrow was just another day you would have to get through all over again. Alone.

CHAPTER TWENTY-ONE

MALCOLM LEFT EARLY Friday afternoon, having arranged for a sub to cover his class for the afternoon. Ithaca wasn't all that far away, but there was a special part to his presentation that night that required some arranging. Before he left, he motioned for Caroline to stay behind as the rest of the class headed out to lunch.

"Are you ready to help your mom with the big bake after school today?" he asked her as he packed his laptop into his messenger bag.

"I think so," Caroline said, sounding uncertain as she twisted a strand of long blond hair around her finger.

"What part are you worried about?" he asked. "I can make notes for you, if you'd like. The agar-agar stuff is tricky."

"No, it's not that." Caroline shook her head. "I already wrote down what I'm going to say. I just—I just wish you were going to do it with us." She looked up at him with pleading in her big blue eyes. "Do you really have to go?"

Ah. Malcolm's heart burst wide open like a fault deep in the Earth's crust. As a teacher, he made a concerted effort not to have favorites among his students. But Caroline was special. This little girl who had been through so much and was still so full of joy and hope. She wasn't anxious about baking with her mom tonight. She was anxious that he was leaving and scared that he might not come back. He knew better than anyone that no matter how much love and support children were surrounded with, being separated from a parent was a trauma that imprinted itself deeply into the soul. Sometimes you didn't even realize it until you were an adult who was so desperate to erase that scar that you ended up doing crazy things like rushing into relationships that weren't right and being too impatient to work for the ones that were.

He put a hand on her shoulder. "I really wish I could be there to watch you and your mom kick baking butt tonight," he said, pleased with the giggle he elicited from her. "But this lecture tonight is really important for getting the dig site up and operational. There are going to be people there I really need to meet in person. But here—" He swiveled in his chair and opened the drawer to his desk. Taking out a chain strung with clear round beads, he closed the drawer and put it in Caroline's hand. "This is a beaded necklace made of rock crystal, a kind of quartz that's been used throughout history for jewelry and decorative vases because it's easy to carve. I got this when I was in China," he said, then bit his lip.

It wasn't necessary to tell her that he got the necklace from a shop next to his birth mother's bakery or that he'd bought it shortly after finding out that she had passed away before he would ever get the chance to tell her that he was okay, healthy, loved. Someday, hopefully, he would tell her all of it and also that he had gotten the necklace vowing only to take it out of its package when he had a family to pass it down to.

"In Chinese culture, gemstones are very important. Different stones have different energies. Crystals like this are used to help with focus, concentration and overcoming obstacles. You can wear this for tonight, but it's only a loan," he said, pointing a finger at her and making a jokingly stern face. "When I come back on Saturday, the very first thing I'm going to do is stop by the bakery and pick this up, all right?"

Relief brightened her features. Caroline nodded and held the necklace reverently in her hands. "I'll take good care of it, I promise."

"Make sure you do," he replied just as solemnly, then held out his arms for a hug. "Hugs?"

Malcolm asked before dropping his arms and holding out his knuckles. "Or fist bumps?"

She barreled into his midsection and wrapped her arms around him so tightly, it knocked the wind from his lungs.

Malcolm swallowed and returned the squeeze, albeit a bit more gently.

After he packed up and left, he turned onto Jane Street and slowed to a stop on the corner in front of the bakery. He parked and got out, waving at one of his students' parents who ran the dry cleaner across the street as he went around the car. The scene taking place inside the large lace curtain–framed window paused him the way you freeze at finding your favorite movie at your favorite scene in the middle of channel surfing.

Georgia was behind the counter of the bakery with the film crew set up around her. She wore her usual diaphanous clothing, a flowing skirt and buttoned blouse in a matching petal pink that made her cheeks glow. Her hair was pushed back from her face with a matching pink headband, and the whole effect was timeless elegance. A modern-day Grace Kelly who had refused the prince's hand to open her own kingdom of sweets here in Crystal Hill. She was in her element, chatting animatedly with the crew in between shots and handing out powdered sugar doughnuts on little napkins regardless of the sweet snowfall that fell on her yellow-checkered apron every time.

A shadow fell over him as the clouds enveloped the sun and his own reflection smiled back at him from the window. He hadn't even realized he was grinning, a face-splitting, goofy expression that was a mix of lovesick and proud. So many people would get to see her work her magic, and he was just happy to have been a small part of making it happen. This was her moment, though, hers and Caroline's. They had walked through their own shadow together, and while he knew there was no other side to make it to, they had found a way to create light in the darkness. As much as he wanted to share in it, Malcolm finally understood that his forever family was going to have to wait until the right time for him to be a part of it. Georgia had made it clear on Monday that she wasn't there. She might never be, and as much as that thought destroyed him, he wasn't throwing in the towel just yet. He had one chance to get her to see they were meant to be together. Tonight he would get his answer.

He whipped his head to the side when the door opened and Silas stepped out.

"Hey, Mr. G, you coming in?"

Malcolm shook his head, casting one more glance at the window. "No, I've got to get going.

But you've got everything ready for tonight after she's done filming, right?"

Silas bobbed his head and crossed his arms over his chest. "Yup. Got it covered." He twisted around to follow Malcolm's gaze, then looked back at him with a sigh. "I'd love nothing more than for you guys to have a big Hollywood ending with her falling into your arms as the whole cast dances around you— Okay, she may be right about me watching too many musicals," he added with a chuckle before his face turned serious. "But Georgia's been holding on to her memories like a life preserver for a long time. I just hope you know that this plan of yours might not have a happy-ever-after."

"I know," Malcolm agreed as he dragged his eyes away from Georgia. "My priorities have changed. It's not about sprinting to the finish line anymore. It's not about what I want for my life anymore. My plans are so much bigger than that now."

"Don't give up on her, though," Silas said hastily. He jerked his head back toward the window. "She's taken to you more than I've ever seen her with any other man since Mike. There were honestly times I thought she had given up on men entirely, but you've gotten through those defenses. It may not seem like it, but you mean a great deal to her and Caroline."

"I'm not giving up on her," Malcolm said. "I'm discovering my own pocket." Silas's face wrinkled with confusion and Malcolm scratched his chin, trying to explain. Then the sun came out from behind the clouds, hitting him full on with a beam of light, and it came to him. "Do you know what rockhounds hate most of all?"

"Rock cats?" Silas quipped with a shrug.

"Nope." Malcolm let out a rueful chuckle. "That's good, though, I'm stealing that one. Rockhounds hate clouds. One of our best tools is the sunlight. It catches sparkle inside the dark pockets, and the sparkle, or druzy, is what tells you there might be a goony i.e., a big gem," he added as explanation, "in that hole. We need the light to find the shiny objects we're hunting, and for the past six weeks, I've been thinking of my future, of Georgia, as the shiny object."

"She's not?"

Malcolm walked around the car, and before he ducked inside, he leaned a hand on the roof and smiled at Silas. "She's the light guiding me."

CHAPTER TWENTY-TWO

GEORGIA LIKED TO think of herself as fairly unflappable, but the second the cameras trained on her, she felt well and truly flapped.

"Gigi, can you tilt your head to the left a little as you hold up that plate?" the woman operating the camera asked as she looked down to examine the last shot on her lens.

"Um, sure." Georgia moved her head and tried to ignore the cramp in her jaw from the smile pasted onto her face.

"That's actually your right," the woman behind the camera said gently. "Other way, hon."

"I'm so sorry." Georgia set the plate down and rubbed her forehead. "This is all way out of my comfort zone. I'm used to hiding in the kitchen, not stepping out into the spotlight."

"That's all right," the camerawoman said. "You're doing great. You, uh, you did, however, get some chocolate on your forehead just now. Trudy, can you get that for Gigi, please?"

Trudy, the makeup artist with long violet hair

and impressive tattoo sleeves covering both arms, rushed behind the counter. Using a soft cloth, she swiped at Georgia's forehead, then gave her a wide grin. "You're doing great, babe," she said in a strong British accent. "So much better than the guy we did yesterday. Total knob. His whole thing is baking outdoors, like recipes you can do with a camping stove, so we spent the entire shoot outside in Florida, fending off mosquitoes." She shuddered. "Beastly. His food is quite good, though, and he's got all the single ladies voting for him because he's, like, model hot." She patted Georgia on the arm and repeated, "You're doing great."

No matter how comfortingly lyrical the words sounded, Georgia didn't feel like she was doing great. She felt off balance, like the top tier of a multilevel cake that had been placed a few degrees from the center and could be displaced from its perch with the slightest motion. She inhaled deeply and puffed out her breath through puckered lips.

She could do this. It was just another day of baking, something she had been doing her entire life. It was like breathing. Instinctive, natural. Yet despite the cameraperson, makeup artist, producer and someone called a gaffer, Georgia felt acutely aware of the fact that she was alone. It seemed wrong. For her, baking wasn't a solitary activity. Whether she was with her mom, Silas, Caroline or Malcolm, it had always been her favorite way of connecting with other people. When words failed her, when the world stopped making sense after Mike's death, baking anchored her to the people who mattered most. She didn't want to do any of this alone.

Baking or life.

As if reading her melancholy thoughts, the producer walked to the counter and leaned on one hand to ask quietly, "Gigi, is your partner, Mr. G, going to be joining us for this shoot? If so, we'd love to get some film of the two of you doing that classic banter the viewers loved so much. You know, the whole science formula versus free-form creative, yin and yang stuff." He tapped some notes on his phone, then looked back up at her. "Just so we know for editing in post, are you two an item in real life or is that just part of the act? It's fine, but if you two aren't really together, you're both in the wrong profession, because most Oscar winners couldn't fake that kind of chemistry. Pardon the science pun—I know that's more his thing."

"We're actually..." Georgia trailed off. What were they? It was the question that had kept her tossing and turning every night this week. They weren't dating, but the potential thorny aspects of a relationship with her daughter's teacher seemed negated by the fact that Caroline adored spending time with him. The producer wasn't wrong about their chemistry, either. Denying she was attracted to him seemed like an exercise in futility when she blushed every time he looked her way. Explaining to a television producer that she couldn't date a gorgeous, smart, kind man who was great with her daughter because she hadn't gotten the heavenly thumbs-up from her late husband wasn't something she was prepared to do today, however. Fortunately, they were interrupted by Silas's booming voice as he held open the door to the kitchen.

"Miss Caroline is ready for her close-up," he announced. After Silas swept his hand through the doorway, Caroline emerged in a miniature version of her mom's apron and her hair pulled back in double French braids. Hopping atop a stool behind the counter, she posed with a hand under her chin like she had been born in front of the camera.

"I'm doing the science part of the bake today," she declared as the producer tapped more notes onto his phone and nodded approvingly. "Mr. G and I went over all the notes for the recipe, and he gave me some fun facts about the moon. Did you know that there's not actually water on the moon? It's water ice, but not like the fruit slushies, like a glacier. I think I might want to be an astronaut and a veterinarian now. People might bring their dogs to space someday, and I can take care of them."

Georgia nearly burst with pride at how completely confident and self-assured Caroline sounded. So different than the little girl who less than two months ago was barely saying more than two words whenever the subject came up. Her dad would be so proud.

A lightning bolt shot through her at the thought. Was that the sign? Her little girl dreaming of a career in the sciences? It wasn't like a giant green flag, and she didn't get the same goose-bump feeling on the back of her arms the way she had in the past, the same certainty that this was him. Still, it wasn't nothing.

There wasn't really time to worry about it, though, because in the next second the producer was hustling them and the crew into the kitchen behind the bakery for the taping of their final bake.

As Georgia shuffled the prepared ingredients around on the gleaming counter, she looked down at Caroline. "How are you doing, sweetheart? Are you nervous? You can tell me if you are. We've never done this with an actual TV crew before. *I'm* nervous."

"Nope, I'm rcady," Caroline said, bobbing up and down on her heels before turning to face

Georgia. "I know what will help. Fist bump, hug or dance?"

"What?"

"Like we do in Mr. G's class," Caroline explained. "He told me once he does it because he knows that some kids get nervous going into a classroom. Giving them a choice of how they start their day makes them feel powerful, and when you're powerful, you don't feel nervous anymore."

I love that man. The thought floated in Georgia's head like a plane skywriting in the clouds.

It startled her so much it took Caroline prodding her in the arm several times to prompt Georgia into responding. "What— Oh, um, hugs. A hug from you is exactly what I need, baby girl."

As she held her daughter close and breathed in the sweet floral smell of shampoo from the top of her head, the ground beneath her feet became solid once again. This, this feeling right here, was everything. Spotlights were ephemeral and fickle, romance might come and go, but she would be a mother forever. No matter what.

"Ladies, I'm going to give you a countdown," the woman behind the camera said in a loud, firm voice. "Watch my fingers and when we get to one, be ready to start. Okay?"

Georgia straightened up as the crew rustled

behind her with lights and a large circular filmy thing. She checked the microphone tucked under her hair to make sure it was secure, then inhaled deeply as the camerawoman's fingers counted down from five in what felt like slow motion.

"Hi, everybody," she said brightly once the cameras began to roll and the lights came up behind her. "I'm Gigi, and filling in for Mr. G today is my daughter, Caroline. She's been baking with me since she could hold a spatula, so I guess she's the OG."

Caroline twisted her head around and squinted at her mom. "Huh?"

Georgia shook her head. "Never mind. That one's for my generation. Today's recipe is a special twist on a Chinese mooncake. Mooncakes are a traditional gift given among Chinese families to celebrate the Mid-Autumn Festival. Shaped like the moon in honor of the goddess waiting there for her earthbound true love, the mooncake symbolizes family and unity."

"Mooncakes are filled with a kind of paste—not the kind we use in class for projects," Caroline said, shaking her finger at the camera and provoking silent laughter from the crew. "It's paste made out of ingredients like sesame or lotus seeds. Mr. G told me that in China they fill the cakes with duck eggs, but our mooncakes are a little different."

"Here in Crystal Hill, there is a special kind of quartz crystal that proliferates in the region because of ancient lakes that dried up millions of years ago," Georgia continued. Taking off her pendant, she held it up for the camera. "Like this one that my late husband found for me years ago on one of our special walks through the woods. He loved learning about the science of our area, like what plants are native and could be used to add new, delicious flavors to my recipes. In that spirit, we're putting a hidden treasure in our mooncakes, a kind of candy called kohatku-tou that looks just like the crystals our town is named for." Georgia hung the necklace around her neck, the familiar weight having the same relaxing effect as her daughter's embrace.

As she and Caroline assembled the ingredients and rolled out their premade pastry sheets, Georgia's muscle memory took over. She and Caroline had baked together so often, it was almost like someone had turned on the autopilot switch inside her and allowed her to sit back and watch the bake take place. Somewhere in this space, she heard the echoes of her mother baking with her when she was a child, the quiet hum of her modern equipment replaced with the loud churning of her mother's handheld mixer. When she picked up the mooncake press embossed with Chinese characters, she felt the love and care of all the women who had used it before her to make pastries others would give to friends and families during this special time.

Caroline blew a strand of hair out of her face, then wrinkled her nose at the sensation, and in that motion, Georgia saw herself and Mike reflected in their child. He was there, with them, the same way Georgia would always be with Caroline even when she grew old enough to have children of her own. The love of family was a connection that could never be broken. Not by distance, not by time. Not even by death. She didn't need a sign from above to tell her that. It was right here in her daughter's smile.

It was as if she blinked and they had finished the taping, holding up their golden mooncakes with the stamp imprinted on the top before cutting them open to reveal the sweet gem hidden inside.

"Cut," the director yelled, then shook his head. "I mean, cut the film. You've already cut the cake. I hate my job."

Georgia exhaled and laughed at the same time, a mixture of relief and anxiety over what the actual result would be. She put her hands on her hips and turned to the producer. "What happens now?"

"Well, the bake we just shot will go live immediately to the website and our official Food

Network social media sites," the producer said, picking up one of the sliced cakes and examining the candy inside. "The shots we took earlier we'll use as promo for the episode with Chase and Anthony if you win." He took a bite and his eyes widened. "This is really good."

"Mom, this is so exciting," Caroline squealed, jumping up and down. "We might get to meet Chase and Anthony!"

"Mmm-hmm." Georgia nodded distractedly. That had been one of the initial reasons she had even thought about entering the contest, yet now that it was within reach, the chance of being on TV and meeting some of her favorite personalities seemed small and almost silly. What was important was the things happening right here and now. BeeBee's wedding. Caroline's renewed interest in science. Malcolm's mining project. So much joy on the road ahead, and she had been spending all her time looking back to where she had been before.

At the sound of heavy footsteps behind her, she whirled around to find Silas with a box in his arms. "This is for you. From Malcolm."

A lump gathered in her throat as she lifted the lid to see a bright blue apron with the words *Food Network Regional Baking Champion* embroidered on it in pink cursive script. "Oh."

It was all she could say. One syllable, and even

that took all of her breath. What was she waiting for? Even if things didn't work out and it got messy, she and Caroline would be all right. They had survived the worst thing that could happen to a family. The only place to go from here wasn't up, it was on. On to new adventures and new loves.

"There's something else from him," Silas said, pulling a sheet of paper out of his pocket.

Georgia took it from his hands, feeling her eyebrows crease downward. It was an order for one hundred and fifty of the mooncakes to be delivered to a lecture hall at Cornell University that evening. Her eyes shot up. "But—but we can't do this. I don't have enough time to make this many."

"You don't have to." Silas's smile widened as a mischievous twinkle glinted in his eyes. "I already made them. Between Malcolm's notes and watching you bake them all week, I got the hang of it pretty quick. Poor Ed. I've been making these for two days now and haven't let him touch a single one." He set the box down on the counter and gestured to the back of the kitchen. "They're in the pantry now. Hurry up and change before it's too late."

"Change?" Georgia looked down at her clothes. "What's wrong with what I'm wearing?"

"Honey, this is a black-tie kind of event at

a prestigious university." He shook his head. "Honestly, what would you do without me?"

"Have a lot more cream cheese brownies in stock, but also be a lot more lonely?" She reached out and touched Silas's arm. "Thanks for bringing me back to life, Si. I mean it."

"Anything for you and your girl," he said, his eyes shining behind his glasses. "I'll get the crew out and finish cleaning up. You and Caroline go back to the house and get dressed quickly or I'm going to start eating these mooncakes I've been holding back from all week and you'll have to explain to Mr. G why there's only one hundred and forty-eight instead of one hundred and fifty."

Feeling dazed, Georgia headed to the door, grabbed her purse and her coat off the hook, then looked down at Caroline, who followed behind her. "You're coming along for the ride with me, right, sweetheart?"

Caroline beamed. "Silas helped me pick out a dress last night while you were working late."

"Of course he did." Georgia threw her purse onto her shoulder and held out a hand to her daughter. "We've got a geology convention to feed. Let's rock and roll."

Caroline snorted. "Oh, Mom," she said with a sigh far too weary for a nine-year-old. "You and Mr. G are perfect for each other."

CHAPTER TWENTY-THREE

MALCOLM SCROLLED DOWN the notes on his phone even though he had read through his speech so many times he had basically memorized it.

Sure, he could entertain a bunch of eight- and nine-year-olds with his silly dances and geology jokes. But this was a room full of some of the most respected experts in the field, not to mention just as many amateur enthusiasts who would find his opening line—"I hope I'm not off to a rocky start"—less than amusing. He highlighted the remark and deleted it. Of course, the next line was "You get the schist," which made him chuckle, but what if he was the only one? Even worse, what if one of his kid vocabulary words slipped out and he said "inspectigate" instead of "investigate"?

The flutterbies (butterflies, oh no) in his stomach had started churning as soon as he walked through the door of the impressive modern building with rows of glass windows staring him down. Now that he was actually getting ready to stand in front of the podium before all the actual eyes looking at him, judging him, this all seemed like an exercise in hubris that he should never have attempted. The only thing keeping him from barreling out the door before the carts came through to serve dinner to the tables scattered around the cleared lecture hall was the fact that he needed these people—and their money—for his new plan to even have a chance of succeeding.

The only familiar face in the crowd was Felicia's, and she was too busy hanging on a man he assumed was her new boyfriend to make eye contact, so there seemed to be no one out there to support him. Then again, even if he had a room full of people who had known him his entire life, it would still feel empty without a certain baker and her daughter.

Malcolm looked down at his watch for the third time in the last ten minutes. The taping should have finished hours ago, so there would be plenty of time for Georgia to make it up here. The question plaguing him was whether or not she wanted to be here. They both knew it was more than a simple bakery order for an event. The cakes had been an excuse; if he was being honest, his participation in the whole contest had been an excuse to see her again and again. The additional time they had spent together had only confirmed what he had felt the very first time they had met. She was the one. He knew it not through scientific process and discovery, but through intuition, somewhere deep in his bones. And as much as he decried superstitious thinking as a scientist, something in him felt like if she showed up tonight, it was a sign she knew he was the one for her, too.

"Hmm," Malcolm muttered under his breath as he cupped his chin with one hand and squinted at his phone. At rapid-fire speed, he tapped out his feelings in a new introduction to the speech he had planned. The new words seemed to calm the storm roiling in his brain, and after he finished, he looked back up at the crowd and there she was.

Georgia stood in the doorway, her curly hair swept back from her face with a sparkly comb on one side. Not that she needed the help to shine. She glowed, even in a simple strapless blue dress that matched the color of her eyes. Caroline peeked out from behind her and waved at him, then gave a double thumbs-up. They were exactly what he needed, all he needed, forever. Hopefully the fact that they had come all this way meant they felt the same.

He grinned back and did a subdued version of his gallop, stopping only when the head of the event tapped him on the shoulder and nodded at the steps leading up to the small platform. Glancing back at the door one more time, he bit his lower lip before ducking his head and walking up to the podium.

The mic squealed once as he tapped on it, and with the lights shining directly in his face, he couldn't see his girls anymore. Still, he knew they were there, and that was enough to give him the courage to speak.

"Good evening, everyone," he said, the volume of his voice booming from the speaker strange and unfamiliar. "I'm Malcolm Gulleson. I teach third grade at Crystal Hill Elementary School in the Mohawk Valley School District. Teaching is a calling and a privilege, and while I cover everything from English and language arts to social studies in my classroom, science has always been a passion of mine." He looked down at his phone to remember the words he had tapped out just a few moments earlier, then continued. "When I was going to school, I was taught that the scientific method consisted of five steps." Holding out his palm with fingers outstretched, he lowered each finger one at a time into a fist. "Observation, research, hypothesis, experiment, conclusions. Obviously, you all know that the actual process is a little more complex than that and there are several small steps in between each one, including the all-important 'grovel for grant money on your hands and knees.'"

The audience rumbled with laughter, and Malcolm felt suddenly relieved that he had not gone with his first attempt at humor. He joined in with a relieved chuckle and went on with the new addition.

"But I have very recently come to believe that there is a step before even observation. I don't know what to call it, because none of the words for it sound all that scientific, and maybe it's not. It's the hunch, that spark of inspiration that makes you stop in your tracks. The feeling that you're on the road to something important and possibly even paradigm-altering. For all our procedures and formulas, the hunch is a step for which we don't even use our brains at all, because it doesn't come from our conscious mind. It comes from the heart. It's a feeling, an intuition. But that intuition is useless unless we're taught how special it is and what to do with it when it strikes. Otherwise, we're just throwing metaphorical spaghetti at every wall we encounter, hoping something sticks. Intuition has to be honed until we are able to instantly recognize potential game changers versus the everyday. As a teacher, how do I give this kind of experience to my students?" He bent forward and gave his best "are you paying attention" face. "That's right, folks. There's a pop quiz in this speech. Lucky for you, I'm going to go ahead and give you the answer. It's experience."

Malcolm cleared his throat and paused for a moment. "I don't know much about my biological parents, but I was raised and loved by parents who were both accomplished scientists. That lived experience formed me as much as the inherited molecules that make up my DNA. I know who I am and what I want in life because of that experience. I want the students I teach and children from all over to be able to have practical, hands-on experience with the incredibly unique geography of the region I'm proud to call my new home. Buried within the dolomite shales of upstate New York are the crystallized memories of seas, earth and life that are no longer around. Only when we take the time to carefully process and sift through the layers of rock are we able to uncover the beauty that is the Herkimer diamond."

Reaching into the pocket of his navy blue suit, he pulled out the best find of his most recent dig. It was a crystal about the size of quarter. Inside was what looked like a small bubble, and as he turned the crystal, the water inside that bubble shifted almost imperceptibly. He held it up to the light between his thumb and teenager finger—index finger in kid-speak.

"I'm sure most of you know what this is. It's an enhydro crystal, a quartz with a pocket of ancient water that was trapped inside as the quartz formed. The water inside is millions of years old. Isn't that incredible?" The murmurs that greeted his find told him that he certainly wasn't alone in that conclusion.

"I dug this out of a pocket from a site I'm excavating right there in Crystal Hill. See, I can talk to my kids about the Cambrian sea that once covered the whole of the Adirondack Mountains a few ice ages ago, or they can see it and hold it for themselves. All our students should have this kind of experience, and I'm hoping that with time and—here's where I circle back to the groveling-for-funding step of the scientific method—sponsorship from people like yourselves who are just as passionate as I am, that we can create a hands-on green mining experience that is accessible to children on every level of the learning and physical ability spectrum. Sluices that are wheelchair friendly, autism-friendly sensory rooms with lighting that shows the different fluorescent properties of the minerals that grow all around us, as well as traditional excavation and recovery that emphasizes respect for the planet we call home.

"And speaking of the place that I call home—" He lifted his chin and nodded at the servers who had recognized the cue he had discussed with the catering director earlier. "I've brought a little treat for all of you that celebrates both my heritage and my future. Mooncakes are a traditional gift during the Mid-Autumn Festival celebrated each year in China, the country where I was born. Brought to you by Georgia's Bakery from Crystal Hill, New York, these cakes have a special surprise when you cut into them. By the way, this recipe is featured on the Food Network's Regional Baking Champion contest final tonight. When you get a chance, please take a moment and vote for our very own baking star, Georgia Wright, and her daughter, Caroline, on the website or any of the Food Network social media pages."

Smiling with what he was quite sure was the same ridiculously besotted expression he'd caught in the window that afternoon and not caring in the least who saw it, he went back to his prepared conclusion. "In summary, interpreting the scientific method is more than following the steps. It takes following your heart."

And with that, he turned and jogged down the steps two at a time to run to the back of the room, where the loves of his life waited for him.

CHAPTER TWENTY-FOUR

As Malcolm spoke, Georgia could barely breathe.

She knew he was a good teacher, that he was charming and charismatic and intelligent. But the way he spoke with such sincerity and vulnerability captured the reverent attention of everyone in the room. She watched as one by one people set down their forks and stopped eating what looked like a nicely prepared filet just so that they didn't miss a word.

The fact that this man cared about her and Caroline was all the sign she needed. In fact, her so desperately seeking a sign should have been a clear enough message that it was time to move forward. To follow her heart, which was still alive and beating. As Malcolm crossed the room and made a beeline for her and Caroline, that same heart leaped in her chest as if to shout *yes* to any choice he offered, whether it was a hug, a fist bump, a dance or even a kiss.

His dark eyes locked with hers, and in their depths was the tangle of emotions she felt fighting to rise to her lips. But before she could reach out for him, Caroline swooped forward and wrapped her arms around his waist.

"That was a really great speech," she said after letting go. Her face beamed with pride as if she was the teacher and one of her students had just aced a test after struggling all year. "Our school is famous now!"

He straightened up, a grin threatening to crack his face in half. "I'm glad you liked it. And hopefully we got a few more votes for you and your mom in the contest out of it. How did the bake go?"

"It was great," Caroline answered for both of them. "I said all the stuff you told me to, about the moon and how we made the candy so it doesn't melt in the oven." Suddenly her eyes lit up at something in the far corner of the room. "Mom, look at that huge geode."

Georgia looked across to the stone taller than her set up in the corner and surrounded by a semicircle of people with a very wary security guard glaring down at them from behind it. It was a shade of purple so dark it looked like the sky at midnight, and under the lights of the tall ceiling, thousands of amethyst crystals glittered like stars.

"That's a neat one, isn't it?" Malcolm turned his head briefly to look at it before smiling back at Caroline. "It's almost identical to the one in the American Museum of Natural History in New York City. My *friend*—" he put emphasis on the word as his eyes flicked meaningfully to Georgia "—Felicia got it on loan from a private collection."

"Can I go look at it?" Caroline clasped her hands in front of her and pleaded with her mom.

"Just for a minute," Georgia warned. "Stay where I can see you, okay?"

Caroline bounded across the room, and Malcolm turned around and took a step back to stand next to Georgia. His arm brushed against hers as he leaned in to whisper, "I don't think even Caroline is charming enough to get that security guard to let her get close enough to touch it, do you?"

Georgia grimaced. "We're about to find out. Caroline's worse than you when it comes to shiny objects."

Malcolm twisted his body to face hers, his hand on his heart in mock offense. "I don't know what you mean." He narrowed his eyes. "Silas told you what I said, didn't he?"

"All Silas said was that I couldn't go to a formal event in my apron with the permanent chocolate stains on it," she teased. Folding her arms, she lifted her chin. "Just what exactly did you say to him? Something about me?"

He turned the rest of the way to face her, taking both her hands in his. "I'll tell you someday." Looking down at her fingers encircled by his, he skated a thumb across her knuckles. "For right now, I'm just happy to see you. Tonight wouldn't have been complete if you and Caroline weren't here."

"Your speech was perfect," Georgia assured him, and his gaze rose. "You had everyone in the palm of your hand. They'll be fighting to sponsor your mining project, I guarantee it." She lifted his hands and held them close to her heart. "What you said…it meant a lot to me, too. Malcolm, I know there's something between us that I've been fighting since the beginning. The feelings I had—have," she corrected herself, "for you came out of nowhere. It made me realize that I was so busy focusing on our recovery that I forgot about the part about actually living my life. So much of life is unexpected, the really bad things and the really good things."

"I'm hoping that I'm one of the really good things?" He tipped his head toward hers with a small smile playing about his full lips.

"You, Mr. G, are one of the best things that has ever happened to me," she murmured so softly no one else in the crowded room could hear but him. "You reminded me that planning for the future doesn't mean forgetting about the past. I think you understand that better than anyone else."

"I do," he whispered. Bringing her hands to his lips, he placed a soft kiss on her fingertips, then reached to cradle her face between the warmth of his palms. "But I'm okay with waiting as long as it takes for the future to get here. Right now feels pretty darn perfect just the way it is."

Tipping her head up, he leaned forward and brought his lips to hers, gently at first, then deepening into something so thrillingly new Georgia felt as though she was floating up among the actual stars instead of the ones made of carbon and earth. He pulled away to place his forehead to hers, then they both turned their heads as Caroline rushed over to them.

"Mom, Mr. G, I got to touch the geode," she squealed. "The security guard's name was Harley and I told him that was my cat's name and that I liked his whiskers too and he laughed really hard."

Georgia and Malcolm exchanged the knowing stare that meant each were thinking the same thing.

"Good for you, sweetheart," she said, reaching out to ruffle Caroline's hair.

"You know, I was afraid you guys might not come to the right place tonight," Malcolm said.

"They changed the lecture room number last minute because there were more people attending than they had expected."

"Huh," Georgia said absently, the memory of the kiss still tingling on her lips. "We didn't even look at the number. We ran into one of the servers on the way in, and he pointed us to the right place."

Caroline leaned back to look at the door, then tugged on Georgia's long skirt. "Mom, look at the number on the door."

Georgia pivoted around, then gasped. The number seventeen was embossed on the door. *Seventeen.* The number stopped Georgia's heart with an all-too-familiar throb. Seventeen, the age she had been when she and Mike had started dating. The number on his football jersey. A number so significant and lucky it became a running inside joke only their family knew, that when they rated something it was never on a scale of one to ten or one to twenty. It was always, always one to seventeen, with seventeen being the highest and best something could be. Seventeen meant that it was perfect. Meant to be.

She looked up beyond the ceiling and whispered a silent thank-you.

Malcolm shrugged, then took Caroline's hand in one of his and Georgia's in the other. Lowering to one knee, he looked up at them with unmistakable love. "While both of you are here on this very special night, I have an important question to ask."

CHAPTER TWENTY-FIVE

As the sound of the Wedding March plucked soulfully on the mountain dulcimer faded into the background, Malcolm stared at Georgia with barely restrained emotion brimming from every corner of his face.

Georgia rolled her eyes.

"You know you didn't have to get down on one knee to ask me and Caroline to be your dates to BeeBee's wedding," she whispered before standing with the rest of assembly gathered in front of the gazebo on Jane Street. "I mean, we were all going anyway. I made the cake."

As BeeBee walked down the aisle, Malcolm leaned down to whisper back, "Okay, so I might have gotten carried away. But I had just given a speech at Cornell University in front of world-class geology experts and also the most beautiful woman in the world. Can you blame me for getting swept up in the drama of it all?"

"Yes," Georgia shot back promptly. "I blame you for making me happier than I have been in a long time. I'm getting smile lines on my face, and it's all your fault."

He wrapped an arm around her waist. "No matter how many wrinkles you get, I'll still think you're the most beautiful woman in the world."

That part was true. What he was leaving out was that two weeks ago as he was kneeling down, he had very much wanted to ask Georgia and Caroline a different question, but for the first time in a long time, he made a choice not to skip right to the happy ending. This was a beginning worth savoring.

"Shh." Georgia elbowed him in the ribs. "You're not supposed to say that about anyone but the bride today. Well, and the flower girl." She reached her hands out to Caroline, who had just finished scattering the flower petals down the white satin aisle runner leading to the gazebo steps.

Caroline raced to their seats in the second row, the light green sash on her dress flying behind her like a cape. The flower crown on her head was slightly askew, which only made her more adorable.

Malcolm bent down to offer a fist bump. "Great job, flower girl."

"Thanks." Her cheeks and the tip of her nose

flushed pink with happiness. "I was trying to make the petals look like constellations."

He straightened up and beamed at Georgia with pride. "That's our science girl right there," he murmured as Caroline nestled into the space between them. "We're going to be getting recruitment calls from NASA for her someday. First veterinarian in space."

"As long as she follows her heart." Georgia echoed the words from his speech, lowering a hand from Caroline's shoulder to give his fingers a squeeze. "The scientific method only works if you start with your intuition, right?"

"Right." He squeezed her hand back. His intuition was telling him that right now he was exactly where he was supposed to be, with the woman who made him happier every single day they spent together than the one before and the child who might not have been his biologically, but whom he would raise with all the love and opportunities he had been given. His parents had given him the road map for this moment, this life with Georgia and her daughter. He would never be able to thank them enough, as well as the people who had made their family happen.

They turned their attention to the gazebo adorned with wildflowers, ferns and sorrel, apparently a nod to BeeBee's water buffaloes' favorite grazing snack. A line of bridesmaids,

BeeBee's sisters in light green satin gowns, each stood on one of the steps. Lucas the cheesemaker, and two older men, one in his sixties and one holding onto a cane who looked at least eighty, stood on the groom's side.

Turning his head, Malcolm looked around at the entire town seated in folding chairs all the way back to the lake. He recognized several students and parents from school, as well as quite a few of the other teachers. It was the messy blending of his work and personal life he had tried so hard to avoid, and yet after everything he'd been through, after making peace with the loose ties of his own past, he'd become okay with things in his life not being neatly organized into separate containers.

Life wasn't a series of steps to be climbed one right after the other. It was more like a meandering walk through the woods, sometimes so dark and shaded by the trees you could barely see one foot in front of the other, but sometimes a shaft of sunlight would penetrate through and illuminate something wonderful and shiny and unexpected.

He and Georgia had spent almost every evening together since the event at Cornell. It felt natural to have her, as a parent and an active member of the PTA, by his side for school events, and since she knew everyone in town, she was able to provide insight into the students that made him look at situations in a whole new way. Their lives combined in a way that might not have been neat, but it blended and rose into something new and beautiful.

In turn, he had helped her prepare the wedding cake. Not that she really needed the help, as her inspiration had come back in full force. After her mooncakes had been overwhelmingly voted as the winning recipe for the Food Network contest, she became a whirling dervish in the kitchen, coming up with new recipes right and left. Her creations were some of the most beautiful and unique pastries he had ever seen, from cookies with icing that looked like sparkling agates to eclairs stuffed with lavender-scented cream and tarts garnished with pomegranate seeds that looked like garnets, another gemstone that could be found in abundance in this amazing geological region. Silas remarked more than once that it was because she was happy again, implying that Malcolm had played a part in the surge of recent inspiration. As much as he hoped that was true, he felt like he hadn't done anything.

Other than fall in love, of course, but that had been inevitable from the beginning. In this case, the hunch and the conclusions had come full circle.

After Bill and BeeBee shared their first kiss,

Georgia wiped joyful tears from her eyes, then looked up at him. "Malcolm, I have something to ask you." Her voice was husky with emotion, and her lips trembled slightly as she reached into the small pocket in the voluminous folds of her skirt.

His heart thundered in his chest. Swallowing hard, he nodded. "What is it, Gigi?"

"Would you…" Georgia's expression suddenly flashed with a twinkle of mischief. "Go to the bakery and put the cake in the back of my car to transport to the reception?" She withdrew her keys from her pocket and jangled them in front of him.

He threw his head back and laughed. "So that's how it's going to be from now on, huh?"

Reaching for her waist, he pulled her close and brought his head to hers for a kiss. A raspy woman's cry from two rows behind them made them break apart instantly, however, and Georgia put a protective arm around Caroline.

Malcolm whipped around, only to see the owner of the bed and breakfast, a distinguished Black woman in her eighties, clutching her chest with one hand and balancing herself on the back of one of the folding chairs in front of her with the other.

"Luigi?" she said, followed by a gasp as the entire wedding party came to a halt on their way down the aisle. "Is that you?"

The very old man with the cane who had been on Bill's side of the wedding party froze after descending the final step and shielded his eyes with one hand, the other wobbling on his cane. "Cecelia? Cecelia Plunkett?"

"Plunkett?" Georgia mouthed almost inaudibly. "She never told any of us her maiden name."

Even Bill and BeeBee tore their eyes away from one another to gape at the pair moving slowly toward each other. People reached out their hands to steady Mrs. Van Ressler as she walked shakily in the man's direction, reaching him first.

The woman sitting on Georgia's other side, Lucas the cheesemaker's wife, Chrysta, whispered to Georgia, "What is happening?" while bouncing her baby up and down gently.

"What are you doing here in my town?" Mrs. Van Ressler asked the man whose face had drained of color and turned as white as the shock of hair on his head. "Don't you live in some castle in Tuscany with your millions of euros and your technology empire?"

He opened his mouth, closed it, then looked down and shook his head. "I—I am here for Bill's wedding. He was the chef on one of my yachts. The last two years I have been teaching him, helping with his business. But he never said that the great actress Cecelia Plunkett lived in his town." The man's eyes lifted, shining with years of unexpressed adoration. "I've thought about you all this time, wondered what became of you."

Mrs. Van Ressler's eyebrows furrowed, and then the corners of her mouth turned up in a small smile. "Well, Hollywood didn't exactly pan out. I married the first rich man I met once I moved back, mostly to spite you for not going after me. The people here know me as Mrs. Van Ressler. I—I haven't been Cecelia Plunkett in a long time."

The man reached out and took her hand. It shook ever so slightly as he lifted it to his lips. "You will always be Cecelia Plunkett to me. The one who got away. The woman who stole my heart when I was only twenty, and I have never gotten it back."

Mrs. Van Ressler, who had once scolded Malcolm for running too close to her prize-winning daylilies, blushed like a schoolgirl. "I've missed you so much. All these years and I never forgot about you, either." She gestured with her free hand back toward the light blue Victorian on the corner behind them. "I run the bed-and-breakfast in town. It's where I keep my collection of Murano glass. I don't know if you remember, but I bought my first piece the summer we met.

Would you—would you like to come back with me to see it?"

"I would love to," he said, releasing her hand and crooking his free elbow toward her arm.

She took it and they walked down the aisle, past the astonished bridesmaids, the groomsmen, and the bride and groom themselves. As they disappeared behind the front door of the inn, murmurs rippled through the town like a stone tossed in a pond.

"Is that the Italian prince she almost married?" one of bridesmaids with long blond hair leaned forward to ask BeeBee.

"He's not a prince, but he's rich enough to be one," BeeBee answered. "We stayed in his villa when we went to Italy to meet Fernando. It's called Villa Celia. He said he named it after the woman he loved who he let go because he thought they were too young." She faced Bill and put her hand on his cheek. "What are the odds us getting married would bring them back together?"

Malcolm tipped his head thoughtfully and scratched his chin. There was probably a formula that could calculate those odds—number of people in the world, relationship statistics in various years, different cultural customs to factor in. Then as he slid his gaze into focus on the people by his side, he caught Georgia smiling at him. At her feet, Caroline was arranging strewn petals into different geometric patterns. For once, he didn't want the scientific answer.

THERE WAS NO method for finding the right person. No formula to quantify falling in love. No number of rules you put in place could govern the heart or protect it from the possibility of loss. This wasn't science, and it wasn't exactly intuition, either. As much as Malcolm enjoyed being able to order and categorize things into neatly labeled boxes, he finally accepted the fact that there was something mysterious, unknowable and chaotic about the way people came together in this world. At times it seemed so random, and yet so many small pieces had to fall into place for love and timing to coincide and make a family. He couldn't help but think that there was something else at work here. Fate, magic or maybe a heavenly assist from a quarterback forever looking out for his family.

From the other side of the aisle, Silas waved to them. "Gigi, you guys go on to the reception. I can bring the cake over. Ed cleared out space in the back of the minivan."

Georgia slipped the keys into Malcolm's hand and lifted her heels off the ground to plant a kiss on his cheek before whispering, "Would you mind helping Silas with the cake while I take Caroline for bridal party pictures?"

Malcolm cupped her chin in one hand and gazed into her eyes for a moment before nodding. "I've got this. You and Caroline go on ahead."

She smiled and took Caroline's hand. "We're so lucky to have Mr. G around, aren't we, sweetheart?" Georgia said to her daughter, who looked over her shoulder and winked at Malcolm before trotting off to find BeeBee and Bill.

Malcolm watched them disappear into the crowd. He was the lucky one, and no matter what forces had brought them together, he would never take a single moment with them for granted. There was no time to waste on guilt. Only gratitude.

After a moment, he turned and sprinted back to the bakery. While the odds of any two people finding their soul mate in a small town in upstate New York might have been dauntingly incalculable, he did, however, know that the odds of Georgia's masterpiece making it to Silas's car without at least one finger dip into the frosting were slim to none.

EPILOGUE

Six months after BeeBee's wedding

"Come on, guys," Georgia called out the kitchen window in the direction of the backyard. "We need to get ready or we're going to be late."

Malcolm and Caroline had been romping out there with their new puppy, Dwayne Johnson—named for actor and former pro wrestler The Rock, of course—most of the afternoon. They had rescued the three-month-old Staffordshire terrier from a shelter last week, and he currently spent the weekdays at Georgia's house and the weekends at Malcolm's. Harley had retreated to the safety of a laundry basket and remained there for the first forty-eight hours, but Dwayne eventually sniffed out the cat's hiding place and won her over with his puppy stare and adorable entreaties for playtime, which consisted of rolling on his back until Harley finally gave in and pounced. One day later, Georgia had found Harley curled in a corner of Dwayne's dog bed, with the puppy snuggled against her into the corner of the square pillow. The unlikely pair had been almost inseparable ever since. Newton the gecko's terrarium would be residing in Caroline's room for the summer, a fact that thrilled Caroline and kept Georgia awake at night with thoughts of the lizard escaping and crawling onto her pillow.

Closing the window and turning around, Georgia took off the blue Food Network Regional Baking Champion apron Malcolm had given her all those months ago. There was no way he could have known she would end up winning the contest, or that hers would be one of the highest-rated episodes of the *Chase and Anthony Eats* show since it began airing almost two years ago. He had simply believed in her, in what she could be, and his faith in her future was strong enough to help her invest in something beyond surviving the next day. She had talked about it on the show, how her journey with grief was a continuing story that wasn't healed overnight by meeting Malcolm. The message had resonated with a lot of people watching who had written to thank her, Malcolm and Caroline for sharing their food and their stories.

That episode was being shown for the town tonight on a big screen in the space where Malcolm's crystal mine and geology center was rapidly taking shape. After his speech, there had been several offers to invest in his project from people just as passionate about geology and education in the sciences as him. With their help, he had secured a loan and had been able to get local and state permits to clear the seven-acre space for excavation and building. They'd gotten a small parking lot paved just before winter set in, and now construction had been completed on the learning center and concession hut that would feature, among other local favorites, Crystal Hill mooncakes.

As she folded her apron and put it back in the drawer neatly labeled "aprons (fun) and pot holders (assorted)," Georgia put her hands on her hips and looked around the room. A year ago, she would have been rushing around, trying to find her shoes beneath the pile of Caroline's school supplies, all while getting Caroline ready at the same time. Now she knew her shoes would be in the shoe cabinet next to the door, and Caroline's schoolbag was hung on the assigned hook below a shelf designated for her dance shoes, rock hammer and miniature telescope.

The sound of the door bursting open was followed by the simultaneous clatter of footsteps and puppy claws skittering on the hardwood floor.

"Good boy, Dwayne," Caroline said above the jingle of the dog's tags on his collar.

A small thump sounded from the living room where Harley had jumped off her cat tree and was now making a beeline for the foyer, where her new best friend came running around the corner.

Georgia laughed. "I would never have imagined these two would get along so well when we decided to get a dog."

Malcolm walked into the kitchen with Dwayne's leash in one hand and a bag of training treats in the other. "That's because they were meant to be," he said, dropping a kiss on Georgia's upturned lips. Turning back around to set the leash and treats on top of the dog crate in the corner, he nodded at Caroline. "Go wash your hands, kiddo. We're out the door for the screening of your mom's show in T-minus five minutes. Setting launch countdown…now." He pushed the buttons on his watch and started the timer.

Caroline squealed with laughter and made rocket ship noises as she ran into the bathroom.

"This mining business had better do well," Malcolm said, strolling back into the kitchen and taking the lid off the red cookie jar to help himself to a miniature black and white. "There's a space camp in Huntsville that NASA does for ages ten and up and Caroline really wants to go next summer. The tuition is more than this poor teacher makes in a month."

Georgia reached up to put her hands on his chest. "It's going to be a success. You've already got great buzz, thanks to the shout-out Chase and Anthony did on their social media pages when they came out to visit."

"I still can't believe that Chase, Anthony and Anthony's mom had a summer house here in Crystal Hill this whole time," Malcolm said after swallowing the rest of his cookie. He wiped his hands on his jeans before wrapping them around her waist. The thrill of his touch had yet to wear off, and every time he looked in her eyes, Georgia fell a little bit more in love with this incredible man.

"It was so funny," she said, her eyes drifting toward the window at the memory. "When I saw Anthony's mom at the shoot, I knew she looked familiar. It was Caroline who pointed out that she had been a bus driver for the elementary school. I mean, she wasn't there long before she and Chase got married and moved to the city permanently for Anthony's piano training at the conservatory, but apparently they're planning on coming back to the house this summer for an extended vacation."

"You know, the more I think about it, the more I think there has to be some method to the universe's madness after all," Malcolm said, bending to rest his forehead to hers. "It's like what you said in the show—love doesn't just happen because you're magically healed from the trauma and the pain. Love is what keeps you moving through it and makes you ready to accept whatever happens in the future."

"I'm so glad you understood what I needed from you," she said softly, lifting her gaze back up to him. "It took a lot of patience for you to wait for the timing to be right. For me and for us."

"Well, time flies when you're having fun, so they say." He pulled back, holding her hands and giving her an appreciative once-over. "And the last six months have been a lot of fun."

Georgia threw her head back and laughed. The last six months *had* been fun, filled with the simple pleasures she had thought were gone forever like their running inside joke of pranking each other with pretending to almost propose. She would get down on one knee only to tie a shoelace or Malcolm's valentine card to her whose cover had read "I would be the happiest man on Earth if you would," and then on the inside it said, "Be my Valentine."

Malcolm jutted his chin at the counter behind her. "By the way, I left a box on the counter. I think it has some of the stuff I was going to bring over to the learning center tonight. Can you open it up while I help Caroline get ready?"

Georgia turned around to see a medium-size box she hadn't noticed before. She frowned. "How could I have missed that?"

From the living room, she heard Caroline giggle. Silly girl must have sneaked behind her and Malcolm while they were embracing and was probably in there playing hide-and-seek with Dwayne. Georgia shook her head as she opened the box, raising her voice as Malcolm moved toward the high-pitched squeals of laughter. "I don't know what I'm going to do with you two goofballs, but..."

The world would never know what she would do with them because inside the cardboard box was not mining tools but a small red leather ring box.

Georgia was as surprised as she had been that night at Cornell when Malcolm had gotten down on one knee, but this time felt different. This time she hoped it wasn't a prank.

This time she hoped it was for real and forever.

Taking the ring box carefully out of its cardboard hiding place, she lifted the lid. Inside was the most beautiful diamond ring in an intricate rose-gold setting. When she took the ring out, she noticed a small sapphire worked into the setting beneath the diamond. Sapphire had been Mike's birthstone.

Georgia turned to see Malcolm kneeling in the middle of the living room floor, with Caroline perched on top of his knee. "Georgia Wright," he said, the words choked with genuine emotion. "I have something to ask you, and it's not whether you want a fist bump, hug or dance."

"Mommy, say yes," Caroline burst out then clapped her hand over her mouth as Malcolm tickled her ribs with one hand.

"I gotta ask her the question first, Care Bear," Malcolm whispered, giving her a tight hug before shifting her off his knee and rising to join Georgia in the kitchen.

"The sapphire—" She held the ring up, tears blurring her vision. "You did that on purpose."

Malcolm nodded as he slid the ring onto her finger and stared down at her with his own eyes shining. "Just because someone's not here anymore, it doesn't mean they stop being a part of us." He squeezed her hand and brought it to his lips for a kiss. "You and Caroline are my family and so is he. And so are all my parents and yours and everyone who came before us to make our future possible. I promise to love you and Caroline the rest of my life, and I will love you through the next million years, through the seas drying up and the next dozen ice ages. Whatever happens in the future, I know that I'll love you both through it all, more than any system or formula could measure. Will you marry me?"

Georgia didn't have to think about it. She knew with her intuition, with her gut, with every fiber of her being that she loved him and would always love him no matter what. "I guess…" she trailed off and bit back a grin. "I'm going to need a new apron that says Mrs. Gigi."

Caroline cheered as Malcolm swept Georgia off her feet and whirled her around the room. He set her down and pressed his lips to hers in a kiss so exhilarating it left her dizzier than the spin. He swept Caroline up next, then the pair exchanged a fist bump before finally breaking into the most absurd version of their galloping dance she had ever seen.

Georgia laughed at the same time the tears poured down her face, because she had learned that joy and sadness could exist at the same time, in the same heart. That moving forward wasn't the same thing as leaving behind. That true love could be just as sweet the second time around.

* * * * *

Be sure to look for Laurie Batzel's
next book in her Crystal Hill series,
Their First Dance,
available in August 2025 wherever
Harlequin Heartwarming books are sold!